P.O. Box 1142

By Lancer Gareth

ISBN: 979-8-3304-7050-1

Printed in the United States of America

Chapter One

Camp Ritchie, Maryland, May 10, 1943

The German army in North Africa was on the verge of surrendering to the British and American forces. In recent days, the sands of the North African desert had been stained with the remnants of fierce battles. For months, the Allies had been relentlessly pushing the Axis forces westward, with the British Eighth Army under General Montgomery advancing from Egypt and the American and British forces under General Eisenhower pressing in from the west.

The once-formidable Afrika Korps, led by Field Marshal Erwin Rommel, had been trapped between these two powerful Allied pincers. Supply lines were cut, morale was low, and the Axis troops were exhausted and outgunned. Town after town fell to the advancing Allies as the Axis forces desperately tried to hold their ground. By early May, it was clear that the end was near for the Axis presence in North Africa.

Despite the imminent victory, there was no respite at Camp Ritchie. The sun had barely risen over the dense Maryland woodlands, yet the camp was already alive with activity. Recruits moved with purpose, their footsteps echoing across the training grounds. Officially known as the Army Specialized Training Program, Military Intelligence Training Center, the camp was a hive of strategic operations. In this secluded corner of America, the sharpest minds were honed to dissect and decipher the secrets of the Axis powers.

Situated in the rolling hills of Maryland, Camp Ritchie was a sprawling installation, its grounds covering hundreds of acres. The camp was a blend of natural beauty and intense military activity. Tall pine trees and thick underbrush surrounded the camp, providing a sense of isolation and focus.

The main entrance, marked by a simple but imposing gate, led to a network of gravel roads that wound through the compound. Rows of wooden barracks lined the streets, their simple structures painted in military olive drab.

Central to the camp was the parade ground, a vast open space where soldiers assembled for drills, ceremonies, and physical training. Flanking the parade ground were various specialized buildings: classrooms for language and interrogation instruction, a gymnasium for physical conditioning, and the administration offices where the camp's operations were coordinated.

Near the edge of the camp, a series of mock villages and obstacle courses were constructed for training purposes. These areas simulated the environments recruits might encounter overseas, complete with faux enemy positions, barbed wire, and trenches. There, soldiers practiced maneuvers, learned to navigate difficult terrain, and rehearsed scenarios they would face in the field.

Within classrooms and training fields, recruits immersed themselves in the intricacies of code-breaking, interrogation, and psychological warfare. Instructors, many of them seasoned veterans and experts in their fields, guided the recruits through rigorous curricula designed to sharpen their mental acuity and tactical skills. The air buzzed with the fervor of relentless study and practice, underpinned by the sobering knowledge that failure was not an option.

Among the new arrivals was Benjamin Steinberg, a second-generation German-American with a personal stake in the conflict. His parents had fled the turmoil of World War I, seeking refuge in New York City. Benjamin stood at around 5'10" with a lean build and a short, dark brown haircut typical of military recruits. His hair had a subtle wave, hinting at a gentle curl that was kept in check by his army styling. His vibrant brown eyes seemed to hold a perpetual intensity as if constantly scanning his surroundings. A small scar above his left eyebrow hinted at a past adventure or mishap.

Fluent in German and driven by a deep sense of justice, Benjamin was determined to contribute to the Allied cause. As he stepped onto the grounds of Camp Ritchie, he couldn't help but feel the weight of his family's history and the urgency of the task ahead.

Upon arriving at Camp Ritchie, Benjamin was greeted by a staff member at the entrance gate who checked his identification and directed him to the administration building for check-in. Following the directions, Benjamin drove through the gate and up one of the gravel driveways, the crunch of the tires on the gravel echoing in the quiet surroundings, until he reached the administration building.

Inside, Benjamin was welcomed by a friendly receptionist who provided him with a welcome packet. "In this packet, you'll find a map of the camp, a list of rules and regulations, and a schedule of orientation activities." The young woman continued, "You'll also find your barracks assignment in there. You should go ahead and pull out that page so that you know where to go next. The first thing you'll need to do after you leave here is check in with your barracks leader."

Benjamin opened the manila envelope and pulled out the first loose page. He thoroughly scanned the document.

The paperwork listed his assigned barracks as "Barracks 12, Bunk 5B." It also included details such as:

- Barracks Address: Barracks 12, Second Floor

- Bunk Assignment: Bunk 5B (Upper Bunk)

- Locker Number: 24

- Barracks Leader: Sergeant Jameson

- Check-in Time: 0800-1000 hours

- Orientation Session: 1100 hours in the Main Hall.

"If you look at your map, you'll find the location of your barracks. Welcome to Camp Ritchie, Private Steinberg," the receptionist added as she stood up to close the filing cabinet behind her.

Benjamin found his way to Barracks 12 and introduced himself to his barracks leader, Sergeant Jameson, who showed him his bunk and locker where he could store his belongings and settle in. His new home for the foreseeable future was situated near the center of the camp, providing easy access to the mess hall, training facilities, and other essential areas.

The barracks were equipped with basic amenities and organized neatly, with rows of bunk beds and lockers for each soldier. Along one wall there was a grouping of small desks where soldiers could write letters home or study their training materials. The air inside was filled with the scents of sweat, boot polish, and the faint aroma of the mess hall's latest offering.

After dropping off his meager belongings, Benjamin departed to attend an orientation session, in the main hall, conducted by a senior officer. The session covered essential information such as the camp's layout, including the locations of the mess hall, training facilities, medical services, and recreational areas. Benjamin learned about the daily routine, including meal times, physical training schedules, and mandatory meetings.

Benjamin also underwent briefings on camp security protocols, emergency procedures, and the importance of following orders and regulations. The orientation aimed to ensure that Benjamin understood his role as a soldier at Camp Ritchie and was prepared to contribute effectively to the camp's mission.

Following the orientation session, Benjamin, along with the other new recruits, were taken to the quartermaster's office. There, Benjamin received his official uniform and equipment, including a standard issue uniform, boots, a helmet, a rifle, and additional gear necessary for training and duties, such as a canteen, web belt, and a field pack. The quartermaster provided instructions on the proper care and maintenance of his equipment.

Next, Benjamin underwent a thorough medical examination to ensure he was in good health and fit for the rigors of training. The examination included checks for any pre-existing conditions, vaccinations, and a general health assessment.

After passing his medical examination, Benjamin and the other recruits attended their first drill and ceremony training session. They learned the fundamentals of military drill, including marching, saluting, and standing at attention. These drills were essential for instilling discipline and fostering unit cohesion.

Following the introductory drill training, Benjamin received a detailed schedule outlining the activities for the upcoming weeks. The schedule included physical training (PT), classroom instruction, and field exercises. Physical training comprised daily exercises designed to enhance stamina, strength, and overall fitness. Classroom instruction covered military intelligence techniques such as map reading, reconnaissance, and enemy identification. Field exercises provided practical training sessions in simulated combat scenarios, allowing recruits to apply their classroom knowledge in real-world settings.

Once the orientation training concluded, Benjamin returned to his assigned quarters to set up his bunk and locker. He meticulously arranged his personal belongings, stowed his issued equipment, and prepared his sleeping area to meet military standards. As he was organizing his space, two fellow recruits, Tom and Jack, approached and began a conversation.

Tom leaned against his bunk, glancing at Benjamin's meticulous arrangement. "Hey there, name's Tom. This your first time in the military?"

Benjamin nodded, offering a small smile. "Yeah, it is. I'm Benjamin. Just finished college before joining up."

Jack, sitting on the edge of his bed, chimed in. "Same here. I studied political science and international relations at Stanford, and I'm hoping I can put my skills to use here. How about you, Benjamin? What did you study?"

"I studied cultural anthropology and history at Brown," Benjamin replied. "I also speak German, French, a bit of Italian. Figured it might come in handy with everything going on."

Tom raised an eyebrow, impressed. "Languages, history, and cultures, huh? You might end up in some interesting places with those skills."

Benjamin shrugged modestly. "I hope so. What about you, Tom? What's your background?"

"Behavioral and experimental psychology," Tom said with a grin. "I'm fresh out of The Ohio State University. Go Bucks!" he cheered enthusiastically. I figured learning to understand the minds of our enemies might help us understand what we're up against, and maybe even how to defeat them."

Jack nodded thoughtfully. "Makes sense. When I signed up, they told me this place was where the real action starts."

Benjamin nodded. "That's what I heard too. So, what do you guys think of the training so far?"

Tom chuckled as he sat on his bunk. "It's intense, but I guess that's to be expected. They really want us to be prepared for anything."

"Yeah," Jack agreed, grinning. "Especially with everything happening out there. Did you hear the latest about North Africa?"

"Not much, just bits and pieces. What's the news?" Benjamin asked, interest piqued.

"Well," Tom said, leaning back, "I heard the Allies are making some serious progress. They've taken back a lot of territory from the Axis. Rommel's not having it easy anymore."

Jack nodded. "Yeah, the Brits and Americans have been pushing hard. Operation Torch was a big success. We're finally turning the tide over there."

Benjamin looked thoughtful. "It's good to hear we're making headway. I've got a buddy in the 1st Infantry Division. Haven't heard from him in a while, but I hope he's doing alright."

Tom gave a sympathetic nod. "I know how you feel. My brother's in the Navy, stationed somewhere in the Pacific. The battles out there are pretty fierce too."

"Yeah, it's tough all around," Jack said, his expression serious. "But that's why we're here, right? To do our part and make sure the good guys come out on top."

"Absolutely," Benjamin said with a smile. "We've got a lot to learn, but I'm ready for it. It's a tough job, but it's worth it if it means helping out our boys overseas."

Tom patted Benjamin on the shoulder. "You've got the right attitude, Benjamin. We'll get through this together."

Jack smirked. "And who knows, maybe we'll get to see some action ourselves once we're done here. Just gotta make it through the training first."

Benjamin laughed. "One step at a time, Jack. One step at a time."

As the day wound down, Benjamin joined his fellow soldiers for the evening meal in the mess hall. The mess hall at Camp Ritchie was a large, utilitarian building designed to accommodate the constant flow of hungry recruits. Its exterior was simple and functional, with weathered wooden walls and a roof that had seen many seasons. Inside, the atmosphere was bustling and lively, with the clatter of metal trays and the murmur of conversations filling the air. Rows of long, sturdy tables and benches stretched across the hall, providing ample seating for the recruits. The tables were lined with salt and pepper shakers, ketchup bottles, and napkin dispensers. At the far end of the room, a series of serving stations formed a well-organized assembly line. Behind the counter, uniformed kitchen staff, moving with practiced efficiency, ladled out portions of food onto trays.

The menu at Camp Ritchie reflected the practical needs of a military training camp, focusing on providing high-energy, nutritious meals to fuel the rigorous physical and mental activities of the day. That evening's meal featured meatloaf served with sides of mashed potatoes, green beans, corn, and bread. There was also a dessert option, apple pie or chocolate pudding.

Benjamin cautiously sampled each of the items on his tray. The meatloaf was dry and a little bland. The vegetables were overcooked, resulting in a mushy texture, but they tasted good. The mashed potatoes were creamy and comforting. Despite the varying quality, Benjamin and his fellow recruits were too hungry to be picky. After long hours of orientation training, they welcomed the opportunity to sit down, eat, and recharge.

After the evening meal, there was some free time for personal activities, such as writing letters home, reading, or socializing with other recruits. The day concluded with "lights out," a designated time when all recruits were required to be in their bunks, and the barracks' lights were turned off. This routine was strictly enforced to ensure everyone got enough rest for the demanding days ahead.

After the lights went out, Benjamin lay quietly in his bunk, his memories drifting back to his childhood in New York City, and the vibrant Jewish neighborhood where he had grown up. The streets were always bustling with activity. Vendors shouted out the day's specials, children played stickball in the alleyways, and the warm, inviting smell of freshly baked challah wafted from the local bakery.

His home was a modest apartment filled with love and laughter. His parents, hardworking immigrants, had instilled in him a strong sense of duty and pride in their heritage.

He remembered Friday nights when the family gathered around the dinner table for Shabbat. The flickering candlelight cast a warm glow on their faces as they recited prayers and shared stories. His mother's tender and aromatic brisket was a staple, and his father would always have a twinkle in his eye as he recounted tales from the old country. These moments were the heart of his childhood, grounding him with a sense of belonging and tradition.

As Benjamin grew older, a restlessness took hold. He felt the weight of expectations and the invisible constraints of his tight-knit community. Despite the love and support, there was an unspoken understanding that certain parts of him—his dreams, his desires—had to remain hidden. The turning point came one evening as he sat on the stoop of their building, watching the sunset over the city. The radio crackled with news of the war in Europe, and Benjamin felt a surge of patriotism mingled with a yearning for something more.

The decision to join the military, immediately after he graduated from Brown University, crystallized at that moment. It was not just about answering the call of duty but also a chance to escape, to find a place where he could redefine himself. He wanted to prove his worth, to contribute to the fight against tyranny, but also to break free from the confines of his small world. He knew it would be difficult, but the promise of a fresh start was a powerful motivator.

Over the following few days, Benjamin's schedule was filled with continuous training, including classroom instruction, team-building exercises, and field trips. The classroom instruction consisted primarily of advanced Intelligence training. Benjamin attended a series of specialized courses in interrogation techniques, language skills, and cryptography. The team-building exercises encompassed activities designed to build trust and coordination among the recruits.

The Field Trips involved visiting simulated enemy encampments and other training sites to practice reconnaissance and intelligence gathering. Through this rigorous training regimen, Benjamin gradually adapted to military life, honing his skills and preparing for his future role in military intelligence.

As Benjamin began to acclimate to life at Camp Ritchie, he often found himself lost in thought during quiet moments. The rigorous training and camaraderie provided a welcome distraction, but the underlying tension remained. He reflected on the difficulty of hiding his true self, and the constant vigilance required to maintain a facade. It was exhausting, and he longed for the day when he could live openly, without fear of judgment or rejection.

The war, in a strange way, felt like an opportunity. Amidst the chaos and uncertainty, there was a chance to rebuild and forge a new identity. Benjamin hoped that through his service, he might find acceptance and a sense of belonging that had eluded him thus far. He dreamt of a future where he could be honest about who he was, where the bonds of brotherhood formed in battle would transcend the prejudices of the past.

In his heart, he held on to the belief that the sacrifices he was making now would pave the way for a better, more inclusive world. The journey was just beginning, and while the path ahead was fraught with challenges, Benjamin felt a renewed sense of purpose. The war would take him far from the familiar streets of his childhood. It offered the hope of a brighter, freer tomorrow.

Chapter Two

Camp Ritchie, Maryland, June 07, 1943

The North African Campaign, a crucial phase of the war, concluded with the surrender of Axis forces in Tunisia. This decisive victory for the Allies marked the end of the conflict in North Africa, securing the region and paving the way for future operations in Europe. Over 250,000 Axis soldiers were taken prisoner, significantly weakening the Axis military presence.

The subsequent weeks saw a shift from defensive operations to more aggressive Allied offensives. The success in North Africa freed up Allied forces for operations in Europe, while the strategic focus also included weakening Japan's hold in the Pacific.

Following the triumph in North Africa, the Allies began detailed planning for the invasion of Sicily (Operation Husky), which would be launched in July. This invasion aimed to knock Italy out of the war and open a new front in Europe.

In the Mediterranean, the Allies conducted operations to secure sea routes and prepare for the invasion of Italy. Naval engagements and air raids targeted Axis supply lines and infrastructure. The Allies also intensified their strategic bombing campaigns against Germany. The Royal Air Force (RAF) Bomber Command and the United States Army Air Forces (USAAF) targeted industrial cities, transportation hubs, and military installations to cripple German war production and morale.

In the Pacific Theater, the Battle of New Georgia in the Solomon Islands began to take shape. This was part of the broader strategy to neutralize the Japanese base at Rabaul and diminish Japan's control over the Pacific. The Allies conducted reconnaissance and preliminary operations to prepare for the New Georgia campaign, which would start in earnest later in June.

At Camp Ritchie, the soft morning light crept over the horizon and cast long shadows over the rugged terrain. Sweat poured from Benjamin's brow, stinging his eyes as he navigated the obstacles. His muscles ached from exertion, but he pushed forward with grim determination.

He hurdled over a series of wooden barriers, his boots pounding against the hard-packed earth. The air was filled with the grunts and shouts of fellow recruits, the clatter of equipment, and the occasional barked commands from instructors. Each obstacle tested a different aspect of their physical prowess and mental fortitude.

Benjamin reached the next challenge—a steep hill of loose gravel. He dug his heels in, using his hands to scramble upward. The gravel shifted treacherously beneath him, threatening to send him sliding back down. He gritted his teeth, focusing on maintaining his balance and momentum.

At the top of the hill, he barely had time to catch his breath before facing a low crawl through a muddy trench. Barbed wire stretched overhead, forcing him to stay low and move quickly. The mud clung to his uniform, weighing him down, but he powered through, his mind set on the end goal.

Emerging from the trench, Benjamin was greeted by the sight of the final stretch—a rope climb up a tall wooden frame. He grabbed the rough rope and began his ascent, hand over hand, his arms burning with the effort. Halfway up, his grip faltered, and he struggled to maintain his hold. Despite his best efforts, exhaustion overtook him. His fingers slipped, and he slid back down, landing on the ground with a thud.

Panting and covered in sweat and mud, Benjamin lay there for a moment, catching his breath. Disappointment washed over him, but he knew this was just one part of his training. He would push himself harder next time, determined to conquer the course and prove his mettle.

After the early morning PT, maintaining hygiene and personal cleanliness was crucial, especially given the intense physical exertion involved. Benjamin was allowed to shower, change into a clean uniform, and head to the mess hall for a quick breakfast. The aroma of freshly brewed coffee and the clatter of trays and utensils provided a brief respite before he was thrust into a rigorous schedule of language classes and lectures on interrogation techniques.

The day's lectures were held in a stark, utilitarian classroom, its walls adorned with maps and diagrams. Benjamin took his seat among the other recruits, notebooks open and pens poised. The instructor, a seasoned intelligence officer with a steely gaze, began the session with a focus on the psychological aspects of interrogation.

"Interrogation is not just about asking questions," the instructor emphasized. "It's about understanding the mind of your subject, exploiting their weaknesses, and gaining their trust."

Benjamin learned about various psychological strategies, such as building rapport, employing deception, and using stress and fear to elicit information. The lectures covered the Reid technique, which involved establishing control over the subject, confronting them with evidence, and encouraging them to confess. They also delved into the use of the Scharff technique, which relied on a more conversational and non-confrontational approach to make the subject feel more comfortable and less guarded.

The sessions were intense and detailed. They included case studies of successful interrogations, highlighting the tactics used and the results achieved. Role-playing exercises were a key part of the training, allowing recruits to practice their skills in realistic scenarios. Benjamin found these exercises particularly challenging, as they required quick thinking and adaptability.

In addition to psychological methods, the lectures covered the legal and ethical considerations of interrogation. The instructor stressed the importance of adhering to the Geneva Conventions and avoiding torture, highlighting the long-term consequences of such actions on both the subject and the interrogator.

Benjamin also learned about cultural sensitivity and the importance of understanding the background and motivations of different nationalities and groups. This was especially crucial when dealing with prisoners from diverse regions, as cultural nuances could significantly influence the effectiveness of interrogation techniques.

The instructor brought in guest speakers who had firsthand experience in the field. These veterans shared their insights and war stories, adding a layer of realism to the theoretical knowledge. Benjamin listened intently as they recounted encounters with enemy soldiers, the challenges of extracting valuable information, and the fine line between coercion and persuasion.

In addition to the psychological and ethical aspects, the lectures included practical skills such as reading body language, detecting lies, and using non-verbal cues to gauge a subject's truthfulness. Recruits were taught how to construct detailed interrogation plans, anticipate potential responses, and adapt their strategies accordingly.

By midday, Benjamin felt mentally exhausted. The sheer volume of information was overwhelming, and he often found himself struggling to absorb it all. Despite this, he remained determined to succeed. He took meticulous notes, reviewed them whenever he had a spare moment, and participated actively in discussions and exercises.

The rigorous training was designed to mold recruits into skilled interrogators who could handle the pressures of wartime intelligence work. Each day brought new challenges and lessons, pushing Benjamin to his limits but also gradually building his confidence and competence.

As the midday lectures wound down, Benjamin realized how far he had come since arriving at Camp Ritchie. The knowledge and skills he was gaining were not just academic; they were tools that could one day save lives and shape the course of the war. The refreshing shower that morning had indeed prepared him for the demanding day, but it was his inner resolve and dedication that carried him through the grueling training.

At lunchtime in the mess hall, Benjamin entered the bustling space, the aroma of hearty food mingling with the hum of conversation. He grabbed a tray and joined the line, scanning the room for a familiar face. Spotting Tom, his bunkmate and fellow recruit, Benjamin felt a spark of relief.

Tom was tall and lean, with a quick smile and a ready laugh that had already endeared him to many of the other recruits. As Benjamin approached, Tom waved him over, making space at the table.

"Hey, Benjamin! How's the brain after those lectures?" Tom asked with a grin, taking a bite of his sandwich.

Benjamin chuckled, sliding his tray onto the table and sitting down. "Feels like it's been put through a meat grinder. So much information, and so fast."

Tom nodded sympathetically. "Yeah, it's intense. But we'll get the hang of it. Just gotta keep pushing, right?"

Around them, the mess hall buzzed with the energy of recruits sharing stories and unwinding from the morning's exertions. Benjamin glanced around, noticing the camaraderie that was beginning to form among the men.

"How did you find the interrogation techniques session?" Benjamin asked, starting on his lunch.

Tom shrugged. "A little overwhelming, but interesting. The whole psychological aspect is right up my alley. Makes you realize how much more there is to interrogation than just asking questions."

"Exactly," Benjamin agreed. "I keep thinking about all the ethical stuff they drilled into us. It's a lot to balance."

"True," Tom said, leaning in a bit closer. "But I think that's what makes it so important. If we don't do it right, we're no better than the enemy."

Benjamin nodded, appreciating Tom's perspective. It was clear that Tom wasn't just there to go through the motions; he cared about the right way to do things, just as Benjamin did. "So, Tom, where are you from? What's your family like?"

Tom's expression softened as he thought for a moment. "I'm from Lancaster, Ohio, born and raised. Got a big extended family there, always buzzing with activity. We've been through a lot together, but they've always had my back."

"If you don't mind me asking," Benjamin prefaced his next question, "Did you enlist or were you drafted?"

"Enlisted," Tom said. "Felt like the right thing to do. My brother's in the Navy. Figured I'd do my part on the ground."

"Same here," Benjamin said. "Except I'm an only child. Feels good to be doing something important, you know?"

Tom nodded. "Absolutely. And who knows, maybe we'll end up making a difference," he chuckled. "Hey, now it's your turn to tell me something about your family."

Benjamin fell quiet for a moment, then shared his own story. "I grew up in New York City, the son of immigrants who worked hard to give me opportunities. Duty and honor were like second nature in our household."

Tom nodded, a thoughtful look crossing his face. "What about after the war? Any plans, dreams?"

Benjamin smiled, a glint of determination in his eyes. "I want to write. Stories that matter, that make people think. Maybe even make a difference."

"That's noble," Tom said, a hint of admiration in his voice. "I just want to make it through this, make a difference where I can. Maybe start a family someday, if that's in the cards."

"Oh? Got a girlfriend back home?" Benjamin asked with a teasing smile.

"Actually, yeah," Tom replied, a soft smile spreading across his face. "Her name's Nancy. We've been together for a few years now. She's back in Columbus, working in a factory to support the war effort. We've talked about starting a family after this is all over, finding a little place to call our own."

Benjamin's teasing smile turned into a warm grin. "Sounds like you've got plans for the future, Tom. Nancy must mean a lot to you."

Tom nodded, his gaze distant for a moment. "She does. We've been through a lot together. I just hope I can make it back to her in one piece. What about you? I'll bet you've got a pretty little Chiquita back home." He stuck out his elbow, playfully nudging Benjamin in the ribs.

Benjamin's demeanor suddenly changed, and a wave of tension flooded through him. "No. I've never been in a relationship before." He diverted his eyes nervously.

Their conversation drifted to lighter topics as they finished their meal, but the mention of loved ones and the future lingered in their thoughts, reminding them of the hopes and dreams they held onto amidst the chaos of war.

As lunchtime wound down, Benjamin felt a renewed sense of determination. The training was tough, but with friends like Tom, he knew he could get through it. They cleared their trays and headed back to the training grounds, ready to face whatever challenges the afternoon would bring, bolstered by the budding friendships that were beginning to form in the mess hall.

The sun hung low in the sky, casting long shadows across the training grounds of Camp Ritchie. Benjamin stood among a group of fellow recruits, his eyes fixed on the rows of rifles lined up before them. The air was thick with anticipation, a mix of excitement and apprehension as they prepared for their afternoon's training in weaponry.

A seasoned sergeant barked commands, his voice cutting through the buzz of conversation. "Attention!" he called out, and instantly, the recruits snapped to attention, their movements crisp and disciplined.

"Today, gentlemen, you'll be familiarizing yourselves with the M1 Garand," the sergeant announced, gesturing toward the rifles. "This here is your best friend on the battlefield. Learn it well, and it'll keep you alive out there."

Benjamin's heart quickened with a mixture of nerves and determination. He had never handled a rifle of this caliber before, but he was eager to prove himself.

The sergeant began the demonstration, showing them how to hold the rifle, load it, and aim with precision. Benjamin followed along, absorbing every detail, his fingers itching to feel the weight of the weapon in his hands.

As the afternoon progressed, they moved from basic drills to live firing exercises. The crack of gunfire echoed through the air, mingling with shouted instructions and the metallic clang of spent cartridges hitting the ground.

Despite the initial jolt of recoil and the sharp smell of gunpowder, Benjamin found himself growing more confident with each shot. He focused on his breathing, steadying his aim as he squeezed the trigger.

The thrill of hitting his target, and the satisfaction of mastering a new skill, fueled Benjamin's determination. At that moment, surrounded by the camaraderie of his fellow recruits, he felt a sense of purpose and readiness for the challenges that lay ahead.

As the sun dipped below the horizon, casting a warm glow over the training grounds, Benjamin couldn't help but smile. That day marked not just a lesson in marksmanship but a step closer to becoming the soldier he aspired to be.

After weapons training, Benjamin headed toward the Administration Building for his scheduled meeting with his mentor, Captain Harris. As he stepped into the office building, his mind still buzzed from the afternoon's weapons training. He glanced around the bustling room before spotting Captain Harris sitting at a desk piled high with paperwork.

"Captain Harris," Benjamin greeted, standing at attention before his superior.

"Sit down, Private Steinberg," Captain Harris said warmly, motioning to a chair opposite him. "How was weapons training today?"

"Challenging, but I'm getting the hang of it," Benjamin replied, taking a seat.

Captain Harris nodded approvingly. "Good to hear. Now, I wanted to talk to you about something important."

Benjamin's curiosity piqued as he leaned forward, giving Captain Harris his full attention.

"I've been keeping an eye on your progress, Private. I want you to know that I think you've been showing a lot of promise, but I feel like your own insecurities are what's keeping you from reaching your full potential. I've been where you are," Captain Harris began, his tone reflective. "When I first joined the Army, I struggled with finding my place, with knowing where I belonged in the world. It wasn't easy."

Benjamin listened intently, sensing that Captain Harris was about to share something significant.

"I was raised in a small town, very sheltered. I never felt like I belonged there, like I was an outsider. I came from a family of immigrants, much like yourself. I was different than the other boys, and they never let me forget that fact. But, then I joined the Army, and it opened up a whole new world for me," Captain Harris continued. "I found something here that I couldn't find anywhere else: acceptance, camaraderie, a sense of purpose. The military became my home."

"I understand, sir," Benjamin replied, nodding thoughtfully. "It's been a journey for me too, trying to find my footing."

Captain Harris smiled reassuringly. "And you will, Private. You've shown potential, determination, and a willingness to learn. Those are qualities that will take you far in this field."

Benjamin felt a surge of gratitude for Captain Harris's words of encouragement. "Thank you, sir. I'll do my best."

"I know you will," Captain Harris said, clapping a hand on Benjamin's shoulder. "Always remember this, just because you're different from the other boys doesn't mean you're weaker or less critical to the war effort. Sometimes the toughest battles are the ones within ourselves. Once you've learned to fully accept who you are, you can draw strength from that. But you're not alone in this. We're a team, and we've got each other's backs."

"Thank you, sir," Benjamin replied, saluting his superior officer.

"That's it for now," Captain Harris returned the salute. "Now, go get yourself some chow and some sleep. You're dismissed."

"Thank you, sir," Benjamin added as he pivoted and left the building.

After dinner, Benjamin lay in his bunk, the thin mattress doing little to cushion him from the hard frame beneath. The words of Captain Harris echoed in his mind, a comforting reminder that he had potential and a place in the military. He felt a flicker of encouragement, a sense of belonging that had been elusive since his arrival.

As he stared at the ceiling, the murmur of conversations from the other recruits filled the barracks. He tried to tune them out, but snippets of dialogue inevitably reached his ears.

"Can't wait to get back to my girl," one soldier said, his voice full of longing. "She sent me the sweetest letter today."

Another laughed. "My wife and I are planning a trip to the mountains once this war is over. Can't wait to hold her again."

Benjamin's heart sank. The talk of wives, girlfriends, and plans with loved ones was a stark reminder of the isolation he felt. He had no one he could openly share his true feelings with, no letters from a sweetheart to cherish.

The conversations took a darker turn as another recruit spoke up. "Did you hear about that guy in the next platoon? Caught him being…you know, not right. They booted him out, gave him a blue ticket."

A chorus of disgusted murmurs followed. "Good riddance. Don't need any of that queer stuff around here."

"That fella got off easy," one recruit added. "I heard about a guy in my brother's company who made a pass at his lieutenant. They gave him a court-martial and sent him to prison."

"Man, if some fella came on to me like that, there wouldn't be any need for a court-martial," a different guy boasted. "They'd be sending him home in a body bag." His comment was rewarded with an eruption of laughter and pats on the back from his bunkmates.

Benjamin's stomach churned. He had hoped for acceptance, but the reality of the homophobia that pervaded even the casual conversations in the barracks was a harsh blow. He felt the walls closing in, the camaraderie that Captain Harris spoke of tainted by prejudice and ignorance.

He turned on his side, facing the wall, and closed his eyes. The sense of belonging he'd felt earlier began to waver, replaced by a growing internal conflict. How could he reconcile his true self with the environment he was in? Could he find a way to fit in without sacrificing who he was?

As sleep eluded him, Benjamin resolved to stay strong. He would take Captain Harris's words to heart, but he would also guard his secret fiercely. In this world, it seemed, survival depended on blending in, even if it meant hiding a part of himself.

Chapter Three

Camp Ritchie, Maryland, July 05, 1943

The Allies were in the final stages of planning for Operation Husky, the invasion of Sicily. Troop movements and logistical preparations were accelerated to ensure readiness for the July 9-10 landings.

Within Italy, there was increasing unrest and dissatisfaction with the war. The Italian populace and some political leaders were becoming more vocal against Mussolini's regime and its alliance with Nazi Germany.

The Allied forces launched Operation Corkscrew. The 99th Pursuit Squadron, colloquially known as the "Tuskegee Airmen", the first all-African-American military aviators in the United States Armed Forces, embarked on their initial combat mission, a sustained air and naval bombardment targeting the strategically vital volcanic island of Pantelleria. The island, strategically important due to its location between Tunisia and Sicily, was heavily fortified by Italian forces. On June 11, after continuous bombardment, the island's garrison surrendered, providing the Allies with a crucial base for future operations in the Mediterranean.

The Allies continued their extensive bombing campaigns against Germany and Italy. Major industrial cities and military targets were relentlessly targeted, aiming to cripple German war production and infrastructure. Lieutenant Charles B. Hall from Brazil, Indiana, achieved a historic milestone by shooting down the 99th Pursuit Squadron's first enemy aircraft. This achievement was particularly significant as it marked the first recorded instance of an African American pilot in a pursuit plane downing an enemy aircraft in aerial combat. Subsequently, the 99th Squadron relocated to Sicily, where they earned a Distinguished Unit Citation for their outstanding combat performance.

In the Solomon Islands, the Allies were engaged in preparations for the New Georgia Campaign. On June 21, they began operations to capture the island of New Georgia from the Japanese, aiming to secure control over the central Solomons.

The Allied forces encountered strong Japanese resistance. These battles were crucial for gaining control over the central Solomon Islands and advancing towards the Japanese stronghold at Rabaul.

The crisp morning air filled Benjamin's lungs as he adjusted the heavy pack on his back, the scent of pine needles and damp earth surrounding him. Recruits were bustling around, checking their gear and tightening their boots, the anticipation palpable as they prepared for the two-day endurance hike.

"Listen up!" Sergeant Callahan's voice cut through the chatter. "Today's hike is going to be tough. We'll cover forty miles over the next two days, with an overnight camp. You'll navigate through various terrains and endure whatever the environment throws at you. Remember, this isn't just about physical endurance; it's about mental toughness. Stay hydrated, keep your pace, and watch out for each other. Move out!"

With that, the hike began. The rhythmic sound of boots hitting the ground echoed through the camp as the line of recruits snaked their way into the dense woods surrounding the facility. Benjamin could feel the weight of his pack pressing down on his shoulders, but he kept his focus on the path ahead.

The first few miles were relatively easy, with the terrain mostly flat. Benjamin found a steady rhythm, his breaths syncing with his steps. He glanced around, noting the determined faces of his comrades. The camaraderie among them was palpable, a silent encouragement to keep moving forward.

As the hike progressed, the terrain became more challenging. The flat paths gave way to rocky inclines and uneven ground. Benjamin's legs burned with the effort of climbing, each step requiring more energy than the last. Sweat trickled down his face, soaking into his uniform, but he pushed on, driven by the thought of proving himself.

They reached a densely forested area, the canopy above blocking out much of the sunlight. The air was cooler here, a small relief from the heat that had started to build. The ground was covered in fallen leaves and underbrush, making each step a careful calculation to avoid tripping or twisting an ankle.

"Keep your eyes open, men," Sergeant Callahan called out. "This is where you need to stay sharp."

Benjamin nodded to himself, his eyes scanning the ground and the surrounding trees. The sounds of nature filled the air—birds chirping, leaves rustling, and the distant sound of a stream. Despite the physical strain, there was something almost peaceful about this part of the hike.

As the sun dipped lower in the sky, the recruits reached a clearing by the stream, their designated campsite for the night. Tired but relieved, they dropped their packs and began setting up a makeshift camp. Without tents, they spread out their bedrolls directly on the ground, using their packs as pillows.

The evening air was cool, and the sound of the flowing stream provided a soothing backdrop. Benjamin and a few others gathered firewood, and soon a small fire crackled, offering warmth and a focal point for the weary soldiers.

They sat around the flames, sharing stories and laughter, the camaraderie growing stronger with each passing hour. The firelight flickered on their faces, casting long shadows and creating a sense of closeness and unity.

As the day slowly turned to night, the clearing by the river was bathed in the soft glow of twilight. The evening air was cool, a welcome respite after the day's grueling march. Benjamin unrolled his bedroll next to Tom's, the two friends settling in close to the flickering campfire. The fire cast dancing shadows on their faces, creating an intimate, almost surreal atmosphere.

The night sounds of the forest enveloped them—the distant hoot of an owl, the rustling of leaves, and the gentle murmur of the stream. The camaraderie around the campfire had dwindled to quiet conversations and the occasional laugh, but a somber mood lingered, the weight of the day's exertion and the realities of war hanging in the air.

Benjamin settled into his bedroll, the earthy scent of the forest mingling with the smoky aroma of the fire. He glanced at Tom, who was staring into the flames, his usually bright demeanor subdued. They sat in companionable silence for a few moments, the firelight casting a warm glow on their faces. The night was peaceful, the sounds of the forest a soothing backdrop. But there was an underlying tension in the air, a weight that both men could feel but had yet to address.

"You alright, Tom?" Benjamin asked, his voice soft but filled with genuine concern. Over the past few weeks, Tom had become one of Benjamin's closest friends, a steady presence in the often chaotic environment of their training.

Tom sighed, not taking his eyes off the fire. "Yeah, just thinking, you know? This war…it gets to you." He paused, then turned to face Benjamin. "Do you ever think about—about what's ahead of us?"

Benjamin smiled, "All the time, Tom. More than I'd like to admit. This war…it's like a dark cloud hanging over us. I try to stay focused on the training, but the thoughts always creep in."

Tom nodded, his expression thoughtful. "It's not just the fear of dying that gets to me. It's the fear of failing—failing the mission, failing my friends…failing my family." He looked back at the fire, his eyes reflecting the flickering flames. "Sometimes I wonder if I'll ever get to go back home and be the husband and father I want to be. What if I can't be that person after all this?"

Benjamin felt a pang of empathy. "I think about that too. Not the husband and father part, but…failing. Letting people down. Not being enough."

Tom gave a sad smile. "It's tough, isn't it?"

Benjamin nodded, feeling a sense of relief that he wasn't alone in his fears. "What scares you the most?"

Tom took a deep breath, the flickering flames reflecting in his eyes. "Death, I suppose. But not just my own. I worry about the men I'll be leading, the friends I've made here. I fear failing them, and not being able to protect them. And then there's the future, if we make it out of this. I worry about being a good husband, and a good father. I don't want to let Nancy down. I want to be everything she needs me to be, but sometimes…sometimes I wonder if I'm enough."

Benjamin felt a lump form in his throat. Tom's vulnerability struck a chord deep within him, bringing his own fears and insecurities to the surface. "Tom, you're one of the bravest people I know. The fact that you care so much, that you think about these things, means you're already a good man. Nancy is lucky to have you."

Tom gave a small, appreciative smile. "Thanks, Ben. That means a lot coming from you. What about you? What keeps you up at night?"

Benjamin hesitated, his heart pounding. This was his chance to open up, to share a piece of the turmoil that had been eating away at him. He took a deep breath, staring into the comforting glow of the fire. "I…I think about failing too. About not living up to the expectations, not just of the army, but of everyone back home. My family, my friends…they all see me as someone strong, someone who can handle anything. But sometimes, I don't feel that way. Sometimes, I feel like I'm barely holding it together."

Tom reached out, placing a reassuring hand on Benjamin's shoulder. "We all have our doubts, Ben. It's what makes us human. But you're stronger than you think. I see it every day. You push through, no matter how tough it gets. That's real strength."

Benjamin felt a wave of gratitude wash over him. He still couldn't bring himself to share his deepest secret, the one that set him apart and made him feel isolated. But talking with Tom, sharing even a small part of his fears, made him feel a little less alone.

"Thanks, Tom. I needed to hear that," Benjamin said, his voice thick with emotion.

"Anytime, Ben. We're in this together," Tom replied, his grip on Benjamin's shoulder firm and reassuring.

As they settled back into their bedrolls, the fire crackling softly beside them, Benjamin felt a sense of peace. The road ahead was still uncertain, but for the first time in a long while, he felt a glimmer of hope. He wasn't alone, and that made all the difference.

"Alright, men, get some rest," Sergeant Callahan instructed. "We've got another twenty miles to cover tomorrow. Stay hydrated and be ready to move out at first light."

Benjamin lay on his bedroll, his muscles aching from the day's exertion. As he stared up at the stars peeking through the canopy above, he found himself thinking of Captain Harris's words about finding a home in the military. He felt a growing sense of belonging, surrounded by comrades, like Tom, who were becoming more like brothers.

As he lay there, the soft murmurs of the campfire and the rhythmic sounds of the forest fading into the background, Benjamin's mind began to drift. The day's exhaustion tugged at him, but his thoughts were relentless, dragging him back to memories he had tried so hard to bury.

He remembered the stolen glances and fleeting touches from his past—moments of connection that had felt both exhilarating and terrifying. There was Samuel, the boy from his hometown, whose laughter had been like music to his ears. They had spent countless afternoons together, their conversations deep and meaningful, but always under the cloak of friendship. Benjamin had felt something more, something profound and frightening, but he had never dared to speak of it. The fear of being discovered, of being rejected or worse, had kept his feelings locked away, a secret even from himself.

Then there had been Daniel, a fellow student from Brown University, whose easy charm and quick wit had drawn Benjamin in. They had shared late-night study sessions, their hands brushing accidentally—yet not. The tension between them had been palpable, a silent acknowledgment of something forbidden. But in a world that demanded conformity, Benjamin had forced himself to pull away, to pretend that what he felt was nothing more than admiration for a friend.

Each memory brought with it a pang of pain, a reminder of the parts of himself he had to keep hidden. He recalled the anxiety of social gatherings, and the constant vigilance to ensure his behavior didn't betray his true self. The fear of being discovered had been a constant companion, shadowing every step, every word, every gesture.

In the quiet of the night, the weight of his secrets felt heavier than ever. He had always known that being honest about who he was would come at a cost, but the price of hiding was equally steep. The loneliness, the isolation, the constant internal conflict—it all wore on him, chipping away at his spirit.

Yet, at this moment, lying next to Tom, Benjamin felt a glimmer of hope. The bond they had formed, the shared fears and insecurities—they were lifelines in a world that often felt hostile and unwelcoming. For the first time in a long while, Benjamin allowed himself to believe that he wasn't entirely alone. Maybe, just maybe, he could find a way to be true to himself without losing everything he held dear.

As sleep finally began to claim him, Benjamin held onto that fragile hope. The road ahead was uncertain, and the fear of discovery still loomed large, but tonight, in the company of a true friend, he felt a little less burdened by his secrets. And for now, that was enough.

Morning came quickly, the first light of dawn rousing the recruits from their makeshift beds. They packed up camp swiftly, ready for the second day of the hike.

The terrain on the second day was even more challenging, with steep hills and rugged paths. Benjamin's legs burned with every step, but the encouragement of his fellow recruits kept him moving forward. The bond they shared, forged through sweat and perseverance, was undeniable.

As they approached the final stretch, the camp's buildings came into view. A surge of relief and determination washed over Benjamin. He quickened his pace, urging his tired body to give just a little more. The sound of cheering reached his ears as they neared the finish line, fellow soldiers and instructors applauding their efforts.

Sergeant Callahan stood at the end, a proud look on his face. "Good work, men. You've proven you have the stamina and determination needed for this job. Remember, this is just one part of your training. Keep pushing yourselves, and you'll be ready for anything."

Benjamin felt a sense of accomplishment wash over him as he dropped his pack and stretched his aching muscles. The hike had been tough, but he had made it. He looked around at his fellow recruits, sharing a moment of silent pride and mutual respect. They were becoming a team, forged through sweat and perseverance.

As he headed back to the barracks, Benjamin couldn't help but feel a growing sense of belonging. The words of Captain Harris echoed in his mind, and for the first time, he truly believed he could find a home in the military.

The following day at Camp Ritchie brought a rare reprieve from the grueling physical training. The recruits were granted a precious extra hour of sleep, a luxury in their demanding schedule. Benjamin welcomed the chance to rest his weary muscles and clear his mind before the day's activities began.

After a hearty breakfast in the mess hall, Benjamin's day unfolded with a sense of purpose and determination. The morning brought him face-to-face with a new challenge: mastering a foreign language. Benjamin was already fluent in German and French, having been taught both languages at home by his mother. He also knew a little Italian, compliments of his inner-city public education. As part of his training, he delved into the intricacies of linguistic nuances, pronunciation, and vocabulary. The language lab buzzed with activity as recruits practiced conversational phrases and translated military texts.

Alongside his language studies, Benjamin delved into the ethical complexities of interrogation techniques. In classroom sessions led by experienced instructors, he grappled with the moral dilemmas inherent in extracting information from prisoners of war. Discussions ranged from the Geneva Conventions to the psychological impact of interrogation tactics. Benjamin absorbed the lessons earnestly, wrestling with the weight of responsibility that came with his training.

Despite the intellectual and ethical challenges, Benjamin found himself excelling academically. His determination to prove himself, coupled with a sharp intellect and diligent study habits, propelled him forward. He absorbed information like a sponge, eager to absorb every detail that would make him a more effective soldier and interrogator.

In the following days, and parallel with his academic progress, Benjamin's physical abilities also improved. The disciplined regimen of PT sessions, combined with a newfound sense of purpose, sharpened his endurance, strength, and agility. He pushed himself during drills, striving to surpass his own limits and earn the respect of his peers.

Beneath the surface, however, lay a constant tension—a deep-seated desire to bury his big secret even further. The weight of concealment pressed on his shoulders, a silent burden that fueled his drive to excel. Benjamin was determined not only to prove his worth as a soldier but also to guard the truth that lay hidden within him.

One afternoon, as he was headed to the mess hall for his last meal of the day, he noticed Captain Harris sitting on a bench observing the comings and goings of recruits and camp staff. He wore a heavy expression on his face. Captain Harris beckoned Benjamin to join him in the quiet alcove. The air crackled with a sense of urgency and purpose, tinged with the gritty determination that defined their work.

"Private Steinberg, join me over here," Captain Harris's voice cut through the evening bustle, firm and commanding.

Benjamin hastened to meet him, his footsteps echoing in the fading light. The backdrop of distant shouts and the clatter of equipment underscored the gravity of their conversation.

"What's on your mind, sir?" Benjamin's voice was edged with a raw intensity, reflecting the gritty reality of their training.

"I need to talk to you about something crucial," Captain Harris began, his tone grave yet resolute. "Come, sit down." He took a moment to collect his thoughts. "Private, our mission here is more than just training interrogators. It's about survival, about gaining an edge in a war that demands everything from us."

Benjamin nodded, his gaze locked on Captain Harris's eyes, mirroring the fierce determination burning within him.

"Our role as interrogators is a tightrope walk," Captain Harris continued, his words weighted with the harsh truth of their reality. "We must extract vital intelligence while grappling with the moral complexities that define our actions. It's not easy, son. It's a gritty, desperate struggle for information that could mean life or death for our comrades."

Benjamin's jaw tensed, his resolve hardening with each word. The weight of their mission pressed down on him like a crushing weight, fueling his determination to succeed at any cost.

"I'm ready, sir," Benjamin declared, his voice low and determined. "I'll push myself beyond limits, do whatever it takes to gain the advantage, and protect our own."

Captain Harris's gaze softened briefly, a silent acknowledgment passing between them. "I've been watching you, Private Steinberg. Your progress is remarkable. But remember, this path demands sacrifices. We tread where others fear, but it's our duty to do so."

As Benjamin walked away, the gritty reality of their mission settled over him like a heavy cloak. Every step forward felt like a battle won, every decision a desperate gamble in the relentless pursuit of their goals. Amid uncertainty and danger, Benjamin's resolve burned bright, a beacon of determination amidst the shadows of war.

Chapter Four

Camp Ritchie, Maryland, August 02, 1943

In the summer of 1943, the tide of World War II was beginning to turn in favor of the Allies, but the conflict remained fierce on multiple fronts. The preceding weeks had seen critical developments that would shape the course of the war.

In the Mediterranean Theater, the Allies launched Operation Husky on July 9-10, 1943, the invasion of Sicily. This operation was a crucial step in the campaign to knock Italy out of the war and open a pathway to the European mainland. American and British forces, under the command of General Dwight D. Eisenhower, landed on the southeastern coast of Sicily.

The operation faced stiff resistance from German and Italian forces, but by late July, the Allies had made significant progress. On July 22, 1943, the key port city of Palermo fell to the Allies. The capture of Sicily provided a vital base for future operations in Italy and caused significant political upheaval in Rome.

The invasion of Sicily had a profound impact on Italian politics. On July 25, 1943, Benito Mussolini was deposed by the Fascist Grand Council and arrested. King Victor Emmanuel III appointed Marshal Pietro Badoglio as the new Prime Minister. Although Badoglio initially declared that Italy would continue to fight alongside Germany, secret negotiations with the Allies began, leading to Italy's eventual surrender later in the year.

High-level Allied conferences and strategic planning sessions took place during this period, focusing on future operations. The Combined Chiefs of Staff, representing the United States and the United Kingdom, continued to plan for the invasion of mainland Europe, which would eventually materialize as Operation Overlord (the Battle of Normandy) in 1944 on the now infamous D-Day. Discussions also centered on increasing coordination between the Western Allies and the Soviet Union to maintain pressure on multiple fronts.

The Allied strategic bombing campaign against Germany intensified during this period. The Royal Air Force (RAF) and the United States Army Air Forces (USAAF) conducted numerous raids on German industrial and military targets.

One notable raid was Operation Gomorrah, which began on July 24, 1943. This operation targeted the city of Hamburg with a series of devastating air raids, resulting in widespread destruction and significant civilian casualties.

The bombings caused a firestorm, leaving much of the city in ruins and marking one of the most destructive bombing campaigns of the war.

In the Battle of the Atlantic, the Allies continued to gain the upper hand against German U-boats. By mid-1943, improved tactics, technology, and increased production of escort vessels and aircraft had turned the tide in favor of the Allies. The Allies' growing ability to protect convoys and hunt U-boats resulted in a significant reduction in shipping losses, which was critical for maintaining the flow of troops, equipment, and supplies to various fronts.

In the Pacific Theater, the Solomon Islands Campaign continued to rage. On July 30, 1943, the Battle of New Georgia concluded with an Allied victory. This campaign was part of the broader effort to secure the Solomon Islands and ultimately isolate the major Japanese base at Rabaul. The success of this campaign allowed the Allies to strengthen their positions in the Pacific and prepare for further offensives.

The period leading up to August 1943 also saw important scientific and technological developments. The Allied codebreakers, led by British mathematician Alan Turing at Bletchley Park, continued to make strides in breaking German Enigma codes, providing crucial intelligence that helped turn the tide of the war. Additionally, work on the Manhattan Project was progressing, with scientists racing to develop the atomic bomb, a project that would ultimately play a decisive role in the war's conclusion.

At Camp Ritchie, the mood was somber. The morning precipitation cast an eerie blanket of fog across the parade ground, its tendrils weaving through the dense canopy of pine trees that surrounded the camp. The air was crisp with the first hints of autumn, carrying the scent of damp earth and pine needles. Benjamin stood at attention, the weight of his freshly pressed uniform a reminder of the journey he had completed and the responsibilities that lay ahead.

The parade ground was meticulously prepared for the graduation ceremony. Rows of folding chairs were arranged with military precision, and a temporary stage had been erected at the front, draped in the stars and stripes. The American flag fluttered gently in the breeze, the fabric rustling softly against the backdrop of solemn anticipation.

As Benjamin stood among his fellow recruits, he could feel the collective energy of the men around him—nervous excitement mingled with a sober sense of duty. The polished brass buttons on their uniforms gleamed in the morning light, and the sharp creases in their trousers spoke of countless hours of drill and discipline. He could hear the faint murmur of hushed conversations, punctuated by the occasional clearing of throats and the scuff of boots on gravel.

The commanding officer, Colonel Andrews, stepped up to the podium, his presence commanding immediate silence. The Colonel's voice was steady and clear, carrying across the assembled men with practiced authority.

"Gentlemen," he began, his eyes scanning the rows of attentive faces, "today we stand at a crossroads of history. The world is engulfed in the flames of war, a conflict that has tested the very fabric of our humanity. Here at Camp Ritchie, you have been trained not just as soldiers, but as warriors of intelligence, bearers of a torch that will pierce the darkness of tyranny and oppression."

He paused, letting the gravity of his words settle over the men. "The training you have undergone is rigorous and demanding, designed to forge you into the sharpest tools in the Allied arsenal. You have learned to dissect the enemy's secrets, to decode their messages, and to turn their own tactics against them. But remember, it is not just knowledge and skill that will see you through this conflict. It is your unwavering dedication to the cause of freedom and justice."

Colonel Andrews' voice grew more impassioned, resonating with a powerful conviction. "We are fighting a war not just of territories and armies, but of ideologies and beliefs. The Axis powers seek to impose a world order built on hatred, intolerance, and subjugation. We, on the other hand, stand for liberty, for the right of all peoples to live free from fear and oppression. Your role in this grand endeavor is to ensure that truth and justice prevail over deception and tyranny."

He leaned forward slightly, his gaze intense. "You will face challenges that will test your courage and resolve. You will encounter enemies who will stop at nothing to protect their secrets. In those moments, remember this: the strength of your character, the integrity of your actions, and the clarity of your purpose will be your greatest weapons. Stand firm in the face of adversity, for you are the vanguard of a new kind of warfare—one that relies not on brute force, but on intellect and perseverance."

The fog seemed to lift slightly as if drawn away by the Colonel's fervor. "As you leave this place and step onto the broader stage of the world, carry with you the lessons you have learned here. Remember the camaraderie, the discipline, and the relentless pursuit of excellence. Let these be your guiding principles as you serve our nation and its Allies."

Colonel Andrews took a deep breath, his voice softening as he concluded. "Today, you graduate as soldiers of intelligence. Tomorrow, you will be the harbingers of hope in a world desperate for redemption. Go forth with the knowledge that your efforts will help shape the future, and that history will remember you not just for your victories, but for the values you upheld."

The Colonel's final words hung in the air, a solemn benediction. "Congratulations, gentlemen. May you carry the torch of freedom with honor and courage."

Benjamin felt a swell of pride as he listened, but it was tempered by the weight of the words. The months of grueling training had transformed him from a civilian into a soldier, yet the real test lay ahead. The gravity of their mission—to outthink, outmaneuver, and outlast the enemy—was not lost on any of them.

The ceremony proceeded with a somber rhythm. Certificates were handed out, each one a tangible acknowledgment of the skills they had acquired and the challenges they had overcome. As Benjamin stepped forward to receive his, the paper felt crisp and cool in his hands, a stark contrast to the warmth of the handshake from Colonel Andrews. "Congratulations, Steinberg," the Colonel said, his eyes meeting Benjamin's with a look that conveyed respect and expectation.

Returning to his place in the ranks, Benjamin scanned the faces of his comrades. Some bore the scars of training—bruises, cuts, and a hardness in their eyes that spoke of sleepless nights and relentless drills. Others, like himself, carried invisible wounds—memories of whispered slurs and the burden of secrets kept hidden.

The ceremony concluded with the playing of the national anthem, the familiar strains filling the air and evoking a powerful sense of unity. As the last notes faded, Benjamin stood at attention, the flag above him a symbol of the ideals they were sworn to protect. Yet, beneath the surface, he couldn't shake the feeling of isolation. The camaraderie of shared experience was tempered by the knowledge that he could never fully reveal who he was to those around him.

The ceremony ended, and the men were dismissed, their conversations rising in a crescendo of relief and anticipation. Benjamin found himself caught in a moment of reflection. The training had been rigorous, the bonds forged through shared hardship strong, but the future remained uncertain. He could hear the laughter and see the smiles, but he felt a gulf between himself and the others, a reminder of the personal battle he fought every day.

As he made his way back to the barracks, the weight of his graduation certificate in his hand, Benjamin knew that the journey was far from over. The path ahead would be fraught with danger and uncertainty, but he was ready to face it, driven by a deep sense of justice and the hope that, someday, the world would be a place where he could live openly and authentically. For now, he steeled himself for the challenges to come, determined to prove that he was more than the sum of his secrets.

After the graduation ceremony was concluded, Benjamin headed to the Administration Building for his final mentor meeting with Captain Harris.

The Administration Building, at that moment, was quiet, save for the occasional rustle of papers and muffled conversations from adjoining offices. The air carried a faint scent of leather and polished wood, mixing with the lingering aroma of coffee.

Benjamin, feeling a mix of anticipation and pride, approached Captain Harris's office, he noticed the door slightly ajar and heard the low murmur of voices inside. He knocked lightly on the doorframe before stepping into the office.

The room was warmly lit by sunlight filtering through the blinds, casting slatted shadows across the floor. Captain Harris stood behind his desk, his posture straight and commanding, a figure of authority and mentorship. Tom was already seated in one of the two chairs in front of the desk, looking up as Benjamin entered.

"Come in, Private Steinberg," Captain Harris said, his voice steady and welcoming. He gestured to the empty chair beside Tom. "Take a seat."

Benjamin sat down, glancing at Tom, who gave him a brief, encouraging nod. The atmosphere in the room was serious but not tense, a mix of formality and the camaraderie that had developed over their training.

"I've called both of you here for a reason," Captain Harris began, leaning slightly forward and clasping his hands on the desk. "You've both shown exceptional skill and dedication throughout your training. The next phase of your service will be critical, not just for your personal development, but for the impact you'll have on our war effort."

Captain Harris paused, allowing his words to sink in. He then reached into a drawer and pulled out two sealed folders, placing them on the desk with deliberate care.

"Private Steinberg, Private Richardson, you've both been selected for a highly specialized assignment at a facility known as P. O. Box 1142. This is a top-secret military intelligence installation where we conduct advanced interrogation and intelligence gathering from high-value POWs. What you'll be doing there is of utmost importance."

Tom shifted slightly in his seat, his curiosity evident. "What exactly will we be doing, sir?"

"You'll be part of a team responsible for extracting critical information from enemy prisoners. Your language skills, psychological training, and interrogation techniques will be put to the test. The information you gather could significantly alter the course of our operations."

Captain Harris opened one of the folders, revealing documents marked with various levels of classification. He picked up a page and handed it to Benjamin.

"This outlines your specific duties and responsibilities. You'll receive further briefings on-site, but I want to emphasize the importance of maintaining the highest level of security and confidentiality. What you'll learn and do at P. O. Box 1142 must stay within its walls."

Benjamin scanned the document, feeling the weight of the responsibility settling on his shoulders. "I understand, sir. We'll do whatever it takes."

"I have no doubt you will," Captain Harris said, his expression one of genuine confidence. "Now, let's go over some critical points you need to be aware of before you arrive."

Captain Harris went on to describe the facility, the nature of the prisoners they would be dealing with, and the specific interrogation techniques they had been trained to use. He highlighted the security protocols, the ethical guidelines, and the importance of teamwork and communication.

"Remember, your work will save lives and bring us closer to victory. It's a heavy burden, but I believe you both are more than capable. Any questions?"

Tom glanced at Benjamin before speaking. "What kind of support will we have if we encounter difficulties, sir?"

"There are experienced officers on-site who will guide you, and you'll have access to psychological support if needed. This is not easy work, but you won't be alone. Lean on each other, and don't hesitate to seek help when necessary."

Benjamin nodded, feeling a sense of resolve. "Thank you, Captain. We're ready."

Captain Harris stood, signaling the end of the meeting. "I'm proud of you both. You've come a long way, and I'm confident you'll excel in this new role. Good luck, and stay safe."

As Benjamin and Tom left the office, the gravity of their new assignment weighed heavily on their minds, but so did the determination to rise to the challenge.

That evening, the barracks were quieter than usual. Benjamin and Tom were packing their belongings and discussing their upcoming assignment. The atmosphere was a mix of excitement, nervousness, and anticipation.

Benjamin sat on his bunk, neatly folding his uniforms and placing them into his duffel bag. The room was dimly lit, with only a few lights casting a soft glow over the rows of bunks. The usual chatter of the barracks had quieted down, replaced by the subdued rustle of packing and the occasional murmur of conversation.

Tom was packing his gear across from Benjamin, his movements purposeful but unhurried. He looked up and caught Benjamin's eye. "Can you believe it's finally happening?" he asked in a hushed tone, a mix of excitement and apprehension in his voice. "Tomorrow, we're heading to P. O. Box 1142."

Benjamin smiled, though he felt a knot of anxiety tightening in his stomach. "Yeah, it's surreal. I mean, we've been training for this moment, but now that it's here, it's…different."

Tom nodded, his expression thoughtful. "I know what you mean. It's one thing to train and another to actually be in the field. But we've got each other's backs, right?"

"Always," Benjamin replied, feeling a surge of camaraderie. "We've been through a lot together. We'll get through this too."

Tom chuckled, the sound a welcome break in the quiet. "And hey, at least we get one more night in these bunks before moving on to who knows what kind of accommodations."

"True," Benjamin agreed, glancing around the familiar barracks. "I'm going to miss this place, in a way. It's been our home for months."

"Yeah, me too," Tom said, a hint of nostalgia in his voice. "But it's time for the next chapter. We've got a job to do."

Benjamin nodded, feeling a renewed sense of purpose. "Let's make sure we do it well."

The two friends continued packing in companionable silence, each lost in their thoughts about the future. As the lights in the barracks dimmed further, signaling lights out, they settled into their bunks for one last night at Camp Ritchie, ready to face whatever lay ahead.

Benjamin lay in his bunk, the rough texture of the military-issue blanket scratchy against his skin. The room was silent except for the occasional creak of a bed or the soft rustle of someone turning in their sleep. He tried to focus on the steady rhythm of his breathing, but his mind kept returning to the day's events and the enormity of what lay ahead.

His assignment to P. O. Box 1142 was an incredible opportunity, a chance to make a real difference in the war effort. He felt a surge of pride at having been chosen, at the recognition of his skills and potential. Captain Harris's words echoed in his mind: "Your work will save lives and bring us closer to victory."

But beneath that pride was a deep, unsettling worry. The weight of his secret—his true self, hidden away—pressed heavily on him. He had managed to navigate the training, keeping his guard up, deflecting questions, and avoiding situations where he might slip. But how long could he keep it up? The thought of being exposed, of the potential consequences, filled him with a cold dread.

His duties as an interrogator added another layer of complexity to his internal turmoil. Extracting information from prisoners, while crucial for the war effort, clashed with his sense of morality. How could he justify prying into others' secrets while hiding such a significant part of himself? The ethical dilemmas weighed heavily on his conscience, casting shadows over his pride and accomplishments.

He turned onto his side, facing the wall, and closed his eyes. His thoughts drifted to his family, to the sacrifices they had made, the values they had instilled in him. They had fled the horrors of one war only to find themselves embroiled in another. He couldn't let them down. He had to be strong and had to stay focused.

Yet, the internal struggle was relentless. The camaraderie he felt with Tom and the other recruits was genuine, but it also highlighted his isolation. They talked about their lives, their hopes, and their fears, but there was always a part of Benjamin he couldn't share, a truth he had to keep hidden. The fear of discovery gnawed at him, a constant reminder of his precarious position.

He let out a slow breath, trying to push the anxiety aside. This was his moment, his chance to contribute something meaningful. He couldn't afford to be distracted. He needed to be sharp, to be the best he could be. But as he drifted towards sleep, the unresolved tension remained a silent companion in the darkness, blending with the moral dilemmas that plagued his every waking hour.

Chapter Five

Fort Hunt, Virginia, August 03, 1943

The land that Fort Hunt occupies was originally part of George Washington's River Farm estate in the 18th century. The area remained largely agricultural until the late 1800s.

In response to the Spanish-American War in 1898, the U.S. government constructed coastal artillery batteries at Fort Hunt as part of the nation's coastal defense system. The fort was named after Brigadier General Henry Jackson Hunt, a Civil War artillery commander.

By the time the 20th century rolled around, the fort's artillery batteries had become obsolete with advancements in military technology, so the fort was largely shuttered, but the site continued to be used for various military purposes.

Since 1942, Fort Hunt has been the site of a top-secret military intelligence operation known only by the address "P.O. Box 1142." This address matched a Post Office box in Alexandria, Virginia where the operation received its mail. The nondescript address was used to maintain the secrecy of the activities conducted there.

As the military jeep bounced along the dirt road, dust billowed up behind it, clouding the clear morning air. Benjamin sat in the passenger seat, his eyes fixed on the dense trees lining the path, their leaves shimmering with dew. Tom gripped the steering wheel, his knuckles white from both the rough terrain and the weight of their mission.

The jeep emerged from the thick forest, and Fort Hunt came into view. A tall chain-link fence topped with barbed wire encircled the facility, its imposing presence a stark contrast to the tranquil surroundings. At the entrance, a heavy iron gate marked the boundary between the outside world and the covert operations within. Guards stood at attention, their uniforms crisp and their faces serious, underscoring the importance of security at this clandestine site.

Tom slowed the jeep to a crawl as they approached the gate. A guard stepped forward, raising a hand to signal them to stop. He scrutinized them with a keen eye, his gaze shifting from their dusty faces to the military insignia on their uniforms. After a brief exchange of identification and orders, the guard nodded and motioned for the gate to be opened. The iron barrier creaked and groaned as it swung inward, revealing the heart of Fort Hunt.

The jeep rolled through the gate and into the compound, where rows of functional, nondescript buildings stood. The structures were built for utility, not comfort—interrogation rooms, administrative offices, barracks, and storage areas. The harsh lines and utilitarian design of the buildings reflected the serious nature of the work conducted within their walls.

Tom navigated the jeep towards the central courtyard, where other military personnel moved with purpose, each immersed in their own duties. Benjamin glanced back at the canvas-covered cargo in the rear of the jeep—all their worldly possessions packed into a few duffel bags and crates. Everything they owned, everything familiar, was now behind them as they stepped into this new chapter of their lives.

The jeep came to a halt, and Tom killed the engine. The silence that followed was filled with an air of anticipation and uncertainty. Benjamin and Tom exchanged a glance, a silent acknowledgment of the challenges that lay ahead. They had arrived at Fort Hunt, a place shrouded in secrecy and laden with the weight of their duty. As they disembarked, the enormity of their mission settled over them like a cloak, both heavy and inexorable.

Benjamin and Tom stepped out of the jeep, their boots crunching on the gravel. The morning air was cool, carrying the scent of pine and earth, a fleeting reminder of the world outside these fences. They stretched their limbs, stiff from the long drive, and then began unloading their gear from the back of the jeep.

A young lieutenant approached, his uniform immaculate, with a clipboard in hand. "Welcome to Fort Hunt, gentlemen," he said, his tone formal. "I'm Lieutenant Harrison. Follow me, and I'll get you settled in."

Benjamin and Tom grabbed their duffel bags, slung them over their shoulders, and fell into step behind Lieutenant Harrison. They moved past the administrative building, where officers and staff were already busy with the day's work, and towards a cluster of barracks.

"Your quarters are just up ahead," Lieutenant Harrison explained as they walked. "You'll have some time to get settled before your orientation and briefings."

They reached a modest barrack at the edge of the compound. It was a simple, wooden structure with a small porch and a few windows. Inside, the barrack was sparsely furnished but clean. There were two cots, each with a footlocker at its end, a small table with a couple of chairs, and a shared wardrobe.

"This barrack, here, is going to be the home of the 'Ritchie boys' for the foreseeable future," Harrison said, handing them each a key. "Mess hall is open until 1900 hours, and you'll find the schedule for the week posted on the bulletin board outside. Your first briefing is at 0900 tomorrow. Get some rest and familiarize yourselves with the facility."

"Thank you, Lieutenant," Tom said, shaking his hand. Benjamin followed suit, appreciating the warmth in Tom's voice that contrasted with the formality of their surroundings.

As the lieutenant departed, Benjamin and Tom began to unpack. The familiar ritual of organizing their belongings brought a small measure of comfort amidst the uncertainty. They worked silently, each lost in his own thoughts.

Tom broke the silence first. "This place is something else, huh? I've never seen anything quite like it."

Benjamin nodded, glancing around their new quarters. "It's different, that's for sure. But I suppose we'll get used to it."

After they had unpacked, they decided to explore the compound. Walking side by side, they passed various buildings and facilities. The interrogation rooms, they noticed, were heavily guarded and off-limits for casual inspection. Analysts and officers moved briskly between offices, carrying files and exchanging information in hushed tones.

They found the mess hall and grabbed a quick meal, sitting at a table with a few other new arrivals. The conversation was light, a mix of introductions and shared stories about their journeys to Fort Hunt.

As evening fell, the compound took on a quieter, more introspective atmosphere. The guards at the perimeter stood vigilant, and the lights from the buildings cast long shadows across the grounds.

Back in their barrack, Benjamin lay on his cot, staring at the ceiling. Tom was reading a letter from home, the soft rustle of paper the only sound in the room. Despite the day's activity, a sense of unease lingered.

"You think we're ready for this?" Benjamin finally asked, breaking the silence.

Tom looked up from his letter, his expression thoughtful. "I think we wouldn't be here if they didn't believe we could handle it. We just need to stay focused and do our best."

Benjamin nodded, comforted by Tom's confidence. He turned off the light and settled into his cot, closing his eyes. Tomorrow, their real work would begin, and with it, the challenges and trials they had both anticipated and feared.

As the first light of dawn filtered through the windows of their barracks at P.O. Box 1142, Benjamin stirred from his sleep. The distant sounds of soldiers starting their day echoed through the camp, a familiar rhythm of military life.

He glanced at the small clock on his bedside table, its hands indicating the early hour of 0530.

Pushing aside his thin blanket, Benjamin swung his legs over the edge of the bunk, his feet meeting the cool wooden floor. Tom was already up, the rustling of his movements signaling his own readiness to face the day ahead.

With practiced efficiency, Benjamin made his way to the communal showers, a row of simple stalls with modesty partitions. The rush of water, steam, and the scent of soap filled the air as he washed away the remnants of sleep, the chill of the water invigorating him for the tasks to come.

Back in the barracks, clad in his olive drab uniform, Benjamin joined Tom on the edge of one of the bunks as they sat there in quiet contemplation, preparing themselves for the morning briefing. The room buzzed with anticipation of the day's activities.

At precisely 0900 hours, the new arrivals gathered in the designated orientation area, a spacious room adorned with maps, charts, and military insignia. Their commanding officer, Colonel Everett Stone of the Army's G-2 Intelligence Division, stood at the front, a figure of authority and purpose.

"Good morning, gentlemen. I'm Colonel Everett Stone, commanding officer of P.O. Box 1142, part of the Army's G-2 Intelligence Division. With me today are Major Thompson, our intelligence operations chief, Captain Reynolds, head of security, and Lieutenant Baker, our interrogation specialist."

Colonel Stone's resonant voice reverberated through the briefing room, instantly capturing attention and commanding respect as he introduced himself and delineated the mission's objectives. "Firstly, I extend a warm welcome to each of you. Our mission here is pivotal to the war effort, and your roles are indispensable to our success." He paused, making deliberate eye contact with every newcomer. "Throughout your tenure here, you will undergo comprehensive training and become integral members of a team dedicated to extracting crucial intelligence from our adversaries."

"Our objectives center around acquiring actionable intelligence to inform strategic maneuvers on the battlefield, contributing significantly to our overall triumph," interjected Major Thompson.

Captain Reynolds chimed in, emphasizing, "Security stands as our utmost priority. You will be briefed extensively on our protocols, secure communication practices, and the criticality of maintaining absolute confidentiality."

Lieutenant Baker emphasized, "As interrogators, your ethical conduct and adherence to protocol are paramount. We will provide training on psychological techniques, establishing rapport with detainees, and managing high-value targets."

Colonel Stone's voice resurfaced with unwavering authority, "Our endeavors here demand discipline, discretion, and unwavering dedication. I expect each of you to exemplify the highest standards of professionalism and integrity. Now, let us proceed with the on-site orientation, encompassing a tour of our facilities and in-depth briefings on mission specifics, security protocols, and ethical guidelines."

The tour began at the main gate, where guards in crisp uniforms saluted as the group arrived at the security checkpoint. As Benjamin approached the main gate, he turned around to see the imposing structure of Fort Hunt in full view. The main gate itself was a formidable sight, a sturdy barrier of metal and wood flanked by armed guards who stood watch with a vigilant gaze. Beyond the gate, a perimeter fence stretched out, marking the boundaries of the military installation.

At strategic points along the perimeter, guard towers rose into the sky, offering commanding views of the surroundings. These towers, manned by alert sentries, were essential for surveillance and defense, ensuring that the base remained secure from any potential threats.

Inside Fort Hunt, a network of buildings and facilities sprawled across the landscape. Barracks for housing soldiers, administrative offices for command operations, the mess hall, and storage areas for equipment and supplies formed the backbone of the base. The architecture was functional and utilitarian, designed to support the operational needs of a military establishment.

Near the main gate, a tall flagpole proudly displayed the American flag, fluttering in the breeze. Other military insignia and banners representing the units stationed at Fort Hunt added a touch of symbolism to the scene, showcasing the unity and purpose of the military presence.

"Good morning, recruits. Again, my name is Captain Reynolds, and I oversee security here at Fort Hunt. As you're aware, security is paramount in our operations," Captain Reynolds explained. "Let's go over the protocols for entering and exiting the fort. Access through the gate is restricted. While there are protocols for personnel to enter and exit the base, these movements are controlled and monitored for security reasons. Access may be granted based on clearance levels, duties, and specific permissions granted by the commanding officers or security personnel."

Captain Reynolds paused for a moment to let his words sink in. "During "liberty days" or leave periods, military personnel typically have the opportunity to leave the base.

However, there are guidelines and protocols regarding leave that you must follow. If you plan to leave the premises, you are required to obtain permission from your commanding officer, adhere to your specific leave durations, and follow any travel restrictions or security protocols in place at the time. Each entry and exit will require proper identification and clearance. Any vehicles must undergo thorough inspections, and personnel will be subject to security checks."

Captain Reynolds continued, "Now, regarding communications, all telephone and radio transmissions to and from the facility are encrypted to ensure secure communication. Regarding letters, if you want to write letters home, give your letters to the designated military postal personnel. Letters are required to be unsealed so they can be inspected for security purposes before being sent out. Make sure to address your letters properly, including your full name and rank and the correct return mailing address. All incoming mail must be addressed to P.O. Box 1142, Alexandria, Virginia, 22301, that's it. Any external communications must be approved and monitored to prevent unauthorized access or information leaks. We take these measures very seriously to maintain operational security and protect classified information."

Next, the group headed toward the main entrance of the P.O. Box 1142 facility. They passed through another security checkpoint guarded by another pair of saluting guards. Inside, they were led through corridors lined with maps and intelligence reports, showcasing the base's strategic importance. They passed by several interrogation rooms equipped with state-of-the-art equipment and observation areas where analysts went diligently about their work.

Major Thompson stepped forward, his voice firm and resolute, commanding the room's attention. "Let's dive into the specifics of our mission here. The primary goal is to gather actionable intelligence that directly supports strategic decisions on the battlefield. Our success depends on the accuracy and timeliness of the information we collect. This intelligence can encompass a wide range of data points, each critical to our operations.

"Firstly, enemy troop movements are a major focus. We need to know where their forces are concentrated, how they're maneuvering, and what their potential targets might be. This information allows our commanders to anticipate enemy actions and position our forces advantageously.

"Secondly, supply routes are of paramount importance. By identifying and understanding the supply lines that sustain enemy operations, we can disrupt their logistics, thereby weakening their ability to wage war. This includes tracking the movement of ammunition, food, medical supplies, and fuel—anything that keeps their war machine running.

"Potential threats also fall under our purview. This isn't limited to large-scale operations but includes identifying sabotage plans, assassination plots, and other subversive activities that could undermine our efforts. Early detection of these threats allows us to take preemptive actions to neutralize them.

"Our intelligence efforts also extend to the political and social dynamics within enemy territory. Understanding the morale of enemy troops, the sentiments of the civilian population, and the internal politics of enemy leadership can provide us with opportunities to exploit weaknesses and foster dissent.

"We achieve these goals through various means: interrogations of prisoners of war, analysis of captured documents, surveillance, and collaboration with resistance groups and other intelligence agencies. Each piece of information, no matter how small, is a potential key to a larger puzzle.

"Our analysts work tirelessly to piece together these fragments of data, creating a comprehensive picture of the enemy's capabilities and intentions. Your role, as part of this team, is crucial. The accuracy of your reports and the diligence with which you conduct your interrogations and investigations can mean the difference between victory and defeat on the battlefield.

"Remember, the information we gather isn't just about immediate tactical advantages; it contributes to our broader strategic goals. By understanding the enemy's long-term plans and capabilities, we can outmaneuver them not just in the next battle, but in the overall war effort. This is the gravity of our mission, and this is why your roles here are so vital."

As the group entered the briefing room, they were struck by the atmosphere of focused intensity. The large maps dominated the room, marked with pins and strings that crisscrossed, illustrating the complexity of the ongoing operations. The overhead projector cast a faint hum, ready to project the latest reconnaissance photos. The telegraph machine in the corner clicked intermittently, sending and receiving coded messages that rippled through the military's vast communication network.

Lieutenant Baker stepped forward, his expression serious and his voice steady, reflecting the gravity of the subject matter. "Ethical guidelines are at the core of our work here," he began, his eyes meeting those of the new arrivals. "As interrogators, you bear a tremendous responsibility not only to your country but also to the principles of justice and human dignity. Your conduct must reflect the highest standards of integrity and professionalism at all times."

He paused, allowing the weight of his words to sink in. "Interrogation is not merely about extracting information;

it's about doing so in a manner that respects the moral and ethical standards we hold dear. You will face immense pressure to deliver results, but it is crucial that you never compromise these standards. The methods we employ must be both effective and humane."

Baker took a step closer to the group, his tone earnest. "We will train you in advanced psychological techniques designed to build rapport and trust with prisoners. These methods are based on understanding human behavior and leveraging it to gather valuable intelligence without resorting to coercion or brutality. You will learn how to read body language, identify stress indicators, and use conversational tactics to encourage cooperation."

"Understanding the cultural backgrounds of those you interrogate is equally important," he continued. "Knowledge of an individual's cultural, religious, and social contexts can be a powerful tool in gaining their trust and eliciting useful information. We will provide you with in-depth training on various cultural norms and sensitivities, helping you to navigate these interactions with respect and effectiveness."

Baker's voice grew more intense as he addressed the handling of high-value prisoners. "High-value prisoners are often the most challenging subjects you will encounter. These individuals are trained to resist interrogation and possess information that could be critical to our war efforts. Handling them requires a unique blend of patience, skill, and psychological insight. You must approach each case with a tailored strategy, always keeping ethical considerations at the forefront."

He then addressed the importance of maintaining mental and emotional balance. "The nature of your work can be taxing. The stress of extracting vital information while adhering to ethical standards can take a toll on your mental health. We provide support systems, including counseling and peer discussion groups, to help you manage this pressure. Never hesitate to seek assistance if you find the burden overwhelming."

Baker paused, his face reflecting the seriousness of the topic. "Remember, the way we conduct ourselves in these rooms does more than gather intelligence; it defines our legacy. Our adherence to ethical guidelines ensures that we can look back on our work with pride, knowing that we upheld the values we are fighting to protect."

"Lastly," he concluded, "integrity is not just about following rules; it's about embodying them. It's about making the right choices even when no one is watching. Every action you take should reflect the core values of honor, respect, and duty. You are the custodians of these principles, and it is through your dedication that we maintain our moral high ground."

With that, Lieutenant Baker stepped back, letting the gravity of his words linger in the air. The recruits sat in thoughtful silence, understanding the immense responsibility that lay before them and the ethical framework within which they must operate.

Colonel Stone stood tall, his presence loomed large as he addressed the recruits with a deep, resonant voice that conveyed both authority and earnestness. "Remember," he began, his gaze sweeping across the faces before him, "every action you take here has a direct impact on our success in the field. What you do within these walls reverberates far beyond them."

He paused, allowing the significance of his words to settle in. "This facility is a crucial nexus in our war effort. The intelligence we gather here can turn the tide of battles, save countless lives, and bring us closer to victory. Each piece of information, each report you compile, each interrogation you conduct—these are not mere tasks. They are pivotal contributions to our overall strategy."

Stone's tone grew more intense as he continued, "Our success depends on the collective efforts of everyone in this room. We are a team, bound by a shared mission and a shared commitment to excellence. Upholding the highest standards in everything we do is not just an expectation—it is a necessity. Whether you are deciphering coded messages, analyzing captured documents, or engaging in face-to-face interrogations, you must strive for precision, diligence, and integrity."

He took a step forward, emphasizing his point. "Our enemies are cunning and relentless. They will exploit any weakness they find. Therefore, we must be equally relentless in our pursuit of excellence. Our protocols and procedures are designed to ensure that we operate with maximum efficiency and effectiveness. Adherence to these standards is not optional; it is a cornerstone of our operations."

Colonel Stone's voice softened slightly, adding a personal touch to his message. "I have seen the impact of our work firsthand. The intelligence gathered here has prevented ambushes, identified key enemy positions, and disrupted supply lines. Our efforts here have saved the lives of our fellow soldiers and contributed to the broader war effort in ways that cannot be overstated. Each of you plays an indispensable role in this endeavor."

He concluded with a powerful call to unity and purpose. "Let us work together, supporting one another and pushing each other to achieve our best. Collaboration and communication are key to our success. If we hold ourselves to the highest standards and remain steadfast in our commitment to our mission, there is no limit to what we can achieve. Together, we will make a difference. Together, we will contribute to the ultimate victory."

With that, Colonel Stone stepped back, his words leaving a lasting impression on the recruits. They sat in silent contemplation, fully grasping the gravity of their responsibilities and the profound impact their actions could have on the war effort.

As Colonel Stone concluded his address, the room remained silent for a moment, each recruit absorbing the weight of his words. The commanding officer nodded to Major Thompson, who stepped forward with a final note.

"Thank you, Colonel Stone," Major Thompson said. "That concludes our orientation tour for this morning. You've been given a comprehensive overview of our facilities, mission specifics, security protocols, and ethical guidelines. I trust you understand the critical nature of your work here."

He glanced at his watch and then addressed the recruits. "We will now break for lunch. You have one hour to eat, rest, and reflect on what you've learned. Lunch is served in the mess hall, which you passed by earlier. Make sure you return here promptly after the break for the next session."

The recruits rose from their seats, the weight of the morning's briefings lingering in their minds. They filed out of the briefing room, exchanging hushed comments and contemplative looks. The hallways buzzed with the low hum of conversation as they made their way towards the mess hall.

The mess hall at Fort Hunt was a spacious, utilitarian room filled with long, sturdy tables and benches. The air was filled with the savory aromas of cooked meals, a welcome respite after the intense morning briefings. Large windows along one wall let in natural light, creating a bright and open atmosphere.

At the entrance, recruits lined up to receive their food from a serving line manned by efficient, no-nonsense kitchen staff. The menu, while simple, was hearty: trays laden with roast beef, mashed potatoes, green beans, and fresh rolls, along with coffee and tea to drink.

Benjamin and Tom, having just received their trays, found a spot at one of the long tables near a window. The sunlight streaming in provided a warm contrast to the serious tones of the morning.

Tom took a bite of his roast beef and looked over at Benjamin. "That was quite the orientation, huh? I knew this place was important, but hearing it all laid out like that really drives it home."

Benjamin nodded, still processing everything. "Yeah, it does. The responsibility feels immense. Every little detail could mean life or death out there."

Tom's expression softened. "We'll get through it. We just have to stay focused and support each other."

Around them, other recruits were similarly engaged in subdued conversations, the weight of their new responsibilities hanging in the air. The mess hall, usually a place for light-hearted chatter and camaraderie, was quieter than usual, with many recruits lost in thought.

After a few moments of silence, Benjamin spoke up again. "I'm glad we have this break. It's a lot to take in all at once."

Tom smiled while biting off a piece of his roll. "Me too."

As they continued their meal, the recruits gradually began to relax, the camaraderie slowly returning as they shared their thoughts and feelings about the morning's intense sessions. By the end of the lunch hour, they felt more prepared to tackle the challenges ahead, bolstered by the sense of unity and shared purpose that the orientation had instilled.

With the sound of the bell signaling the end of their break, the recruits rose from their seats, ready to continue their training and contribute to the vital mission of P.O. Box 1142.

As the recruits returned from lunch, the atmosphere in the mess hall began to shift from the intense focus of the morning's briefings to a more relaxed and conversational mood. Benjamin took a deep breath, ready to dive into the next phase of his integration into P.O. Box 1142's operations.

As the new arrivals returned to the briefing room and sat down, Colonel Stone was ready to continue with the briefing, "As new interrogators, you will not be immediately assigned to handle high-ranking officers or high-value technical detainees. Such prisoners possess critical information that can significantly impact our operations and strategy. Handling them requires a level of experience and finesse that must be developed over time."

He looked around the room, making sure the recruits understood the gravity of the situation. "Your initial assignments will involve working with lower-level detainees. These individuals may include regular enemy soldiers, logistical support personnel, and others who, while still valuable, do not carry the same level of risk or complexity as high-value targets. This phase of your training is crucial for building your interrogation skills, understanding psychological techniques, and gaining confidence in your abilities."

"You will be closely supervised by senior interrogators," Colonel Stone explained. "They will provide guidance, feedback, and support as you navigate these early stages. Pay close attention to their advice and learn from their experience. Each interrogation, no matter how seemingly insignificant, is an opportunity to refine your methods and grow as a professional."

He continued with emphasis, "Once you have demonstrated proficiency and reliability in handling these initial assignments, you may gradually be entrusted with more sensitive interrogations. This progression ensures that by the time you are faced with high-value prisoners, you will have the necessary skills and judgment to conduct these interrogations effectively and ethically. Now, we're going to move over to the main hall, where you will get to meet some of the other members of the team that you will be working with." Colonel Stone gestured toward the doorway connecting the briefing room to the main hall. The young men stood up and made their way into the adjacent room.

Benjamin found himself in a large common room where new recruits and experienced staff mingled. The room buzzed with activity as people chatted in small groups, sharing stories and experiences. Benjamin noticed a bulletin board covered with notices, schedules, and various announcements—a snapshot of life at P.O. Box 1142.

Benjamin spotted Tom across the room, already engaged in a lively conversation with a group of men. As he approached, Tom waved him over. "Ben, come meet the guys!"

Joining the group, Benjamin was introduced to several new faces. There was Staff Sergeant Lewis, a grizzled veteran with sharp eyes and a no-nonsense demeanor, and Corporal Davies, a cheerful and talkative man who seemed to know everyone. Also present were two other young recruits, Private Jenkins and Private Ortega, who like Benjamin and Tom, were just beginning their journey at P.O. Box 1142.

"Good to meet you all," Benjamin said, shaking hands with each of them. He felt a mix of nervousness and curiosity. As the conversation flowed around him, he tried to get a sense of the group dynamics.

Staff Sergeant Lewis was recounting a tale from his early days in the Army, eliciting laughs and nods of agreement. Benjamin listened attentively, appreciating the camaraderie but also searching for any subtle hints that might indicate someone shared his secret. It was a delicate dance—showing interest and openness without revealing too much about himself.

Corporal Davies turned to Benjamin with a friendly grin. "So, Ben, where are you from?"

"New York," Benjamin replied. "It's quite a change coming here, but I'm looking forward to the work."

Private Ortega chimed in. "New York, huh? Must be nice. I'm from El Paso, Texas. This place is a whole different world compared to home."

As the conversation continued, Benjamin felt a growing sense of belonging. The men around him were welcoming and seemed genuinely interested in getting to know each other. Yet, beneath the surface, he couldn't shake the anxiety about his secret. He carefully observed their reactions, their jokes, and their offhand comments, trying to gauge their attitudes and beliefs.

In the midst of the camaraderie, Benjamin's thoughts drifted inward. He knew the stakes were high—not just for the mission but for his personal safety and acceptance. Every laugh, every shared story, was a reminder of what he stood to gain or lose.

He wondered if any of the men around him might be like him, hiding behind the same mask. Did Staff Sergeant Lewis's sharp eyes see more than they let on? Was there a reason Corporal Davies was so friendly and approachable? Could he find an ally in Private Jenkins or Private Ortega?

Benjamin resolved to remain cautious but open. He needed to build trust and find his place within this team. As they continued to talk, he contributed more to the conversation, sharing anecdotes from New York City and listening to the other's stories. He laughed at their jokes and asked questions, all the while maintaining a careful balance—revealing enough to be friendly, but not enough to be vulnerable.

By the time the bell rang, signaling the end of the work day, Benjamin felt a tentative sense of optimism. The initial interactions had gone well, and he had begun to feel the dynamics of the group. He still had a long way to go in navigating his dual roles as a dedicated interrogator and a man with a dangerous secret, but the first steps had been promising.

As he headed back to the briefing room with his new colleagues, Benjamin silently vowed to continue observing, learning, and building connections. He knew that in this environment, camaraderie and trust would be his most valuable assets.

Returning to the barrack after the day's events, Benjamin sat on his bunk, his mind swirling with thoughts and emotions. The day had been a whirlwind—a mix of excitement, apprehension, and determination.

As he gazed at the dimly lit ceiling, Benjamin reflected on his journey so far. From the moment he arrived at P.O. Box 1142, he knew he was stepping into a world of secrecy, duty, and sacrifice. The weight of his concealed identity hung heavy on his shoulders, a constant reminder of the delicate balance he must maintain.

He thought about the camaraderie he had experienced during the day—the welcoming gestures, the shared laughter, and the sense of belonging. It was a stark contrast to the isolation he often felt because of his secret. Benjamin longed for genuine connections, but fear held him back. Would they accept him if they knew the truth? Or would he face rejection and suspicion?

Despite the challenges, Benjamin held onto hope. Hope that he could make a difference, not just in the mission at P.O. Box 1142, but in the lives of those around him. He believed in the importance of his work, in gathering intelligence that could save lives and shape the course of the war.

But intertwined with his hopes were doubts and fears. Could he keep his secret hidden indefinitely? Would the constant pressure of deception erode his sense of self? Benjamin knew he had to stay vigilant, to tread carefully in a world where trust was both a precious commodity and a potential liability.

As he closed his eyes, exhaustion washing over him, Benjamin made a silent vow to himself. He would navigate this intricate dance of secrecy and duty with grace and resilience. He would make a difference, one step at a time, even if it meant carrying the weight of his concealed identity alone.

With that resolve firm in his heart, Benjamin drifted into a restless sleep, his mind already racing with plans for the challenges that lay ahead.

Chapter Six

Fort Hunt, Virginia, August 06, 1943

The early morning air was crisp and cool as Benjamin laced up his running shoes, preparing for a jog around the perimeter of Fort Hunt. The sun had just begun to rise, casting a soft golden glow over the landscape. He relished these moments of solitude, finding clarity and focus in the rhythm of his steps.

Starting at the main gate, Benjamin set off at a steady pace, his breath visible in the chilly air. The compound was quiet, with only the occasional guard on patrol or a fellow early riser crossing his path. As he ran, he let his thoughts drift, absorbing the history and significance of the place.

He paused at one of the old gun placements, now just a bare concrete foundation where cannons once stood. The sight made him reflect on the fort's past. Constructed during the Spanish-American War, Fort Hunt was strategically located on the banks of the Potomac River, a crucial defensive position to protect Washington, D.C., from naval threats. The fort's placement ensured control over a vital waterway, guarding the nation's capital against potential enemy incursions.

Benjamin moved on, jogging past the remnants of the fort's original structure. The stone walls, though weathered by time, still stood as a testament to the fort's strategic importance. He could almost hear the echo of commands shouted by officers, the clatter of boots on cobblestones, and the murmur of soldiers sharing stories of home and loved ones. In its heyday, Fort Hunt would have been a bustling hub of military activity, its ramparts bristling with artillery and its grounds teeming with disciplined troops ready to defend their country.

He stopped again at a particularly well-preserved section of the ramparts, running his hand over the rough stone. What must it have been like, he wondered, to be stationed here over a century ago? The tension of awaiting orders, the camaraderie among the troops, the uncertainty of what each day might bring. It was a different era, yet the sense of duty and sacrifice felt timeless.

Continuing his jog, Benjamin reflected on his own journey. Just as the soldiers of the past had faced their challenges, he was navigating his own path, balancing his secret with the demands of his role. The historical significance of the fort provided a poignant backdrop for his thoughts, a reminder that he was part of a long continuum of service and dedication.

As he rounded the final stretch back towards the barrack's shower building, Benjamin felt a renewed sense of purpose. The fort had stood the test of time, adapting to new roles and challenges. He too would find a way to balance his responsibilities and personal truths, drawing strength from the legacy of those who had come before him.

With the sun now fully risen, casting a warm light over Fort Hunt, Benjamin finished his jog, ready to face whatever the day had in store. He was determined to honor the history of the fort and the sacrifices of its past occupants while forging his own path forward.

Benjamin returned to the barracks after his morning shower, eager to get dressed and meet up with Tom for breakfast. As he entered, he saw Tom lying on his back on his cot, reading the "Stars and Stripes" military publication.

Tom glanced up from the newspaper and struck up a conversation. "Can you believe they've got women flying planes now?" he said, shaking his head in mild disbelief. He read aloud from the article, "On August 5, WASP, The Women Airforce Service Pilots, was formed, consolidating two earlier women's aviation groups. This organization has played a crucial role in the war effort by allowing women to serve as pilots, ferrying aircraft and performing other vital duties."

Benjamin, now half-dressed, raised an eyebrow. "It's incredible. Just goes to show how everyone is pitching in for the war effort."

Tom nodded and continued, "And that's not all. Listen to this. Treblinka Uprising (August 2, 1943): Jewish inmates at the Treblinka extermination camp in Poland staged a revolt. They seized weapons and set buildings ablaze. Although many were killed during the escape attempt, around 300 inmates managed to flee, with about 40 surviving the subsequent hunt by the Nazis."

Benjamin's expression turned somber. "That's both horrifying and heroic. Those poor people."

Tom flipped to another page. "Here's more news: Sinking of PT-109 (August 2, 1943). Lieutenant John F. Kennedy's patrol torpedo boat was rammed by the Japanese destroyer Amagiri in the Solomon Islands. Kennedy and the surviving crew swam to a small island and were rescued later. He received the Navy and Marine Corps Medal for his heroism. Can you believe that? This guy is famous now."

Benjamin nodded. "I heard about that. Quite a story. Kennedy's really something—a real American hero."

"And then there's this," Tom said, his voice tinged with disbelief and irritation. "Patton Slapping Incident (August 3, 1943): General George S. Patton struck a soldier suffering from shell shock at the 15th Evacuation Hospital in Nicosia, Cyprus. This incident, along with another similar event, has become a major controversy over the last few days."

Benjamin frowned as he finished buttoning his shirt. "Patton's always been controversial, but that's just...wrong. Those men have been through hell."

Tom sighed, folding the newspaper and placing it beside his cot. "Yeah, the war brings out the best and the worst in people."

Benjamin nodded in agreement. "Come on, let's get some breakfast. We've got a long day ahead."

The two men left the barracks together, the weight of the morning's news lingering in their thoughts as they headed toward the mess hall to grab some breakfast and coffee before their first scheduled interrogation.

Before their scheduled interrogation, Benjamin and Tom went to the briefing room where Lieutenant Baker was waiting to assign the duo their first subject, Hans Richter.

The interrogation room was small and stark, furnished only with a table and two chairs. Benjamin and Tom entered, their expressions a mix of anticipation and nervousness. This was their first real assignment, a chance to put their training into practice.

As they settled into their seats, Hans Richter was escorted in by a guard. He was a middle-aged man, weary but alert, with a look of resignation in his eyes. The German soldier captured during a skirmish near the front lines now found himself facing the scrutiny of his captors.

"Guten Morgen, Herr Richter," Benjamin began in German. "Ich bin Benjamin, und das ist Tom. Haben Sie Verständnis für Englisch?"

Richter nodded. "Ja, ein wenig," he replied in broken English. "I understand English."

"Good," Benjamin switched to English. "We have a few questions for you."

Richter nodded, acknowledging their presence.

"Let's start with something simple," Tom said with a friendly smile. "What was life like for you before the war?"

Richter's expression softened as he began to talk about his life back home, his family, and his hobbies. The conversation flowed naturally as they discussed non-threatening topics, allowing Richter to feel more at ease.

"Ja, before the war, life was…normal," Richter started. "Family, work, nothing special."

"Can you tell us about your background and upbringing before joining the military?" Benjamin inquired, diving into Richter's personal history.

"Ich komme aus einer kleinen Stadt im Norden," Richter explained. "Family had farm, I help, then join military."

"What motivated you to enlist in the armed forces?" Tom added, seeking insights into Richter's decision to join the military.

"Patriotismus, duty," Richter replied. "Germany needed soldiers, so I join."

"How long have you been stationed at your previous outpost?" Benjamin asked, shifting the focus to Richter's military experience.

"Zwei Jahre, etwa," Richter replied. "Two years, around."

"What were your daily duties and responsibilities at the outpost?" Tom inquired, delving into the specifics of Richter's role.

"Observation, reporting enemy movements," Richter explained. "Patrols, maintenance."

"Have you encountered any challenges or difficulties in your role?" Benjamin probed further, exploring Richter's experiences on the field.

"Ja, enemy patrols, harsh weather," Richter admitted. "Supply shortages."

"And what are your thoughts on the conflict? Do you find conviction in the cause for which you fight?" Tom asked, aiming to understand Richter's perspective.

"It is ein complex matter," Richter paused, choosing his words carefully. "Duty often clashes mit doubt."

Throughout the conversation, Benjamin and Tom maintained a delicate balance between authority and empathy, seeking to elicit information without raising suspicion or hostility from Richter. Their questions were strategic, and probing without being confrontational, as they navigated the nuances of interrogation.

"Can you describe the terrain and surroundings of your outpost?" Tom asked, seeking contextual details.

"Hügelig, bewaldet, river nearby," Richter described. "Good cover, but hard to see far."

"Did you have regular communications with your superiors or other units?" Benjamin inquired, delving into Richter's communication channels.

"Ja, radios mostly," Richter replied. "Messages, updates."

As the conversation progressed, Benjamin and Tom gradually introduced more pointed questions about enemy plans, Richter's training and clearance, and any sensitive information he might possess. They maintained a balance between building rapport and gathering valuable intelligence, ensuring that Richter felt heard and respected throughout the interrogation.

"Have you received any specialized training or certifications during your military service?" Tom asked, focusing on Richter's training and expertise.

"Basic training, reconnaissance," Richter explained. "No special certifications."

"Were you involved in any combat engagements before your capture?" Benjamin queried, exploring Richter's combat experience.

"Skirmishes, no major battles," Richter answered. "Few shots fired, but no major action."

Tom, with his keen observation skills, picked up on subtle cues in the prisoner's body language and tone of voice. He directed the conversation towards sensitive topics, gauging the prisoner's reactions to gauge the significance of certain information.

They carefully avoided triggering defensiveness or suspicion, framing their questions in a way that encouraged the prisoner to open up voluntarily.

"Did you witness any significant events or operations involving enemy forces?" Tom inquired, seeking insights into Richter's observations.

"Some troop movements, fortifications," Richter recalled. "But nothing major."

"Have you ever been injured or treated for any medical conditions while on duty?" Benjamin asked, addressing Richter's health and well-being during deployment.

"Minor injuries, nothing serious," Richter replied. "Treated at field hospital, back to duty."

"What kind of weapons and equipment did you have access to at your outpost?" Tom inquired, exploring Richter's resources and capabilities.

"Standard issue rifles, grenades, field radio," Richter listed. "No heavy weapons."

"Did you participate in any reconnaissance or intelligence-gathering missions?" Benjamin continued, eager for any valuable intelligence.

"Ja, occasionally," Richter answered. "Mostly routine patrols, keine großen Geheimnisse."

"Were there any notable changes or developments in your unit's activities recently?" Tom asked, his curiosity piqued.

"More patrols, tighter security," Richter replied. "Command was…nervous."

"Can you share any information about troop movements or deployments in your area?" Benjamin asked, leaning forward slightly.

"Some units moved south," Richter said, struggling to find the right words. "Others went…towards the front."

"Did you have interactions with civilians or local populations during your deployment?" Tom inquired, shifting the focus.

"Ja, sometimes," Richter replied. "Mostly farmers, traders. No trouble."

"Would you like to take a break?" Benjamin asked. "If you need, I can have the guard outside escort you to the toilette. Also, if you'd like, I can get you something to drink. Would you like a Coca-Cola?"

Richter seemed excited by the offer, "Ja, danke. Do you have a cigarette?" He made a gesture reminiscent of lighting a cigarette in his mouth. Tom reached into his pocket and pulled out a pack of Lucky Strikes and a Zippo, pushing them across the table toward Richter.

Benjamin opened the door of the interrogation room to ask the guard to bring Richter a bottle of Coca-Cola. Once the guard returned and handed Richter the bottle, Benjamin resumed his questioning.

"Have you been briefed on any strategic objectives or plans by your commanding officers?" Benjamin asked, seeking insight into the enemy's strategy.

"Only general plans," Richter admitted. "Hold positions, keine genauen Details."

"Did you have access to classified documents or sensitive information?" Tom questioned, probing for any potential intelligence leaks.

"Nein," Richter said firmly. "No access to high-level documents."

"What were your interactions like with other soldiers and personnel at the outpost?" Benjamin asked, exploring the social dynamics within Richter's unit.

"Normal camaraderie," Richter replied. "We work together, share duties."

"Did you encounter any language barriers or communication challenges during your deployment?" Tom asked, curious about the practical aspects of Richter's service.

"Sometimes with locals," Richter said. "But among soldiers, nein."

"Can you describe the chain of command and organizational structure within your unit?" Benjamin inquired, trying to understand the hierarchy.

"Captain, then lieutenants, then us," Richter explained. "Simple structure."

"Were there any incidents or events that stood out to you during your time at the outpost?" Tom asked, seeking memorable experiences.

"Couple of close calls," Richter recalled. "Enemy patrols, skirmishes."

"Have you observed any logistical or supply operations in your area of operation?" Benjamin asked, shifting to practical aspects.

"Supply convoys, regular," Richter replied. "Food, ammunition, basics."

"Did you have contact with any allied forces or personnel during your deployment?" Tom inquired, exploring potential alliances.

"Nein, no allies," Richter said. "Only our own forces."

"Can you provide details about the fortifications or defensive positions in your sector?" Benjamin asked, seeking tactical information.

"Mostly trenches, sandbags," Richter explained. "Some bunkers, not much."

"Were there any surveillance or reconnaissance activities conducted by your unit?" Tom questioned, curious about their operational activities.

"Ja, regular patrols," Richter replied. "Keep watch on enemy movements."

"Did you receive any intelligence briefings or updates from higher command?" Benjamin asked, probing for any valuable information.

"Occasionally, not often," Richter said. "Only general updates."

"Have you heard any rumors or discussions among your fellow soldiers about enemy tactics?" Tom asked, hoping for some insight into enemy strategies.

"Some talk, mostly speculation," Richter replied. "Nothing concrete."

"Can you recall any specific engagements or skirmishes involving enemy forces?" Benjamin queried, looking for detailed accounts.

"A few, yes," Richter said. "Mostly small-scale, no large battles."

"Were there any casualties or losses suffered by your unit during your deployment?" Tom asked, seeking to understand the toll of the conflict.

"Ja, some losses," Richter admitted. "Friends, comrades."

"Have you been briefed on any upcoming operations or offensive plans?" Benjamin asked, his tone serious.

"No detailed plans," Richter replied. "Only to hold positions."

"Can you share your thoughts on the overall morale and mood within your unit?" Tom inquired, curious about the psychological state of Richter's comrades.

"Mixed feelings," Richter said. "Some confident, others…wary."

"Were there any disciplinary actions or incidents involving misconduct among soldiers?" Benjamin asked, delving into the unit's internal dynamics.

"Minor issues, nothing major," Richter replied. "Mostly discipline."

"Did you encounter any challenges in terms of logistics, supplies, or equipment?" Tom asked, focusing on practical difficulties.

"Supply shortages, ja," Richter said. "Sometimes lacking essentials."

"Have you been involved in any training exercises or drills recently?" Benjamin questioned, curious about their preparedness.

"Regular drills," Richter replied. "Maintain readiness."

"Can you describe the communication systems and protocols used by your unit?" Tom inquired, seeking technical details.

"Mostly radios, coded messages," Richter explained. "Standard protocol."

"Were there any instances of cooperation or coordination with other military branches?" Benjamin asked, exploring inter-branch dynamics.

"Occasionally with Luftwaffe," Richter said. "Not often."

"Did you have access to medical facilities or support services during your deployment?" Tom inquired, shifting focus.

"Field hospital nearby," Richter replied. "Basic medical support."

"Can you provide information about enemy positions or movements that you observed?" Benjamin asked, keen for any actionable intelligence.

"Some positions, ja," Richter said. "Mostly static, some movement."

"Were there any interactions with local authorities or civilian leaders in your area?" Tom asked, seeking broader context.

"Rarely," Richter replied. "Mostly military interactions."

The hours passed as they navigated through the extensive list of inquiries, striving to extract as much valuable information as possible from their captive.

By the end of the session, they had established a level of trust with Richter, allowing for a fruitful exchange of information that could prove invaluable for their mission at P.O. Box 1142. They had a comprehensive understanding of Richter's background, his role within the German forces, and potential insights into enemy operations and plans.

Outside the interrogation room, Benjamin and Tom debriefed on their approach, reflecting on the effectiveness of their interrogation strategy, the wealth of intelligence they had gathered, and its significance for their mission.

After their interrogation, Benjamin and Tom returned to the briefing room. Lieutenant Baker was waiting to debrief them. Staff Sergeant Lewis and Corporal Davies were there as well to sit in on the debrief and offer their constructive criticism.

Lieutenant Baker leaned forward, looking at the duo with interest. "How did it go?" he asked.

Benjamin took a deep breath. "We managed to get quite a bit of information. Richter was cooperative, and provided details about his background, duties, and some tactical observations."

Staff Sergeant Lewis nodded. "Good start. What did you think of his demeanor?"

"He seemed resigned but willing to talk," Tom replied. "He didn't offer much resistance, but he was cautious with specific details."

Corporal Davies chimed in. "Did you notice any patterns or shifts in his behavior that indicated he was holding back?"

Benjamin thought for a moment. "He seemed more guarded when we asked about future plans and high-level intelligence. He might know more than he's letting on."

Lieutenant Baker nodded. "That's a good observation. Sometimes they hold back the most important information. You need to dig deeper, build more rapport."

"Your questions were thorough, but you can always probe a bit more," Staff Sergeant Lewis added. "Get them talking about something personal, something they care about. It can lead to more valuable intel."

Corporal Davies gave a half-smile. "And remember, not every piece of information will be a goldmine. Sometimes it's about piecing together the small details."

As they continued discussing their interrogation techniques, Benjamin noticed subtle hints of homophobia in some remarks from Staff Sergeant Lewis.

"Just be careful," Lewis said with a chuckle. "These Germans can be slippery. You never know what they might be hiding. And watch out for the pretty boys. They can be the most dangerous."

Benjamin tensed slightly, glancing at Tom, who gave a barely perceptible nod. They both knew they had to be cautious, not just with the prisoners but with their own colleagues.

Lieutenant Baker wrapped up the debrief. "Good work today, both of you. Keep refining your techniques, and remember, every detail counts. Dismissed."

As Benjamin and Tom left the briefing room, they exchanged a look of understanding. They had to stay vigilant, not just in their duties but in guarding their own secrets.

Chapter Seven

Fort Hunt, Virginia, August 16, 1943

The Allied invasion of Sicily, known as Operation Husky, saw crucial developments in early August, culminating in a significant event on August 11. The U.S. 3rd Infantry Division conducted an amphibious landing at Brolo Beach, aimed at accelerating the advance towards Messina and cutting off the Axis forces' retreat to the Italian mainland.

This operation consisted of multiple waves of landings. The first wave touched down at 0243 hours, encountering no initial resistance and quickly moving inland to secure key positions, including lemon groves and railroad embankments. Subsequent waves followed shortly, bringing additional infantry, tanks, and artillery. Despite logistical challenges, such as maneuvering tanks around obstacles, the operation initially maintained the element of surprise.

However, as the American forces progressed further inland, they met German resistance. A German half-track and a small sedan engaged American troops, leading to an exchange of fire that alerted German forces in the area. German machine guns and 20-mm cannons responded, resulting in casualties on both sides. Despite this, U.S. forces managed to establish a foothold, block key routes, and prepare for further advances.

The landing at Brolo Beach was part of the broader Allied strategy to expel Axis forces from Sicily and ultimately pave the way for an invasion of the Italian mainland.

The Allied air forces were notably active in August, conducting several significant bombing raids aimed at crippling Axis resources and infrastructure. Among these, Operation Tidal Wave stands out as a particularly impactful mission. Taking place on August 1, this operation involved a daring low-level bombing raid by U.S. bombers targeting the vital oil refineries in Ploiești, Romania.

The Ploiești oil fields were a critical source of fuel for the Axis powers, producing a significant portion of Germany's petroleum needs. By disrupting this supply, the Allies aimed to severely hinder the German war machine. The mission was ambitious and fraught with danger, involving a long-range flight of over 2,400 miles from bases in North Africa to the heavily defended target.

Over 170 B-24 Liberators participated in the raid, flying at dangerously low altitudes to evade radar detection and anti-aircraft defenses. Despite meticulous planning, the operation faced numerous challenges. Navigation errors and strong defenses led to heavy losses; of the bombers that took part, 54 were lost and many others were damaged. The crews faced intense anti-aircraft fire, fighter interceptions, and the hazardous nature of flying at such low altitudes over industrial targets.

Nevertheless, the raid caused significant damage to the Ploieşti refineries, temporarily reducing the output of vital fuel supplies for the Axis powers. The impact of the raid was a mixed outcome: while it achieved its objective of damaging the refineries, the high cost in aircraft and lives made it one of the most costly missions for the U.S. Army Air Forces during the war.

Operation Tidal Wave demonstrated the strategic importance of targeting industrial resources and highlighted the bravery and sacrifices of the aircrews involved. It underscored the Allies' commitment to crippling the Axis war effort by attacking critical supply lines and infrastructure.

Morning rain had been pouring down over Fort Hunt, casting a dreary shadow over the facility. Benjamin and Tom entered the interrogation room, their expressions focused and determined. Over the course of the past ten days, Benjamin and Todd conducted eight more interrogations. By this time, they had been given an ample amount of practice honing their skills. Across from them sat Karl Schmidt, a low-level SS officer and engineer, captured during a recent operation. They recognized the potential value in extracting insights about German military technology from such individuals.

Benjamin initiated the conversation with general questions about Karl's background and SS responsibilities. "Can you tell us a bit about yourself and your background before joining the military?"

Karl, with a stoic expression, began to reveal fragments of his past. "I grew up in a small town near Berlin. My father was a mechanic, so I was always tinkering with machines as a kid. Joining the SS was a way to contribute to something bigger than myself."

Tom, sensing an opportunity to delve deeper, interjected, "How did your family background and upbringing shape your values and decision to join the SS?"

Karl paused, a brief flicker of introspection crossing his face before he replied, "My family instilled a sense of duty and loyalty, which influenced my choice to join."

As the conversation progressed, Benjamin and Tom posed more questions, aiming to unravel Karl's motivations and experiences.

Benjamin leaned forward, his tone measured but probing. "Can you share any memorable experiences or challenges you faced during your training and early years in the military?"

Karl hesitated, choosing his words carefully. "Training was rigorous and focused, with challenges that tested our abilities."

Tom followed up, "What inspired you to pursue a career in engineering within the military context?"

Karl replied, "Engineering allowed me to apply my skills strategically for the greater cause."

Benjamin continued, "Were there any influential figures or mentors who guided your career path and choices?"

Karl nodded, a hint of admiration in his tone. "I greatly admired Wernher von Braun. His work in rocketry and engineering was groundbreaking, and I aspired to follow in his footsteps."

Tom sought broader insights, asking, "How do you view the intersection of your engineering expertise and the broader goals of the German military during the war?"

Karl responded, "Engineering plays a crucial role in advancing military capabilities and strategies."

Benjamin then asked, "Can you describe a moment when your engineering skills were put to the test in a critical situation or project?"

Karl recounted, "There were moments of intense pressure, but that's expected in our line of work."

Tom delved into ethical considerations, inquiring, "Were there any ethical dilemmas or considerations you encountered in your engineering work, especially regarding military projects?"

Karl acknowledged, "Engineering work requires adherence to protocols and standards, which sometimes raise ethical questions."

Having built some rapport and understanding, Benjamin shifted the conversation towards more sensitive topics related to wartime technology.

"Can you provide insights into the locations of strategic facilities or research centers where advanced weapons are being developed?" Benjamin probed, his tone measured.

Karl paused, choosing his words carefully. "I am aware of several facilities scattered across Germany, but their exact locations are classified and closely guarded."

Tom nodded, following up with, "Are there specific scientists, engineers, or military personnel known for their involvement in secret weapons projects?"

Karl's expression remained neutral. "There are experts in various fields working on these projects, but their identities and roles are strictly confidential."

Benjamin continued, "Have you been briefed on any upcoming deployments or tests of new weapons systems? Any notable developments or breakthroughs you can share?"

Karl's response was measured. "I receive operational updates, but specific details on deployments or breakthroughs are restricted to authorized personnel."

Tom probed further, "Can you share any information about the timelines or milestones for the development and deployment of these advanced weapons?"

Karl's response was guarded. "Timelines are fluid, contingent on testing outcomes, logistical considerations, and strategic priorities."

Benjamin posed another question, "Have you encountered any challenges or setbacks in the development of new weapons systems that you are aware of?"

Karl acknowledged, "Technical challenges are expected in such projects, but our teams are resilient and adaptive."

Tom, seeking broader insights, inquired, "Are there any rumors or speculations within military circles about secret weapons projects or facilities?"

Karl's response was diplomatic. "Rumors are common, but distinguishing fact from fiction is difficult in the realm of classified projects."

After suggesting a break, Benjamin stepped outside the interrogation room and approached the guard. "Could you bring us some light beers and a carton of smokes?" he requested, noting that Karl had unknowingly revealed a clue by admitting his admiration for Wernher von Braun and rockets.

Returning to the room with a six-pack of Coors Light beer and a case of Lucky Strike cigarettes, Benjamin resumed the interrogation, probing relentlessly in the direction of Karl's relationship with Wernher von Braun and their potential meetings. "Have you ever had the opportunity to meet Wernher von Braun in person? If so, where and under what circumstances?"

Karl, slightly taken aback by the shift in questioning, hesitated before responding. "I was part of the team that helped design Wernher von Braun's new laboratory."

Benjamin seized on this admission, pushing further. "Can you elaborate on your involvement in designing the laboratory?

Karl, visibly cautious now, measured his words carefully. "I was involved in the structural planning and logistical aspects of the laboratory."

Benjamin leaned forward, his tone measured yet probing. "What were some of the challenges you encountered while designing the laboratory?"

Karl hesitated, choosing his words cautiously. "The location on an island posed unique challenges in terms of transportation and infrastructure development."

Sensing Karl's guardedness, Tom interjected, "Could you describe the island where the laboratory is located? How did its geography impact the construction?"

Karl's responses remained vague, hinting at the complexity of the project without divulging specific details. "The island is surrounded by water, making construction and supply logistics quite intricate."

As the interrogation progressed, Benjamin maintained a steady line of questioning, trying to navigate through Karl's evasiveness. "Karl, let's talk about the rockets that were recently test-launched over the Baltic Sea. Were they developed and produced at this laboratory?"

Karl's expression tightened slightly, a subtle sign of discomfort. "The laboratory was involved in various projects, including rocket development."

Benjamin pressed further, "Can you confirm whether the rockets that were tested over the Baltic Sea originated from this island?"

Karl hesitated, weighing his words carefully. "I am aware of projects involving advanced weaponry, but specifics are restricted information."

Tom, sensing Karl's reluctance to disclose critical details, tried a different approach. "Karl, can you share any insights into the testing or deployment processes for these rockets?"

Karl's response was guarded. "Operational details are closely guarded and restricted to authorized personnel."

Hours passed as Benjamin and Tom continued their relentless questioning, probing into Karl's involvement, his knowledge of the laboratory's operations, and the specifics of the rocket projects. Each question was met with cautious responses, revealing fragments of information while withholding critical details.

Benjamin leaned back momentarily, studying Karl's demeanor. "Karl, you've mentioned that you greatly admire Wernher von Braun. Have you ever had personal interactions with him? Perhaps during your work at the laboratory?"

Karl's expression softened slightly at the mention of Wernher von Braun. "I had the opportunity to observe his work and contributions closely."

Tom saw an opening and pursued it. "Could you share any specific insights or experiences you gained from working alongside Wernher von Braun?"

Karl's response was guarded yet revealing. "Working with him provided valuable insights into rocketry and advanced engineering principles."

Benjamin, sensing a shift in Karl's disposition, pressed on. "Karl, we understand the complexity of your situation. However, we believe that cooperation can benefit everyone involved. Can you disclose any details about the testing sites or launch procedures for these rockets?"

Karl's demeanor remained composed, but a flicker of hesitation crossed his face. "Such information is classified and restricted."

The interrogation stretched into the night, with Benjamin and Tom meticulously navigating through Karl's guarded responses, probing for any cracks in his defenses. The dim light cast shadows on the walls, adding to the tension in the room. Hours had passed, the clock ticking incessantly, each second a reminder of their diminishing patience.

Tom rubbed his temples and leaned over to Benjamin. "We're getting nowhere," he whispered. "I think it's time we change tactics."

Benjamin nodded, recognizing the futility of their current approach. Tom stood up, his chair scraping loudly against the concrete floor, and left the room without a word. Karl's eyes followed him, a flicker of curiosity crossing his face.

Tom strode down the corridor, his steps echoing in the silence. He approached a guard and spoke in hushed tones, instructing him to arrange for a prisoner transfer vehicle to be brought to the rear entrance of the facility. The guard nodded and hurried off to carry out the order.

Minutes later, Tom returned to the interrogation room, his face set in a grim expression. He looked at Karl with cold determination. "We've decided you're being transferred," he said flatly. "You're not being cooperative, and we have no further use for you."

Karl's stoic facade cracked ever so slightly, a hint of uncertainty in his eyes. Benjamin and Tom led him out of the room, his hands bound and a blindfold placed over his eyes. The corridor seemed endless as they guided him through the labyrinthine halls of the facility.

Outside, the night air was cool and biting. They loaded Karl into the back of the prisoner transfer vehicle, its engine rumbling to life. The vehicle began to move, weaving through the darkened pathways around the facility. Karl sat in tense silence, the blindfold heightening his other senses, making every bump and turn more jarring.

They drove for what felt like hours, the monotonous drone of the engine and the endless loops around the facility adding to Karl's disorientation. Finally, they pulled up to an unused and dilapidated area of the old Fort Hunt, the buildings there long abandoned and crumbling.

The vehicle came to a halt, and the door was flung open. Karl was roughly pulled out, his feet hitting the gravel with a crunch. The blindfold was ripped away, and he blinked against the sudden light of a single, flickering lamppost.

Standing before him was an American soldier dressed in a Soviet military uniform, the red star glaring ominously in the dim light. Benjamin stepped forward, his voice steady and cold. "This is your new handler," he said, gesturing to the soldier. "Since you're of no use to us, we're trading you to the Russians. Maybe they'll find a way to get the information out of you."

Karl's eyes widened, panic setting in. He knew the Soviets' reputation for brutality, their methods far more ruthless than anything he had faced so far. "Wait," he stammered, his voice shaking. "You can't do this."

Benjamin and Tom exchanged a look but remained silent, their expressions unforgiving. The Soviet soldier stepped forward, his presence menacing. "Let's go," he said in heavily accented English, grabbing Karl's arm.

Karl resisted, his desperation palpable. "No, please," he pleaded. "I'll tell you what you want to know. Just don't hand me over to them."

Benjamin folded his arms, his expression inscrutable. "Start talking," he demanded.

Karl swallowed hard, his composure shattered. "The rockets," he began, his voice trembling, "The rockets that you're referring to, the V-1, a pulsejet-powered cruise missile, and the V-2, a liquid-fueled ballistic missile, are being developed and built by Wernher von Braun at the Peenemünde laboratory."

Tom nodded slightly, a signal to the Soviet soldier, who released Karl's arm. Benjamin stepped closer, his voice still stern. "If we find out you're lying or holding back, this trade will go through. Understood?"

Karl nodded frantically, relief washing over him as he realized he had bought himself some time, even if only temporarily. The information had been extracted, and the night's efforts had finally paid off. The tension slowly ebbed from the air as they led Karl back to his cell, the weight of the night's revelations settling in.

The next steps were clear. They had a crucial piece of the puzzle, and it was time to act on it.

With this breakthrough admission, Benjamin and Tom had achieved a significant victory in their investigation. Peenemünde's involvement in developing the devastating rockets was now confirmed, marking a crucial turning point in their pursuit of vital intelligence.

The rain continued to pour as Benjamin and Tom made their way to the briefing room, their minds racing with the implications of Karl Schmidt's guarded responses. The debriefing room, illuminated by a dim overhead light, was filled with maps and documents detailing the ongoing efforts of the intelligence unit.

Lieutenant Baker stood at the head of the table, his stern expression softening slightly as he saw Benjamin and Tom enter the room. Staff Sergeant Lewis and Corporal Davies were already seated, awaiting the report with a mixture of anticipation and concern.

"Gentlemen," Lieutenant Baker began, his voice steady, "let's get started. What did you manage to extract from Schmidt?"

Benjamin took a deep breath, collecting his thoughts before he spoke. "Karl Schmidt was cautious, but we managed to get some valuable information. He mentioned his admiration for Wernher von Braun and his involvement in designing a new laboratory for him."

Tom nodded, adding, "Schmidt revealed that the laboratory is located on an island, which posed significant logistical challenges. He also confirmed the involvement of this facility in rocket development."

Lieutenant Baker's eyes narrowed with interest. "Did he mention any specific projects or weapons systems?"

"Yes," Benjamin replied, "Schmidt confirmed that the V-1 and V-2 rockets are being developed at the Peenemünde laboratory. This confirms our suspicions about the lab's role in advanced weaponry."

Staff Sergeant Lewis leaned forward, his expression serious. "Did he provide any details about the testing or deployment of these rockets?"

Tom shook his head. "He was very guarded about operational specifics. He acknowledged knowing about the projects but didn't provide concrete details on testing sites or launch procedures."

Corporal Davies, who had been silently listening, finally spoke. "What about the broader context? Did he reveal anything about the strategic importance of these projects or any upcoming plans?"

Benjamin exchanged a glance with Tom before responding. "Schmidt didn't provide specific timelines or strategic plans, but his hesitation suggested that these projects are high-priority and closely monitored by the German military."

Lieutenant Baker nodded thoughtfully, absorbing the information. "This aligns with other intelligence we've gathered. Peenemünde's involvement in rocket development is a critical piece of the puzzle. Your interrogation has provided us with valuable insights."

Benjamin leaned forward, his tone earnest. "We need to analyze this information and integrate it with other intelligence reports. Schmidt's guarded responses suggest there's more to uncover about Peenemünde's operations and their strategic plans."

Lieutenant Baker agreed. "We'll need to intensify our efforts and collaborate with other units to piece together the full picture. This breakthrough is significant, but it's just the beginning."

Staff Sergeant Lewis spoke up again, his voice resolute. "We should also consider the ethical implications of our interrogation methods. Schmidt's guardedness indicates he's aware of the stakes. We need to balance our pursuit of information with maintaining our moral standards."

Tom nodded in agreement. "Building rapport and gaining trust is crucial. We should continue to approach these interrogations with a focus on ethical conduct and strategic questioning."

Lieutenant Baker concluded the debriefing, his tone firm yet encouraging. "You've done excellent work today, both of you. Let's continue to push forward, gather more intelligence, and ensure that our efforts contribute to the broader war effort."

As the debriefing ended, Benjamin and Tom felt a sense of accomplishment mixed with the weight of the challenges ahead. They had made a significant breakthrough, but the path to uncovering the full extent of Peenemünde's operations and its implications for the war was still long and fraught with complexity.

The mess hall was abuzz with the chatter of soldiers winding down after a long day. The aroma of hot food mingled with the sound of clinking utensils and the hum of conversations. Benjamin and Tom, still processing the gravity of their breakthrough, made their way to the serving line.

Grabbing trays, they loaded up on the evening's offerings: roasted chicken, mashed potatoes, and steamed vegetables. With plates in hand, they found a quiet corner away from the din of the main hall, eager to discuss the day's events in relative privacy.

Tom took a bite of his roasted chicken, savoring the rare moment of stillness. "Can you believe it? We actually got him to admit Peenemünde's involvement in the V-1 and V-2 rockets."

Benjamin nodded, his eyes reflecting the weight of their achievement. "It was a hard-fought interrogation, but we did it. Confirming that information is a major step forward. It feels surreal, thinking about the impact this could have."

Tom leaned back in his chair, a thoughtful expression on his face. "Just knowing that our work might save lives...it makes all the effort worth it. Those rockets have caused so much devastation. Stopping them, or at least disrupting their development, could turn the tide."

Benjamin took a deep breath, the exhaustion of the day beginning to catch up with him. "We've still got a lot of work ahead, but today was a victory. We've got to keep pushing, keep digging. Every piece of information we uncover brings us closer to ending this war."

Tom nodded, a determined look in his eyes. "Yeah, you're right. It's not just about gathering intelligence; it's about using it to make a difference. We've got to keep our focus and remember why we're doing this."

A brief silence settled between them as they ate, each lost in their thoughts. The mess hall continued to buzz around them, but in their corner, a sense of quiet pride and resolve took hold.

Benjamin finally broke the silence. "We make a good team, Tom. Today proved that."

Tom smiled, a hint of camaraderie in his eyes. "We do, Benjamin. And we'll keep pushing forward together. Here's to many more victories."

They clinked their forks together in a makeshift toast, a small gesture of celebration amidst the chaos of war. As they finished their meal, the enormity of their accomplishment settled in. They had taken a significant step in their mission, and the sense of pride they felt was palpable.

With renewed determination, Benjamin and Tom left the mess hall, ready to face whatever challenges lay ahead, knowing that their efforts were making a real difference.

Chapter Eight

Fort Hunt, Virginia, September 09, 1943

In the preceding weeks, Allied forces achieved a pivotal milestone in their campaign to liberate the island of Sicily from Axis control. The conquest of Sicily, a meticulously planned and fiercely executed operation, culminated in the surrender of Italian forces on the island. The relentless push by Allied troops, comprising American, British, and Canadian forces under the operational command of General Bernard Montgomery, had gradually worn down the Axis defenses.

The final stages of the invasion saw intense fighting as Allied troops battled through rugged terrain, fortified positions, and determined resistance from German and Italian forces. The conquest of key cities such as Palermo, Catania, and Messina showcased the strategic prowess and coordinated efforts of the Allied command. Air superiority, naval support, and innovative tactics played crucial roles in overcoming entrenched defenses and securing vital objectives.

The surrender of Italian forces on Sicily not only marked a significant territorial gain for the Allies but also foreshadowed the imminent collapse of Italy's military alliance with Nazi Germany. The stage was set for the next phase of the Allied campaign—the invasion of mainland Italy.

Amidst the tumultuous battlefield successes and strategic strikes, world leaders convened in the serene setting of Quebec City, Canada, for a pivotal conference that would shape the course of the war. Winston Churchill, the resolute Prime Minister of Great Britain, and Franklin D. Roosevelt, the steadfast President of the United States, engaged in intense deliberations.

The Quebec Conference served as a crucible for forging crucial decisions and laying out grand strategies for the Allied powers. Discussions revolved around pivotal topics such as the impending invasion of France, codenamed Operation Overlord, which aimed to establish a Western front against Nazi Germany. The intricate planning, logistical considerations, and diplomatic negotiations formed the backbone of Operation Overlord's preparations, setting the stage for one of the most decisive campaigns of the war.

Additionally, the conference delved into increased operations in the Pacific Theater, addressing the multifaceted challenges posed by Imperial Japan's expansive ambitions and relentless aggression in the

Pacific region. Coordination of resources, military deployments, and strategic alliances formed the crux of discussions, emphasizing the global nature of the conflict and the collaborative efforts required for victory.

The Quebec Conference, held behind closed doors yet reverberating with historical significance, laid the groundwork for pivotal campaigns and diplomatic maneuvers that would shape the trajectory of the war.

In the dark hours of August 17, a fleet of Allied bombers soared through the skies toward a secretive complex nestled along the Baltic coast of northern Germany—the Peenemünde Army Research Center. This clandestine facility, shrouded in mystery and buzzing with activity, was at the forefront of Nazi Germany's advanced weapons program, spearheaded by figures like Wernher von Braun.

The Allies, well aware of the devastating potential of the V-1 and V-2 rockets being developed and tested at Peenemünde, launched a daring and massive bombing raid. The objective was clear: disrupt and dismantle Nazi Germany's capabilities to unleash these deadly weapons upon Allied territories.

As the bombers unleashed their payloads, the night sky was illuminated with explosions, unleashing chaos and destruction upon the Peenemünde complex. The strategic bombing aimed at key infrastructure, production facilities, and research laboratories, aiming to cripple the progress of the V-weapons program.

While the raid caused significant damage and temporarily disrupted production, the aftermath revealed a grim reality—the Germans swiftly adapted by moving much of their rocket development underground. This strategic shift mitigated the immediate impact of the bombing raid on their operations, highlighting the resilience and resourcefulness of Nazi Germany's war machine.

Wernher von Braun was present at the Peenemünde laboratory during the time of the Allied bombing raid. He, along with most of his key personnel, survived the bombing.

Benjamin and Tom stood at attention in Colonel Everett Stone's office, the heavy air of anticipation filling the room. The colonel, seated behind his imposing desk, shuffled through a stack of papers before finally looking up, his deep and robust voice breaking the silence.

"Gentlemen, I have reviewed the reports from your recent interrogation of Karl Schmidt," Colonel Stone began, his eyes steady on them. "The information you extracted is invaluable. You both performed exceptionally well under pressure."

Tom exchanged a quick, triumphant glance with Benjamin, who maintained his composed demeanor despite the swell of pride within him.

"Given your success," Colonel Stone continued, "it is my honor to inform you that you are both being promoted. Private Richardson, you are now to be addressed as Sergeant, and Private Steinberg, you will assume the rank of Corporal. Congratulations."

The weight of the promotion settled over them like a tangible cloak of responsibility and recognition. They snapped a crisp salute, which the colonel returned with a nod of approval.

"At ease," he said, leaning back in his chair. "Staff Sergeant Lewis and Corporal Davies have been swamped with high-level prisoners, and frankly, they could use the support. Effective immediately, you two will be taking over the handling of several prisoners that have proven particularly challenging. Because of your new ranks, you'll be given more leeway in your tactics and techniques, as well as more resources available to you during interrogations to assist in the effective extraction of intelligence."

As Colonel Stone finished speaking, Staff Sergeant Lewis entered the office, his expression sour. He saluted perfunctorily before addressing the colonel. "Sir, I'm more than happy to hand over the 'pretty boy' prisoner to these two," he said, his tone dripping with disdain. "That one's been giving us a particularly hard time—slippery, manipulative, and downright degenerate."

Lewis's eyes flicked to Benjamin and Tom, a sneer tugging at his lips. "Good luck with that one," he added with a mocking tone.

Tom bristled at Lewis's words but kept his face neutral. Benjamin, too, felt a surge of anger but reined it in, focusing on the task at hand. Colonel Stone's face hardened.

"Staff Sergeant Lewis," the Colonel said sternly, "such language and attitude towards prisoners, regardless of their behavior, is unprofessional and unbecoming of your rank. I expect better."

Lewis's sneer faltered slightly, and he mumbled an acknowledgment before turning to leave.

Once Lewis was gone, Colonel Stone addressed them again. "The prisoner in question is indeed difficult, but I have confidence in your abilities. Approach him with the same strategic thinking and persistence you demonstrated with Schmidt. We need whatever information he might be holding."

Benjamin and Tom nodded, understanding the gravity of their new assignment. As they left the colonel's office, their minds were already turning over strategies for handling this new challenge. The weight of their promotions and the responsibility it entailed pressed down on them, but it was a burden they were ready to bear. They knew the road ahead would be fraught with difficulties, but with each other's support, they were determined to succeed.

As they walked down the corridor, Tom broke the silence. "Looks like we're in for another tough one."

Benjamin nodded, his eyes focused ahead. "We'll handle it, just like we did with Schmidt. Together."

And with that, they steeled themselves for the next chapter in their mission, knowing that the stakes had never been higher.

Benjamin and Tom walked down the corridor toward the interrogation room, the fluorescent lights flickering slightly as they went. The air was thick with anticipation; today marked their first meeting with Erik Müller, the 'pretty boy' prisoner who had given Sergeant Lewis such a hard time.

Tom, now a Sergeant, had the details in hand. "Colonel Stone said this guy is smart. Real smart. We need to be careful, Ben."

Benjamin nodded, his thoughts occupied by the unusual task ahead. They entered the room to find Erik already seated, hands shackled but posture relaxed. He was striking, with dark blond hair neatly trimmed, and icy blue eyes that seemed to see right through them. Despite his imprisonment, he exuded an unsettling calm.

Benjamin took his seat opposite Erik, trying to push aside the unsettling mixture of fascination and fear that Erik's presence stirred in him. Tom stood behind Benjamin, observing silently.

"Good morning, Herr Müller," Benjamin began, his voice steady. "I trust you've been made comfortable?"

Erik's lips curled into a sardonic smile. "As comfortable as one can be in such circumstances. But I appreciate the courtesy."

"I'm Corporal Benjamin Steinberg, and this is Sergeant Tom Richardson. We'll be conducting your interrogation for the foreseeable future."

Erik gave Benjamin a faint smirk. "Ah, fresh faces. How delightful," he said, his voice smooth and untroubled. "Let's see what you can do that your predecessors couldn't."

Benjamin, eager to get into his flow, began with some personal questions and remarks aimed at building a rapport with his new subject. He said, "According to your report, it says that your father is a high-ranking official in the German government. What was that like for you, growing up?"

Erik's eyes flickered with a hint of amusement, but his voice remained measured. "My father is indeed a significant figure. It brought a certain…prestige and pressure to our family life. Expectations were always high."

Benjamin nodded, sensing an opportunity to delve deeper. "I imagine that must have influenced your career path significantly. You studied physics at a prestigious university, correct?"

"That's correct," Erik replied, his tone calm and collected. "Physics was my passion, and I was fortunate enough to pursue it at one of the finest institutions in Germany."

"Before the war," Benjamin continued, "you were working on advancing military technology. Can you tell us more about your work and how you became involved in it?"

Erik leaned back slightly, a small smile playing on his lips. "My expertise in physics naturally led to my involvement in military projects. Before the war, I was involved in more conventional military technology projects. It was a stepping stone of sorts, laying the groundwork for more specialized endeavors later on. But it was not by choice; it was more of a…duty imposed by my circumstances and family expectations."

Benjamin noted Erik's careful choice of words and decided to probe a bit further. "Did you have any influential mentors during your career? Anyone who particularly guided or inspired you?"

Erik's expression softened for a moment. "Yes, there were several. But one senior scientist, in particular, was like a mentor to me. He taught me a great deal about both science and the intricacies of our work."

Benjamin made a mental note of this, recognizing a potential lead for further questioning. "And your personal life, Erik? Did you have any significant relationships before the war?"

A shadow passed over Erik's face, and he paused before responding. "There was someone, yes. But those are matters of the past, Corporal."

Benjamin sensed the weight of Erik's words and the personal pain behind them.

Benjamin leaned back in his chair, a thoughtful expression on his face. "Believe it or not, Erik, I know a little something about family expectations." He paused, gathering his thoughts before continuing. "My family has a history that goes back to Germany as well. They left their entire life behind to immigrate to the United States during the 'Great War.'"

Erik's interest piqued as he listened intently to Benjamin's personal story.

"My parents instilled in me the responsibility to do my duty to this country in return for all of the blessings and opportunities that America had given us," Benjamin recounted. "They sacrificed everything to make sure that I would grow up to become an honorable man, one who upholds the values of integrity and service."

There was a brief silence in the room as Erik absorbed Benjamin's words. It was a moment of connection, bridging the gap between interrogator and prisoner with a shared understanding of family, duty, and sacrifice.

"Family expectations can be a heavy burden," Benjamin added, his voice carrying a mix of reflection and determination. "But they also shape who we are and what we strive for."

Erik nodded slowly, a hint of acknowledgment in his eyes. Despite their opposing roles in the interrogation, there was a growing sense of respect and recognition between them, forged through shared experiences and a deeper understanding of the complexities of duty and loyalty.

Tom pulled out a fresh pack of cigarettes and began slapping the box in his hand to pack the tobacco. He pulled the cellophane wrapper off and pulled out a cigarette. Pressing the cigarette butt between his lips, he extended his arm, offering the pack to Erik, who graciously accepted and pulled out a cigarette for himself. Tom raised out of his seat, leaning across the table to light

Erik's cigarette, and then his own. He took a strong drag off his cigarette as he settled back into his chair.

Tom asked, "You mentioned that your involvement in the development of military technology was not by choice, that it was a duty imposed by your circumstances and family expectations. Did you not want to be involved in the military technology field? Did you experience ethical issues with the types of weapons you were developing?"

Tom's question cut through the tension in the room, adding a layer of depth to the interrogation. Erik's eyes narrowed slightly, considering his response carefully before speaking.

"I didn't have the luxury of choice," Erik replied, his tone carrying a hint of resignation. "My family's expectations and the circumstances of the time dictated my path. It was a duty, as you say, one that I couldn't easily shirk."

Tom nodded, acknowledging the weight of Erik's words. "But did you find yourself conflicted with the work you were doing? Developing weapons, especially those with destructive capabilities, must have raised ethical questions."

Erik's gaze drifted for a moment, a flicker of introspection crossing his features. "Ethics are a complex matter, Sergeant," he began, his voice measured. "In wartime, lines blur, and choices are often made in shades of gray. I won't deny that there were moments of moral ambiguity, but duty and loyalty overshadowed personal reservations."

Benjamin observed the exchange, noting the subtle shift in Erik's demeanor. It was clear that beneath Erik's confident facade lay layers of inner conflict and doubt.

Tom leaned forward slightly, his tone gentle yet probing. "Can you elaborate on one of those moments, Erik? A situation where your moral compass clashed with your obligations?"

Erik hesitated briefly, the weight of the question palpable in the air. "There was a project," he began slowly, choosing his words with care. "A weapon system that I had reservations about, both ethically and strategically. But dissent wasn't tolerated, and my concerns were brushed aside in the name of progress."

Benjamin caught the implication in Erik's words, recognizing the significance of this admission. It was a delicate balance between extracting information and navigating Erik's emotional vulnerabilities.

As the interrogation continued, Tom and Benjamin delved deeper into Erik's experiences, probing for insights into his moral dilemmas and the inner workings of the Nazi war machine. Each question peeled back another layer of Erik's psyche, revealing a complex and conflicted individual caught in the tumult of war and duty.

Benjamin acknowledges, "It must have been incredibly challenging to work on a project that conflicted with your ethics. The emotional toll must have been significant. I can only imagine how difficult that must have been for you."

Erik's demeanor shifted subtly. His initial calmness evolved into a more assertive stance, and he began to challenge Benjamin's interrogation methods with his own sharp wit.

Erik leaned forward, his ice-blue eyes locking with Benjamin's. "You're trying to build rapport, Corporal," he remarked, his voice carrying a confident yet measured tone. "But don't mistake camaraderie for compliance. I know what you're after, and I won't make it easy for you."

Benjamin met Erik's gaze steadily, unfazed by the challenge. "I appreciate your candor, Erik," he responded evenly. "But I'm not here to play games. We both know the gravity of the situation."

The dynamic between them shifted into a subtle battle of intellects. Erik skillfully deflected personal questions, steering the conversation toward neutral topics while dropping hints of his own intelligence and resourcefulness. Benjamin, on the other hand, maintained a composed yet probing approach, subtly guiding the dialogue back to areas of interest without appearing confrontational.

Their exchange was a dance of words, each move calculated and strategic. Erik's wit tested Benjamin's patience and perseverance, while Benjamin's probing questions prodded at the edges of Erik's defenses.

Despite the tension in the air, there was an underlying respect between them, born from a mutual recognition of each other's capabilities. It was a unique dynamic, one that set the stage for a battle of minds as they navigated through layers of deception and secrecy.

Erik recounted, "You know, when Staff Sergeant Lewis wanted to talk, he would always bring me an ice-cold bottle of Jägermeister and a rocks glass to drink it out of." He glanced down at the cuffs and chains anchoring him to the table, shaking his wrists to make the chains rattle loudly. "He would also remove my restraints."

Tom, sensing the elevated tension in the room, stood up and said, "How about we take a break? Would you like to use the toilet, Erik?" Erik politely declined. Tom gestured to Benjamin to step outside with him.

As they stepped out of the interrogation room, Tom turned to Benjamin with a thoughtful expression. "He's not like the others, Ben. There's more to him than meets the eye."

Benjamin nodded, his mind already racing with possibilities. "I noticed. He's sharp, and there's a certain defiance in him."

"He's playing a game," Tom observed, "but I don't think it's just for show. There's something he's holding back. We need to dig deeper, find out what he's hiding."

"I agree," Benjamin replied, leaning against the wall. He felt a pang in his stomach at the suggestion. The thought of relentlessly digging into someone's deep, personal secrets hit close to home, and made him feel a little sick. "But we need to do it delicately and respectfully."

Tom crossed his arms, deep in thought. "Do you think we should get him some Jägermeister?"

"If that's what Staff Sergeant Lewis was doing—I guess it couldn't hurt. I'll see what I can scrounge up."

Benjamin vanished down the hallway for a brief interval. Upon his return, he carried an ice-cold bottle of Jägermeister accompanied by a rocks glass. Stepping back into the interrogation room, he observed Tom had already liberated Erik from his restraints, earning a surprised glance from Tom. Benjamin's smirk conveyed his mischief as he announced, "I stumbled upon this in the officer's lounge. They've got a fully stocked bar in there." Tom's eyebrows lifted in astonishment.

Benjamin enthusiastically set the bottle and glass down in front of Erik with a flourish.

"Wonderbar!" Erik smiled widely, his perfect white teeth gleaming under the light of the interrogation room. He pulled out another cigarette, motioning for Tom to light it as he poured himself a heavy shot of the thick, dark liqueur.

Benjamin decided to shift the conversation back to their immediate interests. "Let's talk about the military technology that you were working on before your capture. What can you tell us about its development and capabilities?"

Erik's demeanor shifted back to a more guarded stance. "I'm sure you understand that such information is highly sensitive. But I can tell you that it was designed with the intention of reaching targets far beyond Europe."

Benjamin leaned in slightly, his voice steady. "We need specifics, Erik. Locations, technical details, anything that can help us understand and counter these threats."

Erik met Benjamin's gaze, his icy blue eyes unwavering. "And why should I divulge such information to you, Corporal?"

Benjamin held his gaze, trying to project confidence and authority. "Because, Erik, cooperation could be beneficial for both of us. It's in your best interest to help us."

A tense silence filled the room as Erik weighed his options. Benjamin could feel the complexity of the situation deepening, but he was determined to find a way through Erik's defenses. The interrogation had only just begun, and already, Benjamin sensed that this was going to be unlike any other he had conducted before.

The hours passed with little progress. Erik deftly deflected their questions, turning each one back on them with a mix of sarcasm and wit. His intelligence was evident, and his ability to maintain control over the conversation was impressive.

Benjamin found himself both frustrated and intrigued. Erik's calm, almost playful demeanor was a stark contrast to the guarded responses they usually encountered. As they continued, Benjamin couldn't help but feel a growing sense of fascination, mingled with an unease he couldn't quite place.

Erik's eyes flicked to Benjamin, noting the slight furrow in his brow. "You seem distracted, Corporal. Is there something on your mind?"

Benjamin stiffened, his professional façade slipping momentarily. "Just trying to understand you, Erik. You're quite the enigma."

Erik chuckled softly. "An enigma, am I? That's quite flattering. But perhaps it's you who should be the focus of understanding. What drives you, Corporal? What makes you tick?"

Tom shot Benjamin a concerned glance, but Benjamin waved him off. "We're not here to talk about me, Erik. This is about you and what you know."

"Of course," Erik said, his voice smooth as silk. "But isn't it more interesting when conversations are a two-way street? You ask your questions, and I might just answer. But in return, I'd like to know a bit about you."

As the interrogation stretched into the night, Benjamin and Tom found themselves caught in a delicate dance of words and wits. Erik's responses were elusive, yet each exchange seemed to peel back another layer of his enigmatic persona.

Tom suddenly realized how late it had gotten, so he decided it was time to call it quits for the night. The Colonel had left hours ago, so their debriefing on the day's progress would have to wait until morning. He stepped outside to notify the guard that Erik was ready to be taken back to the detention building.

As Tom stepped outside to speak with the guard, Erik leaned across the table, bringing his face so close to Benjamin's that their noses were nearly touching. Benjamin could feel the warmth of Erik's breath on his lips, an unexpected and disconcerting sensation.

Erik's voice dropped to a whisper, smooth and suggestive. "Detainees are free to move around the detention building between 1500 and 2000 in the afternoon," he murmured, his ice-blue eyes locked onto Benjamin's. "There's a library in the east wing, on the second floor. Inside, there's a quiet, cozy spot I like to visit. You should come to see me there. We can talk some more, just the two of us. Leave your friend behind."

The closeness of Erik's presence, the intimacy of his suggestion, sent a shiver down Benjamin's spine. He felt a jolt of surprise and an uneasy thrill at Erik's unexpected closeness. The warmth of Erik's breath on his lips, combined with the intensity of those ice-blue eyes, left him momentarily speechless. His heart raced, a mix of curiosity and confusion flooding his mind.

He swallowed hard, trying to maintain his composure as the guard entered the room to take Erik away. Once Erik was escorted out, Benjamin and Tom took deep breaths and headed back to the barracks, ready to crash for the night.

Chapter Nine

Fort Hunt, Virginia, September 10, 1943

In the last twenty-four hours, the Allies launched Operation Avalanche, which involved landings at Salerno on the Italian mainland. This operation aimed to establish a beachhead and push inland despite fierce German resistance. The initial landings were met with intense opposition, particularly from the German 16th Panzer Division, resulting in heavy fighting over the subsequent days.

The German forces launched strong counterattacks against the Allied beachhead at Salerno, which temporarily threatened the integrity of the Allied position. However, the Allies managed to hold their ground, thanks to naval and air support, and continued to expand their beachhead over the following days.

These operations marked the beginning of a prolonged and challenging campaign in Italy, which eventually led to the Allies advancing further into the country and relieving pressure on the Soviet Union by opening a new front in Europe.

General Pietro Badoglio, the Prime Minister of Italy made a public radio announcement of the Italian Armistice, which had been secretly signed on September 3. This announcement led to widespread confusion and chaos in Italy as German forces rapidly moved to disarm Italian troops and occupy key positions. The Italian government, led by King Victor Emmanuel III and General Pietro Badoglio, fled Rome, effectively leaving the country without central leadership and resulting in a power vacuum that the Germans quickly exploited.

In addition to the landings at Salerno, the Allies also executed Operation Slapstick, which involved British forces landing at the port of Taranto in southeastern Italy. This operation was intended to secure additional ports and facilitate further advances into the Italian mainland.

The German 10th Army, under the command of General Heinrich von Vietinghoff, launched a series of coordinated counterattacks against the Allied forces at Salerno. Despite the intensity of these attacks, the Allies managed to maintain their beachhead, largely due to naval bombardments and air support that helped repel the German assaults. The ability of the Allies to withstand these attacks marked a crucial point in the campaign and ensured the continued progress of the Italian Campaign.

Benjamin and Tom stood in the Colonel's office, the early morning light streaming through the windows. Colonel Stone, sitting behind his cluttered desk, glanced up from the reports spread out before him. He gave a nod of acknowledgment, motioning for them to take a seat.

"Gentlemen," Colonel Stone began, his deep voice carrying a mix of authority and fatigue, "I've been reviewing the notes from yesterday's session with Müller. Did he give us anything useful?"

Tom shook his head. "No, sir. He's very tight-lipped. We established some rapport, but he hasn't provided any concrete information yet."

Colonel Stone's eyes narrowed slightly. "I see. These high-value targets are trained to resist interrogation. Did he show any signs of weakening?"

Benjamin leaned forward, choosing his words carefully. "He hinted at dissatisfaction with his work and mentioned ethical conflicts. It's a potential angle we could explore further, but he's still very cautious."

The Colonel sighed, rubbing his temples. "That's to be expected. You'll need to find a way to get him to open up. Did you notice anything we could use to our advantage?"

Tom hesitated, then glanced at Benjamin. "He seemed more relaxed when we treated him with a bit more…respect. We removed his restraints and offered him some comforts."

Colonel Stone nodded thoughtfully. "Good. Use whatever leverage you can. These men are not just soldiers; they're human beings with vulnerabilities. Find those weaknesses and exploit them."

Benjamin shifted in his seat, remembering Erik's unexpected closeness and his whispered invitation. He decided to keep that detail to himself for now. "We'll keep working on it, sir. We're confident we can get more out of him."

Colonel Stone studied them both for a moment, then leaned back in his chair. "Alright. Keep pushing, but be careful. Müller is dangerous, and we can't afford any mistakes. Dismissed."

As they stood to leave, Colonel Stone added, "And Benjamin, Tom, keep up the good work. The information we're seeking is crucial."

They nodded in acknowledgment, leaving the office. Once outside, Tom glanced at Benjamin. "Anything you didn't mention in there?"

Benjamin shook his head, his mind still on Erik's invitation. "No, just what you heard."

Tom gave him a searching look but didn't press further. They had a job to do, and for now, that was all that mattered.

On their way out of the briefing room, Benjamin and Tom crossed paths with Staff Sergeant Lewis. "How did your interrogation go yesterday?" he asked with a sardonic grin.

"Not too well at first," Tom replied, "but then we decided to borrow a trick out of your playbook and brought him some Jägermeister. That seemed to loosen him up a bit."

Staff Sergeant Lewis gave them a confused look. "What are you talking about? You think I'd waste good booze on that deviant?"

Tom and Benjamin locked eyes briefly as the Staff Sergeant pushed through them and continued down the hallway.

"How about we take a break from interrogations today?" Tom suggested with a heavy sigh. "We put in a lot of hours yesterday, and I'm a little behind on my report writing."

"Ok," Benjamin nodded in agreement. "Meet you in the mess hall for supper?"

"Yep," Tom replied as he sauntered off toward the officer's lounge.

Benjamin decided to take a walk to get some fresh air and to clear his mind. As he strolled along the perimeter, the sprawling complex revealed itself. The detention building loomed like a colossal structure, reminiscent of a New York City hospital. Previously off-limits as a Private, now as a Corporal, he wandered freely.

His thoughts gravitated inexorably to Erik, confined within those walls. Erik's presence flooded Benjamin's thoughts, an enigma he couldn't decipher. The echo of Erik's whispered words seemed to awaken an uncharted part of Benjamin, primal and restless.

Confusion and curiosity intertwined in Benjamin's mind. Erik's composed demeanor, striking features, and unexpected proposition lingered, etching a profound mark. Benjamin grappled with a mix of fascination and fear, questioning the depths of Erik's impact on him.

With a deep breath, Benjamin tried to dispel the haunting image of Erik, yet it clung to his thoughts, a silent allure that refused to fade.

Benjamin's longing to reconnect with Erik pulled him toward the detention building. Step by step, he closed the distance, driven by a desperate need to see him again. However, as he advanced a few yards, a wave of panic crashed over him, freezing him in place. What if someone spotted him there? The thought of arousing suspicion or worse, exposing his carefully guarded secret, sent shivers down his spine.

Benjamin's resolve crumbled, and he made his way toward the daunting detention building. Approaching the entrance, he confronted the reality of the security checkpoint. With a mix of nerves and determination, he presented his military identification, knowing that each step closer to Erik could unravel everything he had worked so hard to conceal.

Inside the building, Benjamin projected an air of purpose, concealing the tumult of emotions churning within him. He navigated the hallway with determined strides, his eyes scanning for the staircase. Locating it, he ascended to the second floor, each step a blend of anticipation and apprehension.

With a keen eye, Benjamin searched the corridors until a familiar sight caught his attention—a book trolley slightly protruding into the hallway. Following this subtle clue, he made his way toward the library, heart racing with the anticipation of what he might discover within its walls.

Checking his watch, Benjamin noted the time—only 1400 hours. He realized Erik wouldn't be accessible yet, as detainees were granted freedom within the building only after 1500 hours. With a mix of disappointment and resolve, Benjamin decided to bide his time, knowing that patience would be key in this clandestine endeavor.

As Benjamin explored the library, he was struck by the extensive collection and diverse subjects available to the detainees. His curiosity led him to a secluded corner, nestled behind intersecting bookshelves, creating a hidden alcove. Here, amidst science and engineering books, Benjamin felt a pang of recognition—it was undoubtedly Erik's sanctuary. The selection of books mirrored Erik's interests, confirming Benjamin's intuition about this being Erik's retreat within the confines of the detention building.

In Erik's secluded corner, Benjamin settled into what he knew was Erik's chair and delved into "The Meaning of Relativity" by Albert Einstein. Immersed in the profound concepts of space, time, and gravity, Benjamin read quietly, captivated by the world of physics unfolding before him. The words on the pages seemed to bridge the gap between his own reality and the enigmatic allure of Erik's world. Before he knew it, the hour had passed by.

"Einstein's revelations about the fabric of the cosmos, how time and space intertwine, are truly profound," Erik commented, his voice carrying a depth of understanding that resonated with Benjamin's own fascination with the subject. "I enjoyed that one." Eric slowly entered the secluded nook, staring at Benjamin intensely.

Benjamin, slightly startled by Erik's stealthy arrival, softly closed the book and silently met Erik's gaze. "You tricked me, Erik."

"Aww, don't take it personality, Benji. I just wanted to toss one back," Erik replied with a playful smile.

Benjamin bristled slightly, "Please don't call me that," he requested firmly. "Let's make a deal. In the future, if there is something that you want, within reason, just ask me and I will try to get it for you if I can."

"Fair enough," Eric agreed.

Benjamin began to rise from Erik's chair, but Erik interjected, "No, please. I'll fetch another chair." With swift movements, Erik disappeared around the corner and soon returned, placing the chair beside Benjamin, ensuring his comfort.

Erik broke the ice with a question that delved into their shared interest, his eyes glinting with curiosity. "Are you interested in the theory of relativity?" He inquired, his voice carrying a blend of genuine interest and a desire to connect on a deeper level through their mutual fascination with scientific concepts.

Benjamin nodded, a spark of enthusiasm igniting in his eyes. "Absolutely, I find it incredibly fascinating. The way Einstein revolutionized our understanding of the universe is simply mind-blowing."

Erik's smile widened, pleased by Benjamin's response. "I couldn't agree more," he replied. "The concepts of spacetime, gravity, and the bending of light have such profound implications."

As Benjamin and Erik delved deeper into their discussion, they explored the intricate nuances of Einstein's theories. Erik brought up the concept of gravitational waves, explaining how they ripple through spacetime, a phenomenon that had profound implications for astrophysics.

Benjamin listened intently, absorbing every detail with keen interest. "It's amazing how something as subtle as a gravitational wave can reveal so much about the universe," he remarked, marveling at the interconnectedness of space, time, and matter.

Erik nodded in agreement, adding, "And the implications for our understanding of black holes and the origins of the universe are immense. It's like peeling back the layers of a cosmic onion, revealing more mysteries with each discovery."

As their conversation deepened, Erik glanced at the book in Benjamin's hands. "You know," he said quietly, "Einstein's works were banned in Nazi Germany. The regime dismissed his theories as 'Jewish physics.'"

Benjamin looked at Erik with a mixture of surprise and respect. "I didn't know that," he admitted. "It's tragic how much knowledge and progress has been suppressed because of their ideology."

Erik nodded, his expression somber. "Yes, it's a stark reminder of how dangerous ignorance and prejudice can be. But it's also why these ideas are so important—they represent the triumph of truth and reason over bigotry and hatred."

Their discussion flowed seamlessly from one topic to another, from the curvature of spacetime to the implications of Einstein's theories on modern physics. In that quiet corner of the library, they found a connection that transcended their circumstances, united by a shared passion for knowledge and discovery.

At that moment, Benjamin gleaned an important detail about Erik's opinions of the Nazi regime. Erik's somber expression and the weight of his words revealed a deep-seated disdain for the regime's oppressive ideologies. Benjamin realized that Erik valued truth, reason, and intellectual freedom—principles diametrically opposed to the Nazis' doctrines. This newfound understanding of Erik's moral stance added another layer of complexity to their growing connection, deepening Benjamin's respect and admiration for him.

As they sat in the library, classical music softly played in the background. Benjamin noticed Erik humming along with the music, seemingly unaware that he was doing it.

This small, unguarded moment further endeared Erik to Benjamin, showing a gentler, more personal side to the man who was becoming increasingly important to him.

Erik, wanting to know a little more about Benjamin, asked, "Tell me about a book that you love. I want to read it. Something American."

Benjamin's interest piqued, he smiled and replied, "I have just the book in mind." With a spring in his step, he quickly scoured the library shelves until he found the book he was looking for. Returning to where Erik was waiting, he handed him "For Whom the Bell Tolls" by Ernest Hemingway.

"This is a powerful novel set against the backdrop of the Spanish Civil War," Benjamin began, responding to Erik's curiosity. "The story follows Robert Jordan, an American dynamiter who joins a Republican guerrilla unit fighting against Franco's Nationalists. As Jordan prepares to blow up a bridge crucial to the enemy's operations, he grapples with questions of morality, sacrifice, and the human cost of war."

Benjamin's enthusiasm for the book was evident as he delved into its themes. "One of the central themes is the exploration of love in wartime. Jordan's deepening relationship with Maria, a Spanish woman who has suffered greatly at the hands of the enemy, serves as a poignant portrayal of love blossoming amidst chaos and danger. Their love is contrasted with the brutality of war, highlighting the fragile beauty that can still exist in the darkest of times."

He continued, "The novel also delves into themes of loyalty and duty. Jordan's loyalty to his cause and his comrades is tested as he navigates the complexities of guerrilla warfare and confronts the harsh realities of his mission. Hemingway portrays the bonds forged in battle, as well as the sacrifices required for a greater cause."

Erik listened intently, absorbing Benjamin's words and eager to delve into the world of Hemingway for himself.

As Erik flipped through the pages, his brows furrowed momentarily. "This book was also banned in Nazi Germany," he remarked, pointing out the intriguing historical fact about Hemingway's work.

Benjamin nodded, impressed by Erik's knowledge. "Yes, you're right. The Nazis consider Hemingway's writing to be 'degenerate literature' due to its anti-fascist themes and realistic portrayal of war."

Their conversation continued, enriched by Erik's astute observation and Benjamin's passion for literature. As the afternoon waned into evening, Benjamin and Erik found themselves engrossed in a world of shared interests and meaningful exchanges. Erik's keen insights and Benjamin's love for the written word fueled their conversation, leading to discussions about history, philosophy, and the human condition.

In this intimate setting, Benjamin and Erik discovered common ground beyond their initial encounter, laying the foundation for a friendship built on mutual understanding and shared interests. The library's quiet ambiance provided a perfect backdrop for their exploration of ideas and shared appreciation for the power of storytelling.

As Benjamin's memory of his promise to meet Tom in the mess hall surfaced, he felt the weight of duty pulling him away from Erik. With a bittersweet farewell, Erik entrusted him with the book by Albert Einstein, a token of their shared moments. Gratitude filled the air as Erik thanked Benjamin for his companionship before they parted ways. Exiting the detention building, Benjamin found himself immersed in deep reflection, his heart stirred by the profound significance of his time with Erik and the emotions it evoked within him.

Benjamin made his way into the lively mess hall. The clinking of trays and chatter filled the air around him. His eyes quickly found Tom, patiently waiting in line with a tray in hand. A wave of relief washed over Benjamin; he hadn't missed his commitment. Hastily grabbing a tray, he joined Tom in line, their footsteps falling in sync on the tiled floor.

Settling down at their usual spot, Tom's gaze fell upon the book Benjamin carried. "Library?" He asked, his tone tinged with curiosity as he nodded toward the book. Unaware of the library's existence within P.O. Box 1142, Tom seemed puzzled.

Benjamin nodded with a slight smile. "Yes, there's a library tucked away in the detention building," he replied, his voice carrying a hint of wonder at the discovery. Tom's surprise prompted Benjamin to share more, describing the unexpected range of books he found there.

Intrigued, Tom leaned closer. "So, what were you doing in the detention building?" he inquired, prompting Benjamin to explain his recent visit to that part of the facility.

Benjamin glanced around the mess hall, making sure they had some privacy. "Alright, I'll tell you," he began, leaning in slightly. "The other day, while you were outside the interrogation room, Erik mentioned something about a library on the second floor of the detention building. Since our new ranks allow us to explore more of the facility, I decided to check it out," he explained, his voice carrying a sense of discovery and excitement.

Tom's expression shifted to a mix of confusion and mild boredom, giving Benjamin a strange look. "Oh, okay," Tom replied nonchalantly. "Why are you acting weird?" he asked, unable to hide his curiosity.

"I'm not," Benjamin rebutted, trying to maintain his composure despite Tom's probing gaze.

Chapter Ten

Fort Hunt, Virginia, September 13, 1943

Following the announcement of the Italian armistice, Germany quickly occupied northern and central Italy. On September 12, German commandos led by Otto Skorzeny carried out a daring rescue mission, known as the Gran Sasso Raid or Operation Eiche. They successfully freed Benito Mussolini from his imprisonment on the Gran Sasso mountain in Italy. Mussolini was then flown to Germany, where he met with Hitler and subsequently was installed as the head of the Italian Social Republic (a puppet state of Nazi Germany) in Northern Italy. This new regime continued to support the Axis powers.

My Dearest Benjamin,

I hope this letter finds you well and in good spirits amidst your duties at P.O. Box 1142. Mazel tov on your promotion! Your father and I are so proud of you, and we are constantly thinking of you, and praying for your safety during these challenging times.

I wanted to share with you some news about the Jewish community here in New York City. While we continue to face various challenges, including instances of discrimination and prejudice, there is also a strong sense of resilience and solidarity among our people. Synagogues, cultural centers, and community organizations are bustling with activity, providing support networks and opportunities for connection and mutual support.

However, it's important to acknowledge the harsh realities of the world outside our community. Antisemitism still rears its ugly head in different forms, from discriminatory practices in employment and housing to hateful speech and even violent attacks. Just last month, there was an incident where a Jewish-owned business was vandalized with antisemitic graffiti, a stark reminder of the hatred that still exists.

These challenges remind us of the importance of standing together and advocating for our rights and dignity. Despite these hardships, our community remains strong and resilient, working tirelessly to combat prejudice and build a better future for all.

On a brighter note, there has been increased awareness and activism in response to the atrocities happening in Europe. Fundraising campaigns, rallies, and advocacy efforts are mobilizing support for refugees and survivors of the Holocaust. Our community is actively engaged in these efforts, showing compassion and solidarity with our fellow Jews in distress.

In conclusion, my dear Benjamin, remember that you are not alone. You have a strong community behind you, supporting you every step of the way. Stay strong, stay resilient, and know that we eagerly await your safe return home.

With all my love,

Mom

Benjamin put down the letter from his mom, the words echoing in his mind. He steeled himself for what lay ahead. The emotions stirred by the letter lingered, a reminder of the personal stakes in the midst of his professional duties. With a deep breath, he headed off to the interrogation room, each step a silent affirmation of his commitment to the task at hand.

As Benjamin entered the interrogation room for the second time, he couldn't shake the unexpected sense of connection he felt with Erik. It was a rare occurrence in his line of work, where detachment was often a shield against emotional entanglements. Yet, this connection deepened Benjamin's internal conflict. On one hand, he empathized with Erik's predicament, understanding the weight of loyalty and the fear of consequences. On the other hand, Benjamin knew he had a duty to fulfill, a job that demanded perseverance and resolve, even in the face of such personal revelations. So, he pushed his own feelings and emotions deep within himself, locking them away behind a mask of professionalism and determination.

The atmosphere in the interrogation room was thick with unspoken tension that hung in the air like a heavy fog. Benjamin and Tom's expressions were a mix of determination and apprehension, their eyes meeting briefly before returning to focus on Erik.

Erik, seated calmly yet with an underlying sense of unease, exuded a quiet defiance tempered by resignation. His gaze, fixed on Benjamin, held a hint of curiosity mingled with guarded wariness as if he were anticipating his every move and word.

The silence between them was palpable, broken only by the occasional shuffle of papers or the soft hum of the overhead light. Each breath seemed amplified in the confined space, echoing the weight of the conversation that loomed over them like an invisible specter.

Benjamin leaned forward, his gaze fixed on Erik. "Erik, can you tell us about your relationship with your father? How did his beliefs and actions influence your own views?"

Erik's eyes clouded with memories as he spoke. "My father…he was a strong believer in the party's ideals. He saw it as a beacon of hope, a promise of a better future for our country."

Tom, curious, chimed in, "Did you share his beliefs?"

"At first, yes," Erik admitted with a hesitant nod. "I believed in what he taught me, in the vision he painted of a prosperous Germany."

"What changed your perspective?" Benjamin inquired, his tone gentle yet probing.

"I saw the cracks, the injustices masked by propaganda," Erik replied somberly. "My father, he turned a blind eye to them, focused on the bigger picture."

Tom pressed further, "Did you confront him about it?"

Erik shook his head slightly. "No, I couldn't. He was convinced he was doing what was right, that sacrifices were necessary for the greater good."

"And now, how do you see those sacrifices?" Benjamin asked, his voice soft yet intent.

"I see them for what they are," Erik replied quietly. "Lives lost in the name of power and ideology."

Curiosity filled Tom's voice as he continued, "How do you reconcile that with your loyalty to the regime?"

"Loyalty…it's not easy to explain," Erik said, a hint of defensiveness creeping into his tone. "It's ingrained, a part of who I am."

Benjamin, sensing Erik's struggle, spoke gently, "Erik, we're not here to judge. We want to understand."

Erik spoke with a guarded tone, "My father believed in the promises of a better future, in the ideals of the party. But he also saw the corruption, the disregard for human life."

Tom, curious, asked, "And what about you, Erik? Do you still believe in those promises?"

Erik hesitated before responding, "I don't know what to believe anymore. Everything is falling apart."

Benjamin, empathetic, interjected, "We understand the complexity of your situation, Erik. But you have to see that loyalty to a corrupt regime is not honorable."

Erik, frustration evident in his voice, retorted, "You don't understand! If I betray my country, it's not just me who suffers. My father would be disgraced. My family, their lives would be in danger."

Tom, adopting a firmer tone, stated, "We're not asking you to betray anyone, Erik. We're asking you to stand against tyranny."

Erik, defiantly, countered, "And what good would that do? It's too late for justice."

Benjamin, remaining optimistic, replied, "It's never too late to make a difference, Erik. To choose a path that aligns with your conscience."

Erik, contemplative, murmured, "Conscience…it's a heavy burden to carry, especially now."

Benjamin's voice carried a sense of urgency as he addressed Erik, "Erik, you must understand the gravity of your situation. The Nazi regime is crumbling, and your allegiance to them only prolongs the suffering."

Erik, steadfast, replied, "I am aware of the regime's downfall, but my loyalty lies with my family and my country, not its leaders."

Tom, interjecting with conviction, added, "Your loyalty should lie with what's right, not blind loyalty and nationalism. Your silence only aids those who perpetrate atrocities."

Erik, guarded, responded, "Loyalty is not always black and white. Betrayal carries consequences beyond oneself."

Benjamin, softening his approach, said, "Erik, we're not asking you to betray your family or your country. We're asking you to stand against tyranny, to choose humanity over blind allegiance."

Erik, resolute, countered, "And I ask you to understand the weight of my choice. The path of duty is not always easy, nor is it always just."

Tom, chiming in with practicality, urged, "Erik, think of the lives you could save by cooperating with us. Your actions now can make a difference."

Erik, hesitant yet thoughtful, admitted, "I…I understand your perspective, but you don't understand the consequences I face. If I betray my country, it's not just me who suffers. My duty is my burden to bear."

Benjamin, speaking earnestly, concluded, "We all carry burdens, Erik. It's how we choose to bear them that defines us."

Erik's voice carried a skeptical tone as he questioned Benjamin, "Benjamin, you speak of choosing what's right, but have you ever faced the consequences of such a choice? Have you risked everything for a belief?"

Benjamin, pausing to consider, replied thoughtfully, "I've faced difficult choices, Erik. Loyalty and duty have often clashed with what I believe is right."

Erik persisted, his skepticism evident, "And which side did you choose in those moments? Did you prioritize duty over conscience?"

Benjamin hesitated before responding, "At times, yes. But I've also learned that blind allegiance can lead to grave injustices."

Erik probed further, "So, where do your loyalties truly lie, Benjamin? With duty, with country, or with something deeper, something more personal?"

Benjamin, choosing his words carefully, answered, "My loyalties lie with what's just and humane. Sometimes that means questioning authority and standing up for what's right."

Erik, challenging Benjamin's stance, remarked, "And yet, here you are, asking me to betray my country. Is that not a contradiction?"

Benjamin's tone turned firm as he clarified, "It's not about betrayal, Erik. It's about standing against tyranny, even if it means challenging the status quo."

Erik persisted in questioning Benjamin's understanding, "But can you truly understand the weight of my choice? The repercussions go beyond myself. They touch my family, my future."

Benjamin, maintaining empathy, responded earnestly, "I understood the stakes, Erik." He paused for a moment, contemplating a change in approach for the interrogation. He then shuffled through the pages of his notebook and said, "In our earlier interrogation, you mentioned something about having a mentor, a high-level Nazi scientist. Could we talk about that?"

Erik, slightly surprised by the change in topic, replied, "Well, I didn't say that he was a high-level Nazi scientist, but sure, we can talk about that if you'd like."

This shift in focus opened up a new avenue for the interrogation, allowing Benjamin to delve into Erik's mentorship experience and potentially gain insights into Erik's motivations and beliefs.

Benjamin, intrigued by Erik's mentorship, asked, "What was it like working with someone whom you admired so greatly?"

Erik, reflecting on his experience, replied, "It was both challenging and inspiring. Reimar Horten is not just a mentor but also a visionary in aviation. His dedication to innovation and his expertise in aircraft design pushed me to excel."

Benjamin nodded, sensing the significance of Erik's words. "Did he influence your approach to your work?"

Erik nodded, a hint of admiration in his voice. "Absolutely. Reimar's emphasis on meticulous research and unconventional thinking shaped my perspective on engineering. He taught me to question norms and explore new possibilities."

As Benjamin listened, he gained a deeper understanding of Erik's professional journey and the impact of mentorship on his development as a scientist and engineer.

"Can you tell us more about this Reimar Horten?" Tom asked, his interest piqued.

Erik reluctantly answered, "Reimar Horten is a visionary in aviation. He and his brother Walter are at the forefront of developing innovative aircraft for the Luftwaffe. Reimar taught me many things including aspects of aeronautical engineering, research methodologies, and even topics such as ethical considerations in wartime research and development."

"So, you were working for Walter and Reimar Horten before your capture?" Tom asked, trying to contain the excitement he felt at finally making some progress, however small.

"Yes." Alex's tone was guarded again as if he were meticulously choosing his words so that he didn't reveal too much information.

"Can you tell us anything about the technology that they are currently developing?" Tom pressed again.

"I'm sure you understand that such topics are highly sensitive," Alex reminded him. "I can not divulge that information."

Benjamin, who had been digging through his notes again, chimed in. "In our last interrogation, you mentioned that the technology you were developing was, quote, 'designed with the intention of reaching targets far beyond Europe.' So, two aviation geniuses with the help of a physicist from a prestigious university in Germany developing a technology with the capability of reaching targets far beyond Europe—the Horten brothers are building an experimental aircraft."

Erik shifted uncomfortably in his chair. "Yes, it is called the Horten H.XVII. That's all I can tell you."

"I think that's a good place to stop for the day," Tom announced. "Erik, thank you for your cooperation. I will have the guard escort you back to the detention building."

On his way out, Erik paused and turned back toward Benjamin. "You said that if there was something that I wanted, I should ask you, and you would get it for me if possible."

"Yes, Erik," Benjamin responded, curious about what Erik might request.

"I would like to be able to listen to music in my quarters. Could you get me a radio?" Erik asked, a hint of longing in his voice.

Benjamin nodded, understanding the request. "I will see what I can do. It'll have to be approved by Colonel Stone, which might take a little time, but I'll do my best to arrange it for you."

Erik nodded gratefully before continuing on his way, a sense of anticipation for the possibility of having music to accompany him in his downtime.

Back in the briefing room, Colonel Stone sat at the head of the table, his expression serious yet attentive. Benjamin and Tom stood before him, ready to debrief on their latest findings.

Benjamin started, "Colonel, we've uncovered new information regarding an experimental aircraft project known as The Horten H.XVIII."

Colonel Stone's eyebrows raised in interest. "Go on."

Tom added, "We don't have specific details about the aircraft itself or its development location yet. However, we've learned that two visionary aviation experts, Walter and Reimar Horten, are heading the project."

The Colonel leaned forward, his gaze focused. "The Horten brothers. They're known for their innovative designs. This could be a significant development."

Benjamin nodded, "Indeed, sir. Erik mentioned their involvement but didn't provide further details. It's clear that this project holds strategic importance for the enemy."

Colonel Stone nodded thoughtfully. "Keep digging. We need to know more about this aircraft and its potential capabilities. Any clues on its timeline or deployment?"

Tom replied, "Not yet, sir. We're working on gathering more intelligence, especially regarding the project's progress and any vulnerabilities we can exploit."

The Colonel's expression hardened slightly. "Continue your efforts. This could be a game-changer if we can gain insights into their experimental aircraft program."

The sense of urgency in the room was palpable as they discussed the implications of The Horten H.XVIII project and the role of Walter and Reimar Horten, knowing that more information could shape their strategic planning and operations.

"Excellent work boys," Stone said, a rare smile breaking his stern expression. "This could save countless lives. I knew I made the right decision putting the Ritchie boys on this assignment. I'm relieving you of some of your other assignments for now. I want you to put everything you've got into this interrogation. Do whatever you need to do, just get me that intel."

"Thank you, sir," Benjamin and Tom snapped to attention, graciously accepting the Colonel's compliment.

Benjamin then cautiously broached the topic of the radio. "Sir, Müller asked about the possibility of obtaining a radio for his quarters…"

Colonel Stone cut him off with a shake of his head. "I'm afraid that's not possible, Corporal. Security protocols prohibit us from allowing radios in detainee quarters."

Benjamin's expression fell slightly, but before he could respond, Colonel Stone continued, "However, there's an old record player in the office's lounge that nobody ever uses. The only records we have are classical music. You can use that one."

Benjamin and Tom exchanged a glance, recognizing the compromise. "Thank you, sir. We'll make do with the record player," Benjamin replied.

Colonel Stone's tone turned serious as he leaned forward. "Besides, if we don't get the location of this experimental aircraft facility, Herr Müller will be shipped out to one of the POW labor camps, or he'll end up in a military prison for the rest of his life. This is your guy's last chance. We can't keep detainees here who are uncooperative."

The weight of the Colonel's words hung in the air, emphasizing the urgency of their mission and the consequences of failure. Benjamin and Tom nodded in understanding, knowing that they had to succeed in extracting crucial information from Erik.

"He's a physicist and a genius. Isn't there something we can do to utilize his knowledge and expertise?" Benjamin asked, hopeful for a way to leverage Erik's skills.

Colonel Stone's expression turned grave. "Not if he won't cooperate and give us the intel we need. Our hands are tied in that regard."

Benjamin's shoulders slumped slightly, realizing the limitations. "But sir, if he works with us, couldn't we offer him something in return?"

Colonel Stone nodded, understanding the implication. "If he agrees to cooperate fully and provide valuable intelligence, we could probably get him citizenship under Operation Overcast. But that decision ultimately rests with him."

Chapter Eleven

Fort Hunt, Virginia, September 17, 1943

In the Aegean Sea, during the Battle of Leros, part of the Dodecanese Campaign, British forces attempted to seize control of the Dodecanese Islands following Italy's armistice with the Allies. The British aimed to use these islands as bases for further operations in the Mediterranean. Leros, with its strategic harbors and airfields, became a focal point.

On September 13, British forces started landing on Leros. However, German forces launched counterattacks to regain control. The battle was characterized by intense air raids and ground assaults, with the Germans eventually gaining the upper hand due to their air superiority and reinforcements. The British and Italian defenders put up a stubborn resistance but were gradually overwhelmed. By September 17, the Germans had secured significant positions on the island, leading to its eventual capture.

In the Pacific Theater, the Allies were preparing for the Bougainville Campaign, part of the larger Solomon Islands campaign. The goal was to neutralize the Japanese stronghold on Bougainville and establish airfields to support further operations. Planning and reconnaissance missions were ongoing.

Allied forces were continuing their operations in New Guinea, where they aimed to push back Japanese forces and secure the region. This included smaller skirmishes and the consolidation of previously captured territories.

Benjamin carried the newly cleaned and polished record player and a stack of classical music records through the dimly lit corridors of P.O. Box 1142. His excitement was palpable; he had spent the last few days ensuring everything was perfect for Erik. He couldn't wait to see Erik's reaction. However, when he reached the cozy nook in the library where Erik usually sat, he found it empty.

Perplexed, Benjamin headed off to find a security officer. After a brief search, he located one near the entrance to the detention area. The officer was a burly man with a stern expression, but Benjamin approached him with determination.

"Excuse me, Officer. I'm looking for Erik Müller. He's not in his usual spot in the library. Can you tell me his detention cell number?" Benjamin asked.

The officer glanced at a clipboard before responding. "Müller is in cell 37. Down that hallway, to the left."

"Thank you," Benjamin said, making his way down the indicated hallway. The air was cooler here, and the walls seemed to close in, creating an oppressive atmosphere. When he reached cell 37, he knocked on the heavy door but received no response. He knocked again, louder this time, but still no answer.

Confused and a bit worried, Benjamin tugged on the door handle. The door was unlocked and slid open slightly. Erik was not there. Benjamin decided to leave the record player and records inside Erik's cell. As he was placing them down, another thought struck him. He needed to find out where Erik was. He turned back and retraced his steps to the security officer.

The officer was still at his post, looking slightly annoyed as Benjamin approached again. "He's not in his cell," Benjamin said, trying to keep the concern out of his voice. "Do you know where he might be?"

The officer's expression softened slightly. "Some of the detainees have been complaining about feeling sick. We've had a few sent to the infirmary. You might want to check there."

Benjamin's heart sank. He hadn't considered that Erik might be ill. "Thank you," he said, hurrying off toward the infirmary, his mind racing with worry. As he walked, he couldn't help but think about the conversations they'd had and the subtle bond that had formed between them. He hoped fervently that Erik was alright.

Upon reaching the infirmary, Benjamin was struck by the sterile smell and the sight of several beds occupied by pale, weak-looking men. He quickly scanned the room and spotted Erik lying on one of the beds, looking gaunt and fragile.

A doctor approached Benjamin, recognizing his concern. "You must be here for Müller."

"Yes," Benjamin replied, his voice tight with worry. "What happened to him?"

The doctor sighed, wiping his hands on a towel. "Erik has dysentery. It's quite severe. He'll need to stay here for several days to receive IV fluids and antibiotics. We're doing everything we can to stabilize him. Hopefully, that will be enough and he won't need a blood transfusion." The doctor briefly checked Erik's vitals and then continued on with his rounds.

Benjamin's heart clenched at the sight of Erik in such a weakened state. He approached the bed and gently took Erik's hand, hoping to convey some comfort. "You're going to be alright, Erik. Just hang in there."

Erik's eyes flickered open, and he managed a weak smile. "I guess I'll have to take a rain check on that second date," he murmured, his voice barely above a whisper.

Benjamin's heart palpitated. His eyes darted around to make sure nobody was within earshot. Squeezing Erik's hand gently, he replied in a hushed tone, "Just focus on getting better right now, okay? I'll be right here. I won't let anything happen to you."

Just then, a surly-looking nurse approached to move Erik into a private room for closer observation. She inspected Benjamin curiously.

"Can I stay with him for a while?" Benjamin politely asked the nurse as she was making notes on her clipboard.

The nurse looked up from her paperwork, her expression stern but understanding. "Are you an immediate family member or a medical officer?"

"No, but I've been working closely with him on…important matters. I need to see him," Benjamin insisted, his voice tinged with urgency.

The nurse hesitated for a moment, then nodded. "Alright, but you'll need to follow strict protocols. Dysentery is highly contagious. You'll have to wear protective gear, and your visit will be supervised and limited in time."

Benjamin agreed, and soon he was donned in a protective gown, gloves, and a mask. He was led to the room where Erik lay on a cot, an IV drip in his arm. The sight of Erik, pale and weak, tugged at Benjamin's heartstrings.

"Erik," Benjamin called softly as he approached the bed. He reached out, his gloved hand lightly touching Erik's arm. "I brought you something. I left it in your cell, but I wanted to tell you about it. An old record player with classical music. I thought it might lift your spirits."

A faint smile crossed Erik's lips. "Thank you, Benji. That means a lot."

The medical officer supervising the visit cleared his throat, reminding Benjamin of the time constraints. "Just a few more minutes," he said.

Benjamin nodded, turning his attention back to Erik. "I'll be back to check on you, I promise. Just focus on getting better, alright?"

Erik's eyes shone with gratitude. "I will. Thank you."

As Benjamin left the infirmary, he couldn't shake the worry gnawing at him. Erik's condition was serious, and he knew that time was of the essence—not just for Erik's health, but for the vital information they still needed.

A few days passed before Benjamin was able to see Erik again. He had kept in contact with the infirmary regarding Erik's improvement and knew that Erik had recently been transferred back to his private cell, though he was still on antibiotics and bed rest. Benjamin had finally earned a pass-day and was excited to spend it with Erik.

Benjamin approached Erik's cell, the familiar sound of the lock turning resonating as the guard let him in. Erik was lying on his cot, looking pale but more alert than the last time Benjamin had seen him in the infirmary. A slice of morning light peeked through the narrow window over Erik's bed and bathed his smooth skin and pale pink lips with warm light.

Erik's eyes fluttered open, and he gave a weak smile. "Benji…you came."

"Yes, I did," Benjamin replied, pulling a chair close to Erik's bed. "How are you feeling?"

Erik's voice was barely above a whisper. "Like I've been hit by a train. But seeing a familiar face helps. I heard you were checking on me."

"I was worried," Benjamin admitted, pulling a chair close to Erik's cot. "I'm glad you're on the mend."

Erik nodded, his eyes softening. "It means a lot to know someone cares.

Erik tried to sit up, but he lacked the strength. Benjamin helped him prop a pillow under his back so that he could lay comfortably on his side. Erik gestured toward the record player that Benjamin had brought him.

"I wanted to play something for you. The record is there, I just can't get up."

"I'll get it," Benjamin said as he got up to turn on the record player and position the needle. He glanced at the thin printed label on the inner circle of the record. "Schumann?"

Erik nodded, a faint smile appearing on his lips. "Yes, Robert Schumann's 'Fantasie in C', 17th Opus, Second Movement. It's one of my favorites. I thought you might appreciate it."

Benjamin carefully placed the needle on the record, and soon the powerful, emotive notes of Schumann's masterpiece filled the room. The intense yet whimsical melodies seemed to create a profound atmosphere, offering a temporary escape from the harsh realities of their world.

"Thank you, Benjamin," Erik said softly, closing his eyes as he listened to the music. "This means a lot to me."

Benjamin sat back down, watching Erik's face relax as he immersed himself in the music. At that moment, he realized how much these small gestures of kindness mattered, even in the midst of war.

"Tell me about that place where you grew up," Benjamin asked softly.

Erik sighed, his thoughts drifting back to his childhood. "I grew up on a country estate in Potsdam. It was a beautiful place, surrounded by nature. My father was a member of the Reichstag during the Weimar Republic. When Hitler began his rise to power, my father joined the Nazis, believing in the promises of a revitalized Germany."

Benjamin listened intently as Erik continued, "Our estate was expansive, with gardens that seemed to stretch on forever. We were relatively affluent, given my father's position. I spent a lot of time exploring the grounds, fascinated by the natural world and later by the engineering marvels my father introduced me to."

Benjamin nodded, picturing the idyllic scenes Erik described. "It sounds like a remarkable place to grow up."

"It was," Erik said, a hint of nostalgia in his voice. "But it was also complicated. My father's political affiliations brought certain expectations and pressures. He believed strongly in the new regime's potential, but he also saw the corruption and the disregard for human life that came with it."

Benjamin could see the conflict in Erik's eyes. "And how did that shape your own views?"

Erik paused, reflecting on the question. "It made me question everything. My father's idealism clashed with the harsh realities I witnessed. I admired his dedication to our country, but I couldn't ignore the moral compromises he made. It's why I find myself in this position now, torn between loyalty to my family and doing what's right."

Benjamin reached out, placing a comforting hand on Erik's arm. "You're not alone in this struggle, Erik. We all have our battles to fight, and sometimes, standing up for what's right means going against everything we've been taught."

Erik nodded slowly, taking in Benjamin's words. "Thank you, Benjamin. It helps to know that someone understands."

Benjamin paused, absorbing Erik's words. He couldn't help but notice how Erik described his dilemma as being 'torn between loyalty to his family and doing what was right.' This indicated that Erik grasped the notion that aiding Benjamin was indeed the morally correct course of action.

"Can you tell me about your mother?" Benjamin inquired.

Erik's eyes softened with a nostalgic gleam. "My mother is a kind-hearted woman," he began, his voice carrying a hint of fondness. "She always puts her family first, no matter the circumstances. I remember her strength during difficult times, her unwavering support for me, shaping my values and sense of duty."

Benjamin hesitated, choosing his words carefully. "So, your mother knows about your…"

"…proclivities for other men?" He smiled briefly at Benjamin's awkwardness. "Yes. She has known since I was a little boy," Erik replied calmly, his expression reflecting a mixture of acceptance and understanding. "As did my father, which is why I was required to join the military after I graduated from the university. My father was well aware of Hitler's views on homosexuality, and he was determined to save his reputation. It would not have looked good to have the Gestapo knocking at his door in the middle of the night to collect his degenerate son. With my education, it was not difficult for him to get me assigned to a laboratory somewhere out of sight and relatively out of harm's way."

Benjamin's empathy deepened as he considered Erik's situation. "It must have been awful," he said softly, "being forced into a life that wasn't of your choosing."

Erik nodded solemnly. "Given the climate of Germany these days, I imagine he probably saved my life," he admitted, acknowledging the harsh realities of their time.

Erik paused, his gaze distant as he spoke softly. "I often feel isolated, Benjamin. It's like I'm torn between two worlds—the duty I must uphold as a soldier and the person I am, especially regarding…well, you understand."

Benjamin nodded, empathy flickering in his eyes. "I do, Erik. It's not easy navigating these personal dilemmas, is it? Balancing what we must do with what we feel is right."

Erik's shoulders relaxed slightly, a mix of relief and vulnerability in his expression. "Exactly. Every decision feels like a battle between duty and conscience."

Taking a deep breath, Benjamin opened up too. "I struggle with acceptance, Erik. Professionally, personally…it's a constant challenge. And the weight of secrets, the inner turmoil—it's exhausting."

Erik's gaze met Benjamin's, a silent understanding passing between them. "You carry so much, Benjamin. I can see it. The pressure, the conflicts…it's a heavy burden."

Internally, Benjamin wrestled with conflicting emotions. His duty demanded a certain distance, but his growing affection for Erik blurred those lines, creating a tangled web of loyalty and desire.

"I wanted so badly to join the armed forces after graduating from the university," Benjamin confessed, his voice tinged with both determination and vulnerability. "I hoped to serve my country, to pay my debt to this nation that gave me a home when my family no longer had one."

Erik listened intently, sensing the depth of Benjamin's emotions as he continued. "All my life, I have felt like an outsider. I thought that this would be my way of earning acceptance—acceptance from my family, acceptance from my peers, as well as from my country. But even now that I have dedicated my life to military service, I still feel like I don't belong—like I have to hide who I truly am."

His voice trembled slightly with the weight of his confession. "I struggle with the notion of sacrificing my future, offering my life to a country that doesn't even want me in it, for one reason or another—because my family are immigrants, because I'm Jewish, because I'm…" His voice choked as his eyes swelled with tears.

Erik reached for Benjamin's hand and gripped it tightly.

The record player's abrupt halt disrupted the moment, drawing Benjamin's attention. The needle lifted and returned itself to its cradle, the sound carrying a hint of amusement and anticipation. He chuckled softly, wiping the tears from his eyes. "Well, let's see what else you've got in this stack of records," he suggested, gesturing towards the collection with a playful smile. "Ooh, here's one I'll bet you haven't heard. Louis Moreau Gottschalk's romantic symphony, 'A Night In The Tropics'. How do you feel about American composers?"

Erik scrunched his nose and stuck out his tongue in mock disapproval. In response, Benjamin glared at him, one eyebrow arched. Erik's serious facade broke, and he burst into a wide smile.

"It's good to see you smile again," Benjamin confessed. "I was really worried about you for a while. The doctor mentioned that you might need a blood transfusion."

"Aww, I think I'll be alright, Benji. I am feeling a little better now," he admitted, the two men locking eyes in an unspoken moment of relief. "The doctor said that a lot of detainees have been getting sick lately due to the declining sanitary conditions caused by the overcrowding in this building. A little fresh air would probably do us all some good."

Erik's eyes twinkled with mischief. "You know, you're so much cuter than my previous interrogator, Staff Sergeant Lewis."

Benjamin laughed loudly, then quickly covered his mouth, reminding himself of the need for discretion. "What happened that made him dislike you so much? I mean, he is a bigot, but he really doesn't like you."

Erik smirked. "I called him a pompous, pig-headed ignoramus with the charm of a damp sock."

Suddenly overcome with longing, Benjamin could no longer contain it. His heart pounded so fast it felt as though it might burst. Leaning in slowly, his eyes remained locked with Erik's. Gently, he pressed his lips against Erik's in a tender, heartfelt kiss.

Erik kissed him back and then suddenly recoiled, "We need to be careful."

"Do you think someone's watching us?" Benjamin asked with concern on his face.

"Nein, schöner Mann, I am contagious. I don't want you to get sick," Erik replied as he ran his fingers across Benjamin's cheek.

"That's the first time you've spoken German to me," Benjamin observed.

"Sprechen sie Deutsch?" Erik asked with a look of intrigue.

Benjamin kissed Erik again, "Ja, ich spreche fließend Deutsch." Switching to French, he said, "Je parle aussi français," and then to Italian, "E sono anche abbastanza bravo con l'italiano."

Erik grabbed Benjamin by the shirt collar and pulled him in for another kiss, "You are so sexy." Switching to French, he said, "Arrive ici, gentil, beau homme," and then to Italian, "Baciami!"

Benjamin was flushed as he exited the detention building, heading for the mess hall to meet Tom for supper.

As he approached, Tom gave him a scrutinizing look. "What's gotten into you?"

"What do you mean?" Benjamin asked, panicking as if he'd been found out.

"You're practically skipping. Why are you so cheerful, weirdo?" Tom teased, flashing a goofy grin as they both stepped into the chow line. "I got another letter from Nancy."

"Oh yeah?" Benjamin asked with genuine excitement. "How is she doing? Is she still working in the factory?"

"Yeah, but they stopped making commercial boilers. Now they're building them for the U.S. Navy," Tom explained. "She's doing well, though. A bit lonely, but at least she has her family there to support her. I sure do miss kissing on her."

"I'm glad she is doing well. I'm sure she misses you, too, Tom," Benjamin said as they sat down to eat. "Hey Tom, I have a proposal. I'd like your assistance in persuading Colonel Stone to authorize a supervised outing for Erik. The overcrowding in the detention building due to new POW arrivals has led to worsening sanitary conditions, affecting Erik's health. I believe some fresh air could improve his well-being and possibly make him more receptive to cooperation. If we can show him a glimpse of freedom and the benefits of cooperation, it might encourage him to share valuable information and expedite his release from this facility."

Tom pondered silently for a moment before responding, "It's an intriguing strategy, but why specifically involve me?"

"This isn't your usual armored van escort with blindfolds and shackles. I'm proposing a compassionate approach—a brief outing without restraints, just for an afternoon," Benjamin clarified, emphasizing the humane nature of the request. "I just think I'll have better odds of getting authorization if you express your support for the plan. You are my superior officer after all."

"I guess it's worth a shot. I mean, the worst that could happen would be that he denies your request," Tom offered.

That night, Benjamin lay wide awake, his mind racing as he relived the afternoon he had spent with Erik. Every detail played out in his mind—the way Erik's eyes sparkled when he smiled, the warmth of his touch, and the depth of their conversation. The kiss lingered in his thoughts, a mix of tenderness and longing that left Benjamin feeling both exhilarated and conflicted.

He couldn't shake the intensity of his feelings, the undeniable connection he felt with Erik. It was more than just attraction; it was a profound sense of understanding and vulnerability that they shared. But with that connection came a wave of fear and uncertainty. The risks were enormous, and the stakes impossibly high.

Benjamin sighed, turning onto his side and staring at the dimly lit room. He knew he couldn't ignore his feelings, yet he also couldn't afford to let them jeopardize his duty. The conflict within him grew stronger, a tumultuous mix of duty and desire, loyalty and love.

As the night wore on, Benjamin's thoughts continued to swirl, each moment with Erik replaying in an endless loop. It was a night of restless reflection, caught between the yearning in his heart and the responsibilities that weighed heavily on his shoulders.

Chapter Twelve

Fort Hunt, Virginia, September 21, 1943

The Massacre of the Acqui Division, also known as the Cephalonia Massacre, began on September 15, after Italy's armistice with the Allies. German forces, viewing the Italian soldiers as traitors, issued an ultimatum to the Italian 33rd Acqui Infantry Division stationed on the Greek island of Cephalonia: join the Germans, surrender, or face combat. The Italians resisted, leading to a brutal confrontation.

Fighting continued for almost a week, until the numerically superior Germans, including mountain troops, overwhelmed the Italians. The German High Command ordered no prisoners to be taken due to the Italians' perceived betrayal. By the end of the battle, around 5,155 Italian soldiers were executed, and another 3,000 drowned when ships transporting them to concentration camps were sunk. This massacre is considered one of the largest prisoner-of-war massacres of World War II.

On September 17, Brigadier Fitzroy Maclean led a British liaison mission to meet Yugoslav partisan leader Josip Broz Tito. This mission, known as the Maclean Mission (Macmis), was crucial in assessing the effectiveness of Tito's forces in resisting the German occupation compared to other resistance groups. The main objective was to determine who was inflicting the most damage on German forces and how the Allies could support their efforts.

Tito's Partisans had emerged as a significant force against the Axis powers, and Maclean's task was to evaluate their operations and recommend support strategies. Churchill's directive was clear: focus on practical military outcomes without concerning themselves with post-war political scenarios. The collaboration between Maclean and Tito led to substantial Allied support for the Partisans, including air drops of supplies and coordinated operations.

Maclean's mission was instrumental in fostering a robust alliance between the British and Yugoslav Partisans, ultimately contributing to significant disruptions of German operations in the Balkans.

In the Pacific Theater during most of September, Allied forces made significant progress in the Solomon Islands, particularly on Vella Lavella. After landing on the island in mid-August, American and New Zealand troops faced fierce Japanese resistance. By mid-September, they continued their offensive to secure the island, which involved intense jungle fighting and overcoming logistical challenges.

Allied forces, including the U.S. Army, Navy, Marine Corps, and New Zealand units, engaged in small-unit actions against well-trained Japanese defenders. Despite the rugged terrain and continuous air raids from nearby Japanese bases, the Allies successfully established supply points and carried out coordinated attacks. The New Zealand troops set up bases and conducted operations from Maravari, utilizing barges to transport supplies and reinforcements due to the lack of roads.

The Battle of Vella Lavella is noted for its strategic importance in the Solomon Islands campaign, demonstrating the Allied tactic of bypassing heavily fortified positions to seize less defended but strategically valuable locations. This approach allowed the Allies to build airfields and strengthen their foothold in the Pacific.

The office of Colonel Stone exuded an aura of authority, its walls adorned with military commendations and strategic maps. Benjamin and Tom stood outside, steeling themselves for the upcoming conversation. Benjamin straightened his uniform and took a deep breath before knocking on the door.

"Enter," Colonel Stone's commanding voice echoed from within.

They entered the office, saluting respectfully as they approached Colonel Stone's desk. The Colonel looked up from his paperwork, his expression a mix of curiosity and sternness.

"At ease, gentlemen. What brings you here?" Colonel Stone inquired, folding his hands on the desk.

Benjamin stepped forward, "Sir, we're here to discuss a proposal regarding one of our detainees, Erik."

"Erik? The German physicist we've been interrogating?" Colonel Stone clarified, studying Benjamin closely.

"Yes, sir. We believe that granting him a supervised outing within the facility's perimeter could be beneficial," Benjamin explained, his tone measured and respectful.

Colonel Stone raised an eyebrow, intrigued. "Explain."

"We've observed a decline in Erik's health due to the overcrowding in the detention building. The unsanitary conditions are taking a toll on him," Tom interjected, adding weight to Benjamin's argument.

Benjamin continued, "A brief outing with no restraints, under strict supervision, could improve his well-being and potentially increase his cooperation. It could serve as an incentive for him to share valuable information."

Colonel Stone listened intently, considering their proposal. "And you believe this is worth the potential risks?"

"We've assessed the security measures thoroughly, sir. The benefits of gaining Erik's trust and cooperation outweigh the risks," Benjamin replied confidently.

After a moment of contemplation, Colonel Stone nodded. "Very well. I'll authorize the supervised outing for Erik Müller. But remember, this is a one-time opportunity. Make sure everything is handled with utmost caution and security. Let me make this very clear to the both of you gentlemen. Herr Müller is to be back inside that detention cell before suppertime."

"Thank you, sir. We'll ensure everything is carried out responsibly," Benjamin expressed gratitude, with Tom nodding in agreement.

As they left Colonel Stone's office, a sense of accomplishment and determination filled Benjamin and Tom. They were one step closer to gaining Erik's trust and extracting crucial information for their mission.

"I guess I'll start making the rounds and let all of the security guards on duty know that we're going to have a detainee out on the grounds this afternoon, Tom said. "I'm assuming that you'll want to be the one to let Erik know."

"Thank you, Tom," Benjamin added as they headed down the hallway.

Benjamin watched the clock on the wall of the small cubicle where he was filling out paperwork. As the hands aligned at 1500 hours, he set his pen down and stood up, a sense of anticipation building within him. He knew this news would be a significant gesture in gaining Erik's trust.

He made his way through the facility to the detention building where Erik was held. The guard at the door acknowledged him with a nod and unlocked Erik's cell. Erik looked up from where he sat on the narrow bed, curiosity evident in his icy blue eyes.

"Erik," Benjamin began with a smile, "I have some exciting news for you."

Erik stood up, his expression a mix of skepticism and interest. "What is it?"

"We've arranged a supervised outing for you," Benjamin announced, watching Erik's reaction closely. "It'll be within the perimeter, but you'll get some fresh air and a change of scenery."

Erik's eyes widened slightly, a glimmer of hope breaking through his usually guarded demeanor. "Really?"

"Yes," Benjamin confirmed. "We've realized that the conditions here in the detention building haven't been ideal, and we believe this could help improve your well-being. Plus, it gives us a chance to talk more openly."

Erik leaned against the cell wall, processing the news. "And when is this outing supposed to take place?"

"Right now," Benjamin replied. "We'll have security measures in place, but I think you'll find it a welcome change. Plus, we'll get to spend another afternoon together! Follow me."

As they walked through the secured doors of P.O. Box 1142, Erik glanced around, taking in the rare opportunity to move freely in the open air within the perimeter.

The sun hung high in the sky, casting a warm glow over Fort Hunt. Benjamin and Erik set off on a slow walk around the perimeter of the facility. Benjamin took it upon himself to show Erik a few of the more interesting historical areas within the compound, hoping to provide some respite from the oppressive confinement of the detention building.

They strolled along the well-worn paths, the crunch of gravel underfoot the only sound accompanying their footsteps for a while. Benjamin pointed out various landmarks and shared snippets of history that he thought might intrigue Erik.

"Over here," Benjamin said, gesturing to a nondescript building, "is one of the original structures from when this place was first built. It served multiple purposes over the years, from a cavalry post to horse stables."

Erik nodded, taking in the surroundings with a sense of quiet appreciation. "It's fascinating how places like this hold so many layers of history."

As Benjamin and Erik walked through the secluded area outside P.O. Box 1142, Erik subtly slipped his hand into his pocket, feeling the reassuring presence of the hidden transmitter he had stuffed into the lining of his detention uniform. He knew he had to be quick and discreet.

Over the past weeks, Erik had managed to gather various components from around the detention building, including the record player Benjamin had given him, which was now in his quarters. His background in physics and engineering had proven invaluable as he had meticulously assembled a small, makeshift radio transmitter using parts from the record player and various other electronics. He had hidden the tiny device within the lining of his detention uniform, always ready for the opportunity he had been anticipating.

Finding a spot where the foliage was denser, offering a bit more cover, Erik slowed his pace, allowing Benjamin to walk a few steps ahead. With a furtive glance around to ensure they were alone, Erik deftly pulled out the small device and activated it. The transmitter emitted a faint, almost imperceptible hum as it powered up.

Erik whispered into the device, sending a message to his undercover allies outside of the facility. He knew the risk he was taking, but desperation had driven him to this point. His message was brief, coded, and filled with urgency.

Just as quickly as he had produced the transmitter, Erik tucked it back into the lining of his uniform. He took a deep breath, trying to calm his racing heart, and resumed walking as if nothing had happened.

Benjamin turned back towards him, a smile on his face. "This place really does have a surprising calming effect, considering it was built for war, doesn't it?"

Erik nodded, forcing a smile. "Yes, it does. It's a welcome respite from everything."

Benjamin's attention was drawn back to the natural beauty surrounding them, completely unaware of Erik's clandestine actions. The transmission had been sent, and now all Erik could do was wait and hope that his message reached its intended destination and that help would come.

Benjamin led Erik to a small, enclosed courtyard with benches and a few patches of greenery. The fresh air and open space were a stark contrast to the confines of his cell.

Erik took a deep breath, savoring the moment. "This day is…unexpected. Thank you, Benjamin. I didn't fully realize how much I needed this until now."

Benjamin felt a sense of accomplishment as he saw Erik's reaction, knowing that this small gesture could make a significant difference in their ongoing efforts to build trust and cooperation.

As the sunlight bathed Erik, Benjamin was struck by how incredibly beautiful he was. If there were such a thing as perfection, Benjamin decided, Erik was its living example. The vibrant streaks of his hair glistened like strands of spun gold in the radiant sunlight, framing his face in a halo of warmth. His eyes, a mesmerizing shade of icy blue, seemed to sparkle with a hidden depth that drew Benjamin in, making it hard for him to divert his gaze.

But it was not just Erik's eyes that captivated him; it was the flawless smoothness of his skin, pale and ethereal in the sunlight. Every curve and angle of his chiseled features cast seductive shadows that seemed to dance with the shifting light, accentuating his allure.

As Benjamin sat there, taking in Erik's beauty, a wave of longing washed over him. It was as if the sunlight had infused Erik's presence with an irresistible magnetism, pulling Benjamin closer with each passing moment. Benjamin found himself lost in the sheer allure of Erik's exquisite form.

The subtle breeze made the fabric of Erik's gray and white striped detention uniform dance along the contours of his lean, athletic chest and abdomen, accentuating the arousing peaks and valleys of his magnificent physical construct. Each movement revealed the sculpted lines of his body, a testament to strength and grace intertwined.

Benjamin couldn't help but notice the way Erik's muscles tensed and relaxed with every breath, a subtle rhythm that added a sensual cadence to his presence. The sunlight played across his skin, highlighting the definition of his shoulders and the curve of his neck, creating a portrait of masculine allure that was impossible to ignore.

It was as if the world around them faded into the background, leaving only Erik's captivating physique and the palpable tension that simmered between them. Benjamin found himself drawn to Erik's gravitational presence, his senses heightened by the sight of such raw, natural beauty.

At that moment, amidst the freedom of the outdoors and the intimacy of their shared space, Benjamin was acutely aware of the desire that pulsed through him, a longing that stirred with each passing second in the presence of Erik's enchanting physicality.

"Benji, you're gawking at me, is something wrong?" Erik asked with an amused expression. "Blink your eyes if you can hear me," he chuckled.

Sitting on a weathered bench, Benjamin and Erik continued their conversation, their voices carrying softly on the breeze. The usual barriers and reservations seemed to melt away in this secluded haven, allowing them to delve deeper into their fears and hopes, sharing pieces of themselves that they had kept hidden.

"I never imagined finding solace in a place like this," Erik admitted, his gaze fixed on the distant horizon. "It's as if the world outside fades away, leaving only us and our thoughts."

Benjamin nodded, a faint smile playing on his lips. "It's moments like these that remind us of our humanity, of the connections that transcend the walls and boundaries imposed upon us."

Erik continued, "Sometimes, I wonder if the choices I've made will lead to regret. The future feels like an uncertain path shrouded in darkness, and I can't shake this feeling of apprehension."

Nodding in understanding, Benjamin replied, "I know what you mean. The weight of responsibilities, the fear of not living up to expectations—it's like a constant battle within myself."

Erik's voice took on a vulnerable tone as he continued, "It's not just the responsibilities. It's the secrets I carry, the parts of myself I've hidden away for so long. Will I ever be free from them?"

Placing a comforting hand on Erik's arm, Benjamin reassured him, "You don't have to face that burden alone, Erik. Sharing your struggles is the first step toward finding peace."

Erik's voice softened as he confessed, "It's hard to let go of the fear, though. Do you think the world will ever accept us for who we truly are?"

With gentle understanding, Benjamin replied, "I hope so, but we can't control how others perceive us, Erik. What matters is accepting ourselves, embracing our flaws and strengths alike."

Erik delved deeper into his introspection, "Do you ever wonder if the choices we make now will define us forever? That we'll be trapped by the consequences?"

Reflectively, Benjamin replied, "It's a possibility. But I believe we also have the power to shape our futures, to learn and grow from our experiences."

Erik's tone turned quiet as he admitted, "I hope you're right. Sometimes, it's hard to see beyond the present moment, to imagine a different path."

In that secluded corner outside P.O. Box 1142, amidst the quiet murmurs of nature and the whispered confessions of two souls intertwining, Benjamin and Erik shared their deepest fears and vulnerabilities, finding solace in the understanding and support they offered each other.

But amidst the weight of their worries, there was also a glimmer of hope, a shared belief in the possibility of something more. They talked about their dreams, the aspirations that whispered to them in moments of solitude, daring them to reach for something beyond the confines of their current reality.

"I never thought I'd find someone I could share these thoughts with," Erik confessed, his voice tinged with a mixture of gratitude and longing. "Someone who understands, who sees beyond the facade we present to the world."

Benjamin reached out, his hand coming to rest on Erik's arm in a gesture of solidarity. "We're in this together, Erik. No matter what the future holds, we'll face it together."

"Everything seems so broken," Erik said, his voice heavy with despair. "Basic human decency has been lost, replaced by idealism, religious extremism, xenophobia. Things have gotten so dark, it's hard to imagine much of a future at all."

"There's still a chance, Erik," Benjamin urged. "There's still a glimmer of hope that we could come out of this together. Maybe, just maybe, we could even find happiness together."

Benjamin took a deep breath, summoning the courage to continue. "This is what I've been trying to figure out how to tell you. Erik, you have to tell us what you know. Colonel Stone has made it clear—they're not going to keep you here much longer. If you continue to be uncooperative, they're going to transfer you to a POW labor camp or a military prison. I will never see you again. You will never be free again. But if you tell us what you know, we can help you get citizenship in this country. You could live a relatively normal life."

Erik shook his head, his expression pained. "Benji, this is what I've been trying to tell you. Your military doesn't want people like us. Your country doesn't want people like us. If I give you what you want, what happens? I might get to live in this country that no more wants or accepts people like us than the Nazis do."

His voice grew more intense, a mixture of frustration and sorrow. "One minute you talk about how the weight of hiding your truth from the world is an overwhelming burden, but then the next minute you're telling me that we could be together and happy. If you're trying to sell me a happily-ever-after fantasy ending, you're not selling it very well. And what would be the cost? The lives and reputation of my family? Benji, I care about you, but I will not betray my family for a fantasy."

Benjamin felt a pang of guilt at Erik's words. He knew Erik was right, and the reality of their situation was stark and unforgiving.

"Erik, I know it's not that simple," Benjamin said, his voice softening. "I understand the risks, and I know that what I'm asking is huge. But I believe in you. I believe that together, we can find a way to navigate this, to build something real despite everything."

Erik sighed, his shoulders sagging with the weight of his burdens. "Benji, it's not just about us. My family...they've already suffered so much. If I give up the secrets I hold, it could destroy them."

Benjamin reached out, placing a hand on Erik's arm. "I don't want to put you in a position where you have to choose between us and your family. But I also can't stand the thought of losing you. If there's even a small chance that we can find a way to make this work, shouldn't we try?"

Erik looked into Benjamin's eyes, searching for something—hope, perhaps, or a promise that everything would be alright. "What if it all falls apart? What if I end up alone, ostracized in a country that doesn't want me, with no way back?"

"Then we'll face that together," Benjamin said firmly. "I won't abandon you. We'll figure it out, step by step. But we need to take that first step, Erik. You need to trust me."

For a moment, they stood in silence, the tension between them palpable. Erik finally nodded, though his expression remained troubled. "Alright, Benji. I'll consider it. But I need to think about how to protect my family too."

Benjamin squeezed Erik's arm gently. "Thank you, Erik. That's all I can ask for. We'll find a way, I promise."

As they continued their walk, Benjamin couldn't shake the feeling of dread and conflict that had settled in his chest. Time was running out, and the road ahead was uncertain, fraught with dangers and difficult choices. But for now, they had each other, and that was enough to keep hope alive.

They walked in silence for a few more moments, the weight of their conversation hanging in the air. The sun dipped lower, casting long shadows across the ground and bathing the surroundings in a warm, golden glow.

"Benji, can I ask you something?" Erik's voice broke the silence, tentative and uncertain.

"Of course, Erik. Anything," Benjamin replied, his heart quickening.

Erik stopped walking and turned to face Benjamin, his expression a mixture of vulnerability and determination. "What if this war never ends for us? What if we're always fighting, always hiding who we are? How do we live like that?"

Benjamin took a deep breath, searching for the right words. "I don't have all the answers, Erik. But I do know that hiding who we are is something we've both been doing for far too long. Maybe we can't change the world overnight, but we can find small pockets of peace, moments where we can be ourselves without fear."

Erik's eyes softened, a flicker of hope igniting within them. "Do you really believe that's possible?"

Benjamin stepped closer, reaching out to gently cradle Erik's face in his hands. "Yes, I do. We can create those moments together. And who knows, maybe we'll find others like us, people who understand and accept us. It's a long road, but we don't have to walk it alone."

Erik closed his eyes, leaning into Benjamin's touch. "I want to believe that, Benji. I really do."

"Then hold on to that belief," Benjamin urged, his voice barely above a whisper. "It's what will get us through the darkest times."

They stood there, the world around them fading into the background as they found solace in each other's presence. The bond between them felt stronger than ever, a lifeline in a sea of uncertainty.

As the sun began to set, painting the sky in hues of pink and orange, Benjamin knew that this moment was fleeting.

But it was enough for now—a promise of what could be, a glimmer of hope amidst the shadows.

"Let's keep walking," Benjamin said softly, his hand still resting on Erik's cheek. "We have a little more time before we have to head back."

Erik nodded, his eyes still closed. "Alright, let's make the most of it."

They continued their walk, side by side, their footsteps in sync as they navigated the quiet paths around the compound. The conversation turned lighter, filled with shared memories and dreams of a future where they could be free.

In that brief respite from the harsh realities of their lives, they found a sense of peace. And for Benjamin, that was enough to keep fighting for a better tomorrow.

Benjamin escorted Erik back to the detention building, his mind replaying their conversation. He glanced at Erik, who seemed to be lost in his thoughts as well. As they reached Erik's containment cell, Erik paused.

"Thank you for today," Erik said softly, trying to convey all the unspoken words through his gaze. He gave a small, appreciative smile. "I needed this, Benji. More than you know."

Benjamin watched as Erik stepped inside the cell. The door closed with a heavy clang, the sound echoing in Benjamin's mind. He waited until the guard locked the door securely, then turned to leave.

As he made his way to the mess hall, Benjamin's thoughts were heavy. He replayed every word Erik had said, every emotion that had flickered across his face. The weight of the secrets they both carried pressed down on him, making his steps feel leaden.

When he entered the mess hall, the air was thick with the mingled scents of dinner, and the low hum of voices filled the space, punctuated by the occasional clink of cutlery against trays. The contrast to the silence of the detention building was striking, a jarring reminder of the duality of his world. He spotted Tom in line, already holding a tray, and quickly grabbed one himself, falling into step beside him.

"Hey, Tom," Benjamin said, trying to shake off the melancholy that clung to him.

"Hey, Ben," Tom replied, noticing the somber look on Benjamin's face. "How did it go with Erik?"

Benjamin sighed, not sure where to begin. "It was...intense. We talked about a lot of things. Fears, hopes, the future...or the lack of it."

Tom nodded, understanding the gravity of the situation. "It sounds like it was a heavy conversation."

"It was," Benjamin admitted. "But I think it was necessary. He needs to know that there's still a chance for something better, even if it seems impossible right now."

They reached the end of the line and found a table in a quieter corner of the mess hall. As they sat down to eat, Benjamin couldn't help but feel the weight of the day pressing down on him. He knew that their journey was far from over and that the path ahead was fraught with uncertainty.

"Tom, do you ever wonder if we're doing the right thing?" Benjamin asked, voicing a question that had been gnawing at him.

Tom looked at him thoughtfully. "All the time, Ben. But we have to believe that what we're doing will make a difference. That it will lead to something better."

Benjamin nodded, taking comfort in Tom's words. "I hope you're right. For all our sakes."

As they ate, Benjamin's thoughts remained with Erik, locked away in his cell, carrying the weight of his secrets and responsibilities. He resolved to find a way to give them both a chance at the future they so desperately needed.

Chapter Thirteen

Fort Hunt, Virginia, September 27, 1943

The tides of war were beginning to shift. On September 21, during Operation Avalanche (the Allied invasion of Italy), British forces, specifically elements of the British 78th Infantry Division, entered the town of Termoli located in the Molise region of Italy.

The capture of Termoli was part of the larger Allied strategy to push northward along the Italian peninsula and gain control of key strategic points.

Following the initial entry of British forces, Canadian troops from the 1st Canadian Division launched an assault on Termoli. Despite facing German resistance, the Canadians successfully captured Termoli on September 23, securing a vital foothold for the Allies in Italy.

On September 25, German forces launched a counterattack against the Allied-held town of Termoli. The German counteroffensive aimed to dislodge the Canadian troops and regain control of the strategic location.

Despite the German counterattack, the Canadian forces, supported by British units, managed to hold their ground and repel the enemy assault. By September 27, British and Canadian forces linked up effectively, reinforcing each other's positions and securing Termoli against further German attacks. The successful defense and consolidation of Termoli marked a significant achievement for the Allies in their Italian campaign, paving the way for further advances northward towards Rome.

During the period of September 21 to September 27, Allied military leaders, including General Dwight D. Eisenhower and his staff, were engaged in intensive strategic planning for Operation Overlord (the Allied invasion of Normandy). Detailed discussions and preparations were underway regarding the timing, location, logistical aspects, troop deployments, and coordination of air, sea, and ground forces for the invasion.

The selection of landing sites along the Normandy coast was a crucial aspect of the planning. Various factors such as beach conditions, defensive fortifications, terrain features, and potential German resistance were taken into account when choosing the landing zones.

Intelligence gathering efforts, including aerial reconnaissance, espionage, and analysis of German defenses, played a vital role in shaping the invasion plans. Allied intelligence gathering operations such as the Army G-2 Intelligence Division's covert facility, P.O. Box 1142, provided valuable information about enemy troop movements, fortifications, minefields, and obstacles on the beaches.

Coordination with French resistance groups, such as the Maquis, was also part of the planning process. Resistance activities, including sabotage operations and gathering intelligence behind enemy lines, were integrated into the overall strategy for weakening German defenses and disrupting their communications.

Measures to maintain secrecy and deceive the Germans about the true nature and timing of the invasion were also underway. Operation Bodyguard, a complex deception plan involving fake military operations and misleading intelligence, was implemented to confuse the enemy and divert their attention from the actual landing sites.

Benjamin stood in the briefing room, his eyes skimming over the recent interrogation notes, trying to make sense of the puzzle laid out before him. The room buzzed with activity, officers, and analysts moving with purpose, maps and intelligence reports scattered across tables, highlighting the gravity of their mission. Colonel Stone's commanding voice cut through the noise, his words carrying the weight of urgency and necessity.

"We need this information, gentlemen. Time is not on our side," Stone's tone brooked no argument, his steely gaze meeting each person's eyes in turn, impressing upon them the critical nature of their task.

Benjamin couldn't help but feel the pressure mounting. Every second counted, every detail in those notes could be the key to unlocking vital intelligence. Yet, amidst the controlled chaos of the briefing room, his thoughts kept drifting back to his last session with Erik.

There had been a change in Erik, subtle yet palpable. A restlessness lingered in his eyes, a hint of something unspoken beneath his calm exterior. Benjamin shook his head, trying to dispel the distractions. He needed to focus, to piece together the fragments of information gathered from Erik's responses.

As he delved deeper into the interrogation notes, Benjamin's determination grew. He knew that the fate of their mission, perhaps even the outcome of the larger war, hinged on their ability to extract actionable intelligence. With Colonel Stone's words echoing in his mind, Benjamin steeled himself for the challenging tasks ahead, ready to confront whatever obstacles lay in their path to obtaining the crucial information they needed. He decided that he would pay another visit to Erik in the detention building later that afternoon.

That afternoon, the detention building's library was unusually lively, a stark contrast to the usual somber atmosphere of confinement. As Benjamin entered, the first thing that caught his attention was a group of detainees gathered in a corner, their heads close together in intense conversation. They cast furtive glances in Benjamin's direction, their voices lowering to whispers as he approached, a sense of secrecy hanging in the air like an unspoken code.

Pretending to browse the books, Benjamin kept a keen eye on the group, his instincts alert to any signs of unusual activity. Erik, not actively engaged in the conversation, caught sight of Benjamin and quickly signaled to the others, their discussion halting abruptly.

"What's going on here, Erik?" Benjamin asked, injecting a casual tone into his voice, though his curiosity and suspicion were evident.

"Just a discussion about…literature," Erik replied, his response sounding rehearsed, but his eyes betrayed a hint of panic, a flicker of nervousness that didn't escape Benjamin's notice.

As the other detainees scattered, leaving Erik alone in the secluded nook with Benjamin, Erik appeared visibly unsettled, his usual calm demeanor replaced by a noticeable agitation. He sat across from Benjamin, his posture tense, his eyes darting towards the windows and doors as if expecting someone or something to interrupt their conversation at any moment.

"Erik, you seem distant today. What's on your mind?" Benjamin probed, his tone gentle yet probing, trying to gauge Erik's mood and uncover the source of his unease.

"Just thinking about…possibilities," Erik replied vaguely, his voice lacking its usual confidence, his words tinged with a sense of apprehension.

Benjamin's suspicion grew stronger with each passing moment. Something was definitely off, and he couldn't shake the feeling that there was more to Erik's behavior than met the eye.

Benjamin asked, "Have you given any more thought to our last discussion?" There was a note of concern in his voice, tempered with a touch of curiosity, as he sought to understand Erik's state of mind.

Erik's response was a little snappy, his agitation evident in the way he replied, "I've had other things on my mind, Benjamin. It's not easy to focus on hypotheticals when reality is pressing down on us."

The tension in the room was palpable, the air heavy with unspoken words and underlying unease. Benjamin noted the change in Erik's demeanor, the sharpness in his tone, and the guardedness in his expression. It was clear that something had shifted since their last conversation, and Benjamin couldn't help but wonder what events or thoughts were weighing on Erik's mind so heavily.

Benjamin sat with Erik for a while longer, trying to ease the tension that hung in the air like a heavy cloud. However, it became increasingly apparent that Erik was not in the mood for conversation. His responses were terse, his attention drifting to distant thoughts that seemed to occupy his mind completely.

Sensing Erik's need for space and understanding that pushing further might only exacerbate the situation, Benjamin decided to take his leave. Standing up from his seat, he offered Erik a nod of understanding and a reassuring smile, silently communicating his respect for Erik's boundaries.

"I'll leave you to your thoughts, Erik," Benjamin said softly, his voice carrying a tone of empathy.

Erik's gaze briefly met Benjamin's, a flicker of gratitude passing through his troubled eyes before they returned to their distant gaze. Benjamin turned and made his way towards the door, leaving Erik to his solitude and the weight of whatever burdens weighed upon him.

As Benjamin exited the room, he couldn't shake off the concern that lingered in his mind. Erik's sudden change in demeanor and the underlying tension hinted at deeper struggles that he was grappling with. Benjamin resolved to give Erik the space he needed while also remaining ready to offer support whenever Erik was ready to open up.

In the mess hall, Benjamin sat with Tom, his mind racing with a torrent of thoughts and uncertainties. The clatter of utensils, the chatter of fellow soldiers, and the aroma of food filled the air, but to Benjamin, it all seemed distant and muffled, as if he were in a bubble of his own thoughts.

Tom's voice broke through Benjamin's reverie, his concern evident in the furrow of his brow and the earnestness in his eyes. "Do you think he's planning something?" Tom's question cut through the ambient noise, drawing Benjamin's attention back to the present moment.

"I don't know," Benjamin replied, his voice tinged with a mix of apprehension and frustration. He stared at his untouched food, his appetite forgotten amidst the weight of the situation with Erik. "But I can't shake this feeling."

Tom leaned in closer, his expression growing more serious. "What kind of feeling?"

Benjamin hesitated, searching for the right words. "It's not just Erik I'm worried about," he began. "I don't think he's planning anything on his own. But he might be assisting others, maybe even considering participating in something bigger."

Tom's eyes widened slightly. "Like what? Do you have any idea?"

Benjamin nodded slowly. "Earlier today, I noticed some suspicious activity in the library. A group of detainees were whispering among themselves, and they went silent the moment I walked in. Erik was with them, and when I asked him what was going on, he said they were just discussing literature. But something felt off."

Tom's concern deepened. "What kind of suspicious activity? Do you think they're plotting something?"

"Possibly," Benjamin replied, his mind replaying the scene in the library. "Erik seemed unusually agitated when I questioned him. His usual calm demeanor was gone, replaced by a nervous energy. It's like he was caught off guard and trying to cover something up."

Tom leaned back, his eyes scanning the mess hall as if he could see the hidden threads of conspiracy Benjamin hinted at. "We need to keep a closer watch on them, then. Maybe alert Colonel Stone, let him know what you saw and felt."

Benjamin nodded, though he felt a pang of reluctance. He didn't want to believe that Erik could be involved in something harmful. But the evidence, however circumstantial, was mounting. "I'll talk to the Colonel. But we need to be careful. If Erik and the others are up to something, we can't afford to tip them off."

The usual camaraderie and banter that filled the mess hall felt distant to Benjamin. He felt oddly isolated as if a barrier had formed between him and the rest of the world. The laughter and conversations around him seemed to echo faintly, the sounds blending into a background hum that only served to emphasize his own inner turmoil.

As Benjamin and Tom continued their conversation, discussing possible scenarios and trying to make sense of Erik's behavior, Benjamin's thoughts kept circling back to their last interaction. The unease that had settled in the pit of his stomach refused to dissipate, leaving him with a sense of foreboding that he couldn't quite shake off.

Benjamin was hesitant to bring his concerns to Colonel Stone's attention. The weight of his uncertainty pressed heavily on his shoulders. If Colonel Stone discovered that Erik was involved in a plot of some kind, Erik would likely be put under even stricter supervision, potentially severing any unsupervised interaction between them. The thought of losing the opportunity to connect with Erik on a more personal level filled Benjamin with a sense of dread. He needed to find out the truth himself before making any drastic decisions.

Determined to uncover the reality of Erik's involvement, Benjamin decided to take a bold step. Later that evening, when the detention facility was quieter and the guards less vigilant, he made his way to Erik's cell. The corridors were dimly lit, casting long shadows that danced eerily along the walls as he walked. His heart pounded with a mix of anticipation and anxiety.

When he reached Erik's cell, he paused, listening for any sounds that might indicate Erik's activities. Hearing nothing but the soft rustle of movement inside, Benjamin took a deep breath and knocked gently on the door before entering unannounced.

Erik looked up, startled, as Benjamin stepped inside. He was crouched beside his bed, his hands busy with something hidden in the shadows. For a moment, their eyes locked, and Benjamin saw a flicker of alarm in Erik's usually composed gaze.

"What are you doing here, Benjamin?" Erik asked, trying to mask his surprise with a casual tone.

"I needed to talk to you," Benjamin replied, his voice steady despite the turmoil within. He glanced around the cell, noting the disarray of papers and the faint glow of a small lamp. "What's going on, Erik? You've been acting strangely, and I need to know why."

Erik hesitated, his fingers twitching nervously. Benjamin's eyes were drawn to a glimpse of metal and wires peeking out from beneath the bed. He moved closer, his curiosity piqued.

"What is that?" Benjamin asked, pointing to the hidden object.

Erik's expression shifted from surprise to resignation. With a sigh, he pulled out the device he had been working on—the makeshift radio transmitter. It was crudely assembled, but the intent behind it was unmistakable. To Benjamin's surprise, Erik was disassembling it, his fingers moving deftly to remove the components.

Benjamin's eyes widened in shock. "Erik, what are you doing with this?"

Erik ran a hand through his hair, clearly conflicted. "It's not what you think, Benjamin. I wasn't planning anything harmful. I just…I needed to hear news from the outside world. To know what's happening out there. I couldn't stand the isolation any longer. But I realized the risk was too great, so I'm taking it apart."

Benjamin felt a mix of relief and apprehension. While Erik's explanation made sense, the risk involved was immense. "You know the consequences if you're caught with this, don't you? They'll tighten security around you, and you'll lose any chance of freedom."

"I know," Erik replied quietly, his eyes pleading with Benjamin to understand. "But I felt like I was suffocating in here, cut off from everything and everyone. This was the only way I could think of to stay connected."

Benjamin thought, "This must be why he was acting weirdly earlier." He took a deep breath, weighing his options. If he reported Erik, it would mean losing the chance to connect with him unsupervised and possibly ruining the fragile trust they had built. On the other hand, by not reporting it, Benjamin was taking a significant risk, one that could jeopardize his own position and credibility if discovered.

With a sigh, he made his decision. "Erik, you need to give me the transmitter," Benjamin said firmly, his voice leaving no room for argument.

"Right now," Benjamin said finally, his decision made. "I won't report this, but you have to give me the transmitter, or what's left of it, right now."

With a nod, Erik handed him the disassembled parts of the transmitter. Benjamin carefully gathered the pieces, feeling a sense of resolution. He knew this was a gamble, but he believed in Erik and his intentions. As he left the cell, the weight of his decision settled over him like a heavy cloak, shrouding his thoughts with the gravity of what he had chosen to do.

Benjamin carefully tucked the disassembled transmitter into his pocket as he left the detention building, his mind swirling with thoughts of what to do next. The weight of the device seemed to press against him, a tangible reminder of the risks he was now entangled in.

Upon reaching his quarters, Benjamin sat down at his desk, the transmitter laid out before him. He studied the pieces carefully, noting their crude construction and the ingenuity behind Erik's attempt to stay connected. Despite the danger it posed, Benjamin couldn't help but admire Erik's determination.

With a deep breath, Benjamin hid the transmitter in a secure compartment within his belongings, ensuring it was well-concealed. With the device safely hidden away, Benjamin breathed a sigh of relief. He was taking a huge risk, but it was a risk he was willing to take for the sake of what he believed was right.

Not much later, Tom returned to the barracks and flopped down into his cot with an audible exhale. "Did you get a chance to talk to Colonel Stone?" he inquired.

"No, I think I might have just been blowing things out of proportion. You know, in this line of work, eventually, you start seeing shadows where there aren't any," Benjamin replied.

That night, Benjamin laid in bed, his mind restless with thoughts of everything that had transpired. The weight of the disassembled transmitter hidden in his belongings seemed to cast a shadow over his thoughts, a constant reminder of the risks he had taken and the precarious situation he found himself in.

As he stared up at the ceiling, Benjamin couldn't shake off the feeling of uncertainty gnawing at him. What had started as a simple act of compassion towards Erik had now evolved into something much more complicated. He wondered if he had underestimated the gravity of the situation, if his desire to protect Erik had clouded his judgment.

The events of the day played out in his mind like a relentless reel, each scene punctuated with moments of tension and apprehension. From his impromptu decision to confiscate the transmitter to the daunting prospect of hiding its existence from Colonel Stone, Benjamin couldn't help but question the consequences of his actions.

What if he had made a mistake? What if his actions led to unforeseen consequences for Erik and himself? The uncertainty of it all weighed heavily on him, filling him with a sense of unease.

Despite the doubts plaguing his mind, Benjamin felt a sense of determination stirring within him. He couldn't undo what had already been done, but he could control how he moved forward. He resolved to be more cautious, to tread carefully, and to think through his decisions before acting impulsively.

With a deep breath, Benjamin closed his eyes, hoping that sleep would bring clarity and a renewed sense of purpose. Tomorrow would bring new challenges, but he was ready to face them head-on, armed with a sense of responsibility and a commitment to do whatever it took to protect those he cared about.

The next morning, Benjamin woke up at his usual 0530. He quickly put on his shorts and jogging shoes, eager to clear his mind with his morning jog. The crisp morning air filled his lungs as he set off, the steady rhythm of his feet hitting the ground helping to organize his thoughts.

After his run, Benjamin hit the showers, letting the warm water wash away the fatigue and tension from his muscles. He felt a bit more centered, ready to face whatever the day might throw at him. Returning to the barracks, he expected to find Tom waiting for their usual breakfast routine. However, when he walked in, Tom was nowhere to be seen.

A slight frown creased Benjamin's forehead. It was unusual for Tom to deviate from their established routine. He glanced around the barracks, hoping to catch a glimpse of his friend, but the place was empty. Concern began to gnaw at him as he made his way to their usual breakfast spot, hoping Tom had gone ahead.

The mess hall was already bustling with soldiers, the clatter of trays and the murmur of conversations filling the air. Benjamin scanned the room, his eyes darting from table to table. When he didn't see Tom, his concern deepened. He grabbed a tray and mechanically filled it with food, his mind preoccupied with thoughts of where Tom could be.

Sitting alone at their usual table, Benjamin's thoughts raced. Had something happened to Tom? Was he called in for an early duty? Or perhaps he had some urgent business to attend to? Each possibility seemed more unsettling than the last. As he poked at his food, his appetite vanished, replaced by a growing sense of unease.

At that same moment, with a heavy heart, Tom made his way to Colonel Stone's office. He knocked and entered, his dread palpable.

"What brings you here, Sergeant?" Stone asked, looking up from his desk.

"Sir, I need to talk to you about some suspicious activity in the detention building. I think some of the detainees are planning something," Tom said, his voice tense.

"What gives you that impression?" Stone inquired, his gaze sharpening.

"Corporal Steinburg has mentioned observing some suspicious activities. Detainees have been congregating and talking in hushed tones, breaking away as soon as someone comes near. And he says that Erik Müller has been acting very strangely lately as if he might have some involvement," Tom explained.

"Is that so?" the Colonel replied, his tone growing serious. "And why hasn't Corporal Steinburg reported this suspicious activity to me himself?"

"Well, sir, I believe that Corporal Steinburg is in so deep with the ongoing interrogation of Müller that he might be suffering from a temporary lack of proper judgment. This interrogation has really taken a toll on him," Tom said, trying to convey the gravity of the situation.

"I understand," the Colonel replied, nodding thoughtfully. "These things can get downright mucky and complicated. Thank you for bringing this to my attention. I will see to it that your suspicions are thoroughly evaluated."

"Thank you, sir," Tom replied, snapping a salute and turning to leave.

Chapter Fourteen

Fort Hunt, Virginia, September 30, 1943

The Axis powers, primarily Germany and Italy, were aware of the growing threat posed by the Allied forces in various theaters of war. In response, they began deploying reserves to key strategic locations. These reserves consisted of well-trained troops, armored units, and artillery, intended to bolster defensive capabilities and provide rapid response to Allied advances. The deployment of reserves aimed to reinforce critical sectors along the front lines and prepare for potential Allied offensives.

Axis forces focused on enhancing their defensive lines, which included fortifications, trenches, bunkers, and obstacles such as barbed wire and minefields. The goal was to create formidable barriers that would impede Allied advancements and force them to engage in costly assaults. Reinforcing defensive lines also involved repairing and strengthening existing structures damaged during previous engagements to maintain a robust defensive posture.

In addition to reinforcing defensive positions, the Axis powers strategically redeployed troops and resources based on intelligence assessments and operational priorities. This involved shifting units from less threatened sectors to areas deemed vulnerable to potential Allied offensives. By reallocating forces in a flexible manner, Axis commanders aimed to maintain a balance between defending critical territories and conserving resources for offensive operations when opportunities arose.

Axis defensive measures also involved integrating advanced defensive technologies into their strategies. This included utilizing anti-tank weapons, improved artillery systems, and mine-laying techniques to create formidable defensive zones. Additionally, they employed camouflage, decoys, and concealment tactics to deceive Allied reconnaissance and disrupt enemy targeting.

At this time, Adolf Hitler was desperately seeking his so-called "Wunderwaffe" or "wonder weapons," experimental military technologies that he hoped would turn the tide of the war back in their favor.

By late 1943, the development and deployment of these wonder weapons had become a significant focus for the Nazi leadership. Hitler and his military strategists were increasingly desperate for breakthroughs that could counteract the growing strength and advances of the Allied forces.

The quest for wonder weapons was driven by a combination of technological ambition, military necessity, and Hitler's personal fascination with advanced weaponry. The Nazi regime poured significant resources into research and development programs, often at great human and economic cost, in the hope that these innovations would provide a decisive advantage.

As dusk settled over P.O. Box 1142, casting long shadows across the compound, a daring escape plan was set into motion. The sky was painted with hues of deep orange and purple, the last remnants of daylight fading into the encroaching darkness. It was a calculated risk, meticulously timed to perfection to exploit the fleeting window of opportunity before the nightly lockdown at 1900 hours descended like an iron curtain, sealing the fate of all within its reach.

Inside the detention building, a tense quiet hung in the air. Guards patrolled the halls with practiced indifference, their routines a monotonous dance that the detainees had studied for weeks. Every shift change, every patrol route, and every surveillance blind spot had been noted and analyzed, forming the blueprint of the escape plan that now hung by a thread of timing and precision.

The conspirators moved into position, their hearts pounding with the weight of what was about to unfold. Each person had a role to play, a critical piece in the elaborate puzzle. They had waited for this moment, coordinating through covert messages and silent signals, their loyalty to the cause unwavering despite the risks.

With swift, practiced motions, they moved through the corridors of the detention building. Surveillance cameras, a technology that was stolen from the Nazis, were avoided, their positions and blind spots exploited with precision. The guards, caught unaware, fell victim to the detainees' well-rehearsed maneuvers. They were overpowered quickly and silently, ensuring no alarm would be raised.

The group of detainees, their nerves taut with anticipation, quietly exited the detention building, gathering in the shadows. They held their breaths as the final minutes ticked away. They had prepared for this night, forging documents, crafting makeshift tools, and memorizing every detail of their escape route.

Timed to coincide with the next shift change and the fading light, the detainees made their move. Outside the compound, their allies initiated the distraction—a well-timed explosion set off near the outer perimeter.

The blast sent a plume of smoke and debris into the air, shattering the evening's tranquility. It was followed by a series of secondary explosions and the screeching of a vehicle's tires, as a truck loaded with supplies was driven erratically towards the gates. The guards, caught off guard by the sudden chaos, rushed to respond, leaving their posts in disarray.

Alarms blared, lights flickered, and the confusion provided the perfect cover for the detainees. The patrol guards, momentarily blinded by the smoke and the flashing lights, missed the figures darting through the shadows toward the fence.

As they reached the outer perimeter, the real challenge lay ahead. The perimeter fence loomed like a menacing barrier, patrolled by armed guards and watchtowers that scanned the area with unyielding vigilance. But the detainees were ready, their plan accounting for every possible contingency.

The diversion outside had worked, pulling guards away from their posts. The detainees, moving like shadows in the dim light, approached the fence with bated breath. The watchtowers, their spotlights cutting through the darkness, were temporarily blinded by a second, well-placed distraction—another explosion set off by their outside allies.

With the guards' attention diverted, the detainees sprinted towards the fence. They moved with the fluidity of well-trained soldiers, using makeshift tools to cut through the wire. Bullets whizzed past, the crackle of gunfire mingling with the shouts of alarm. But their determination was unyielding, fueled by the desperate need for freedom.

One detainee, a Nazi U-boat commander, was the first to attempt to scale the fence. He reached the top just as a spotlight found him. A single shot rang out, and he fell, his escape cut tragically short. But the others pressed on. One by one, three escapees squeezed through the cutout in the fence. Their resolve was steeled by his sacrifice.

Erik, caught in the surge of motion, made his own desperate bid for freedom. He moved swiftly through the shadows, his heart pounding with the rhythm of his hurried footsteps. The perimeter fence loomed ahead, a daunting barrier but also the final obstacle to his freedom. He quickened his pace, the taste of liberation almost within reach.

Suddenly, a hand grabbed his arm, yanking him back into the shadows. Erik spun around, eyes wide with surprise and anger, coming face-to-face with Tom.

"Erik, stop!" Tom hissed, his grip tightening. "What the hell do you think you're doing?"

"Let go of me, Tom!" Erik snarled, wrenching his arm free. "I'm getting out of here. I can't stay locked up any longer."

Tom's eyes flashed with a mixture of concern and determination. "Do you have any idea what you're risking? You'll get yourself killed!"

"Better to die trying than to rot in that cell," Erik shot back, his voice edged with desperation. "You wouldn't understand."

"Try me," Tom challenged, stepping closer. "Why are you doing this? Is it worth throwing everything away?"

Erik's expression hardened, but a flicker of vulnerability crossed his eyes. "I can't stay here, Tom. Every day I'm here, I feel like I'm losing myself. This place is slowly killing me. It's killing my spirit. I don't belong here! I need to be free, to find a way back to who I was before all this."

Tom's grip loosened slightly, his voice softening. "And what about Benjamin? Do you think he wants this for you? Do you think he could stand losing you like this?"

Erik's resolve wavered, the mention of Benjamin striking a chord. "I...I don't want to hurt him. But I can't stay. I can't live like this anymore."

"Running isn't the answer," Tom said firmly. "Think about what you're doing. Think about Benjamin. If you go through with this, you'll be leaving him behind, and for what? A chance that might end in a bullet?"

Erik's shoulders sagged, the weight of Tom's words sinking in. "I don't know what else to do."

Tom looked him in the eye, his expression earnest. "You stay. You fight. Not with guns or escapes, but with your mind, your heart.". He pleaded, "Help us! Tell us what you know! Giving us the information that you're withholding could save thousands of lives! Benjamin believes in you, and so do I. We want to help you. Don't throw it all away!"

The sound of approaching footsteps and the distant shouts of guards cut through the tension. Erik glanced toward the fence, then back at Tom, torn between the lure of freedom and the reality of his situation.

"Please, Erik," Tom implored, his voice steady and sincere. "Stay for him. Stay for yourself."

In a wave of panic, Eric made a sudden lunge toward the perimeter fence and Tom tackled him to the ground. They struggled fiercely, a silent battle of wills in the darkness.

Benjamin, arriving on the scene, saw the two men grappling. He rushed forward, his mind racing. Without thinking, he pulled out his gun, aiming it at Erik. "Stop! Both of you, stop!"

The struggle ceased, the air thick with tension. Erik's eyes were fiery and wild. His intense gaze met Benjamin's, a mixture of fear and defiance. He was panting from the fierce scuffle with Tom.

In that charged moment, as chaos reigned around them, Benjamin's voice trembled with desperation. "Erik, don't do this! I...I can't let you go. I can't lose you!"

Erik, breathing heavily, looked at Benjamin with a mix of confusion and realization. "Benji, put the gun down. You don't want to shoot me. Please, just let me go. Benjamin, please let me go!"

The gun in Benjamin's hand shook. He couldn't pull the trigger. "Erik, stay where you are! Please don't make me do this!"

The sudden crack of gunfire pierced the night, shattering the fragile calm that had settled between Benjamin and Erik. It was a shot from a guard stationed in the distance, a warning that their escape had been noticed. The bullet whizzed past them, missing its mark, but its chilling echo reverberated through the air, a stark reminder of the peril they faced.

Erik froze, his resolve faltering as he took a step back from the fence. Fear etched lines of uncertainty on his face, mirroring the tumultuous emotions raging within him. He turned to look at Benjamin, searching for reassurance in the darkness.

"I can't let you go," Benjamin's voice quivered, his eyes locked on Erik's. The confession hung in the air, unspoken words lingering between them. "I…I'm in love with you."

The weight of Benjamin's admission hung heavy in the tense silence that followed. Erik's breath caught in his throat, his heart pounding with a mixture of disbelief and longing. For a moment, time seemed to stand still, their surroundings fading into insignificance as their feelings for each other took center stage.

"I…" Erik started, his voice barely a whisper. His gaze softened, filled with a depth of emotion that words alone couldn't express. "Benjamin, I…I feel the same way."

Benjamin took a hesitant step closer, his eyes never leaving Erik's. "I didn't want to admit it, not even to myself. But seeing you, knowing what you mean to me…I can't lose you, Erik."

Erik reached out, his hand trembling slightly as he touched Benjamin's cheek. "I never thought I could feel this way, especially here, in this place. But you've shown me something real, something worth holding onto."

Benjamin lowered his gun, his relief palpable. He took Erik's hand in his, their fingers intertwining. "We'll find a way, together. Whatever it takes, we'll make it through this. You're not just another detainee to me, Erik. You're everything."

Erik pulled Benjamin into a tender embrace, their hearts beating in sync. "You've given me hope, Benjamin. And I promise, I won't let go."

The world around them seemed to fade away, the chaos and danger momentarily forgotten. In that embrace, they found solace and strength, a love that transcended the confines of their circumstances.

Tears glistened in Benjamin's eyes as he leaned into Erik's touch. "Every moment we've shared, every word, every glance…they've all led me to this. I can't imagine my life without you."

Erik's eyes shone with unshed tears, his voice breaking. "I was ready to leave, to take my chances out there. But now…knowing how you feel, knowing we're not alone in this…I can't walk away."

The admission hung between them, a fragile bridge connecting their hearts in the midst of chaos. The danger they faced was real, but in that fleeting moment, their love eclipsed everything else. It was a revelation that bound them together, defying the barriers of their circumstances.

As they stood there, caught in the intensity of their emotions, the world around them seemed to blur. The distant shouts of guards and the faint glow of searchlights became background noise to the profound connection they shared.

From the shadows cast by the dimly lit compound, Staff Sergeant Lewis observed the tender moment between Benjamin and Erik. His trained eyes caught every subtle gesture, every whispered word, and his expression hardened with suspicion.

As Benjamin confessed his feelings and Erik reciprocated, a flicker of realization crossed Lewis's face. He knew that such emotions, between detainees and interrogators, were forbidden in the rigid hierarchy of military protocol, especially if they were both men.

Quickly assessing the situation, Lewis ducked behind a nearby corner, his mind racing with the implications of what he had witnessed. The clandestine nature of the encounter only fueled his suspicions further.

With a calculated move, he slipped away, intent on reporting his observations to Colonel Stone. The weight of what he had seen added a new layer of complexity to an already volatile situation. Lewis knew that his next steps could have far-reaching consequences for everyone involved.

Before the commotion had fully de-escalated, Erik was returned to his detention cell, his escape attempt thwarted. One man lay dead, and three others were now on the loose. The consequences of that night rippled through the compound. The echoes of the escape attempt reverberated throughout P.O. Box 1142, leaving behind a trail of shattered plans and exposed hearts.

The dawn broke with a heavy tension hanging over P.O. Box 1142. The air was thick with unease after the previous evening's escape attempt, and everyone on base could feel it. Benjamin woke at his usual 0530, his mind still replaying the night's events. He dressed in his usual shorts and jogging shoes and set off for his morning run, hoping the familiar routine would provide some clarity.

After his run, he showered and returned to the barracks, where Tom was waiting for him as usual. They headed to the mess hall together, the weight of the previous night's chaos pressing on their shoulders but unspoken between them.

As they sat eating their breakfast, the mess hall buzzed with subdued conversations. The atmosphere was charged, and the usual camaraderie was overshadowed by whispers of the escape attempt and the consequences it might bring.

Just as Benjamin was starting to feel the comfort of normalcy, the door to the mess hall swung open with an ominous creak. Colonel Stone, flanked by two stern-faced military police officers, walked in with purposeful strides. Conversations died mid-sentence, and all eyes turned to the commanding officer.

Colonel Stone's eyes locked onto Benjamin, his expression a mask of stern resolve. The room fell into a tense silence, and Benjamin's heart sank as he realized the gravity of the situation. The colonel's voice cut through the air with cold authority.

"Corporal Steinburg, on your feet," Colonel Stone ordered, his tone brooking no argument.

Benjamin stood slowly, his mind racing but his body moving almost mechanically. He exchanged a quick, bewildered glance with Tom, who looked equally shocked and worried.

One of the MPs stepped forward, his expression grim. "Hands behind your back," he commanded, his voice devoid of emotion.

Benjamin complied, feeling the cold steel of the handcuffs snap around his wrists. The sensation was surreal, the finality of the act hitting him like a punch to the gut. He was led out of the mess hall, the weight of the previous night's events crashing down on him with every step.

Tom and the other diners watched in stunned silence, the reality of the situation sinking in. The mess hall, usually filled with the sounds of morning chatter and clinking cutlery, was now eerily quiet. No one dared to speak, their expressions reflecting a mixture of shock, confusion, and a growing sense of dread.

As Benjamin was escorted to the brig, he couldn't shake the feeling of impending doom. His mind was a whirlwind of thoughts—about Erik, the improvised radio transmitter, and the confession he had made in the heat of the moment. The consequences of those actions were now unfolding, and he could only brace himself for what was to come.

Chapter Fifteen

Fort Hunt, Virginia, October 04, 1943

The U.S. Navy had just launched Operation Leader, an air attack on German shipping and installations off the coast of Norway. This operation demonstrated the increasing reach and impact of Allied naval aviation against German maritime interests.

During this time, the Nazis were heavily involved in various operations and activities in Norway which had been occupied by Nazi Germany since April 1940. By 1943, German forces were entrenched in the region.

The Nazis were using Norway's ports and coastline for strategic naval operations, which included securing shipping routes and preventing Allied access to the North Atlantic. Additionally, they were heavily engaged in countering resistance movements and sabotage efforts by the Norwegian resistance, which was notably active in disrupting German operations, including the significant sabotage of heavy water production essential for nuclear research at Rjukan.

The Nazis were actively working on atomic energy in 1943. The German atomic bomb project, known as the Uranverein (Uranium Club), headed by physicists Werner Heisenberg and Otto Hahn, had been active for several years by this time. The project's goal was to explore the potential of nuclear fission for military purposes, specifically the development of an atomic bomb.

In Norway, the efforts included research on nuclear reactors, heavy water production, and uranium enrichment. One of the critical components for this research was heavy water, produced at the Vemork hydroelectric plant in Rjukan, Norway. This facility became a target for Allied sabotage efforts, including the famous Norwegian heavy water sabotage operations, which aimed to disrupt the Nazi atomic program.

Allied bombing raids targeted other facilities involved in nuclear research as well, which were crucial for their reactor experiments. Additionally, the Allies' intelligence efforts, such as the Alsos Mission, disrupted and monitored German progress, capturing key scientists and documents for use in their own atomic programs.
Because of the Allied bombing efforts in Norway, German scientists faced significant technical challenges, including difficulties in obtaining sufficient quantities of enriched

uranium or plutonium, which are critical materials for an atomic bomb.

The tension at P.O. Box 1142 had only intensified following the failed escape attempt. One detainee was dead, and the three others that had managed to breach the perimeter fence, were recaptured within a few hours. By the next morning, repairs to the gate, and perimeter fence, were already underway.

Tom had orders to report to Colonel Stone's office at 0900. His unwavering support for Benjamin placed him in the line of suspicion. He was forced to give a statement, his loyalty now seen as a potential threat to the integrity of the unit.

As Tom arrived at Colonel Stone's office, he felt a mixture of apprehension and determination. He knew that his loyalty to Benjamin had put him in a precarious position, but he was ready to face whatever consequences awaited him. Knocking on the door, he waited for permission to enter, steeling himself for the conversation that would follow.

Colonel Stone's stern voice called out, "Enter." Tom stepped in, his posture reflecting both respect and a hint of unease. Colonel Stone motioned for him to sit, his expression unreadable as he studied Tom.

"Tom," Colonel Stone began, his voice measured, "I understand your loyalty to Corporal Steinberg, but recent events have raised concerns about where that loyalty truly lies."

Tom met the Colonel's gaze steadily. "Sir, my loyalty is to our mission and to the unit. Corporal Steinberg is a valued member of this team, and I stand by him because I believe in his integrity."

Colonel Stone nodded, but there was a tightness around his eyes that betrayed his concern. "I appreciate your candor, Sergeant. However, loyalty must also be balanced with adherence to protocols and the chain of command."

"I understand, sir," Tom replied. "I'm here to cooperate fully and provide any information that may assist in resolving this situation."

The conversation continued, with Colonel Stone probing into Tom's interactions with Benjamin, his knowledge of Benjamin's activities, and his assessment of Benjamin's actions and character. Tom answered each question honestly, mindful of the delicate balance between defending his friend and maintaining the unit's trust.

Colonel Stone leaned back in his chair, his eyes fixed on Tom. "Sergeant, how long have you known Corporal Steinberg?"

"About five months, sir," Tom replied. "We've been through a lot together since we both arrived at Camp Ritchie."

Colonel Stone nodded. "And in that time, have you ever noticed anything unusual about his behavior? Anything that might suggest he was involved in activities outside of his duties?"

Tom shook his head. "No, sir. Ben…Corporal Steinberg has always been dedicated to his work. He's one of the most diligent interrogators we have."

"Did he ever mention Erik Müller to you before the recent events?" Colonel Stone's voice was calm but insistent.

"Not until the initial interrogation, sir," Tom answered. "He did mention feeling a connection with Müller, which he thought might be useful in getting information."

Colonel Stone raised an eyebrow. "A connection? Explain."

"He felt that Erik was someone he could reach on a personal level," Tom said, choosing his words carefully. "He believed that building rapport with Erik could lead to valuable intelligence. It was a strategic move, not an emotional one."

Colonel Stone leaned forward, resting his elbows on the table. "Do you believe Corporal Steinberg's connection with Müller compromised his judgment?"

Tom hesitated, then shook his head. "No, sir. I think Corporal Steinberg was always clear about his objectives. He knew the line between personal feelings and professional duty."

"Have you ever seen Corporal Steinberg act in a way that might be considered…unethical?" Colonel Stone asked, his tone sharp.

Tom took a deep breath. "No, sir. He always adhered to the protocols. He was empathetic, yes, but he never crossed any lines."

"Did he ever express any doubts about his role here? Any conflicts about what we're doing?" Colonel Stone's eyes bore into Tom's.

"He did struggle with the ethics of our work sometimes," Tom admitted. "But who doesn't? It's a tough job, and he was honest about his feelings. That doesn't mean he was disloyal or untrustworthy."

Colonel Stone tapped his fingers on the table thoughtfully. "What's your personal assessment of Corporal Steinberg, Sergeant Richardson? Do you believe he's capable of betrayal?"

"Absolutely not, sir," Tom said firmly. "Corporal Steinberg is loyal to this unit and to his country. He's been put in a difficult position, but he would never betray us."

Colonel Stone regarded Tom for a moment, then nodded. "Very well. I appreciate your candor, Sergeant. The investigators have a few questions for you, so I'm going to turn it over to them."

"Of course, sir," Tom added.

One of the MPs, Sergeant Jack Harper, stood just to the left of Tom in Colonel Stone's office. Tall and broad-shouldered, his sharp features and dark brown gave him an imposing presence. His uniform was immaculate, every button polished to a shine. Despite his stern demeanor, there was a watchful intensity in his eyes.

Sergeant Harper stepped forward, "Sergent Richardson, you were close to Corporal Steinberg. Did you know about the transmitter?"

Tom gave Sergeant Harper a confused expression. "No, I—don't know anything about a transmitter," Tom replied firmly. "If he had a transmitter, he must have confiscated it from Erik Müller. Ben wouldn't know the first thing about building a radio transmitter. Erik would, though. Benjamin is my friend. I trusted him, and I still do. As I said earlier, we trained together at Camp Ritchie. He would never betray the unit. He wouldn't jeopardize everything we've worked for."

Sergeant Harper continued, "Have you noticed any unusual interactions between Colonel Steinburg and Erik Müller? Anything that seemed out of the ordinary?"

Tom shook his head. "Benjamin treated Erik with respect like he would any detainee. I've never seen anything inappropriate."

Colonel Stone pressed further. "Think carefully, Sergeant. Even the smallest detail could be important."

Tom took a deep breath, trying to recall every interaction he had witnessed. "There was nothing inappropriate. Benjamin was doing his job, trying to get information. That's all."

Sergeant Harper's eyes narrowed. "What about Corporal Steinberg's personal life? Did he ever mention anything about his…preferences?"

Tom's heart raced, but he kept his voice steady. "Benjamin's personal life is his own business. It has nothing to do with his ability to perform his duties."

Sergeant Harper leaned in, his tone sharp. "We need to know if there's anything that could compromise his loyalty or judgment. Did he ever confide in you about his sexuality?"

Tom felt a surge of protective anger. "No, he didn't. And even if he had, it wouldn't change my opinion of him. He's dedicated to his work and to this unit."

The MP gave Tom a dissatisfied grimace, clearly not convinced but unsure how to proceed. "Thank you, Tom," Sergeant Harper finally said. "We appreciate your cooperation. We'll be in touch if we need more information."

"Sir," Tom addressed Colonel Stone, standing at attention. "I brought my notes with me from after the first interrogation of Erik Müller, until now."

Colonel Stone looked up from his desk, his eyes narrowing with interest. "Go on, Sergeant."

"After our initial interrogation, Corporal Steinburg and I sat down and devised a strategy for this interrogation. You yourself said that this one would be challenging." Tom took a deep breath, steadying himself. "I'd like for you to read the notes I have kept from our interrogations and conversations. I think you'll find that I keep thorough notes, sir."

He handed the notebook to Colonel Stone, who took it and began to flip through the pages. The room was silent except for the rustle of paper. Tom watched the Colonel's expression, hoping that his detailed observations and carefully planned strategy would reflect their diligence and professionalism.

"Sir," Tom interjected, addressing Colonel Stone again. "I believe if we continue to follow this strategy, we can gain valuable information from Müller without compromising our principles. Please, just let me prove it. If you give me the opportunity, I will get you your intel."

Colonel Stone's eyes scanned the notes, his brow furrowing in concentration. After a few minutes, he looked up, his expression unreadable. "Thank you, Sergeant. You are dismissed."

Tom left the office with a heavy heart, knowing that his loyalty had placed him at a crossroads where the path ahead was uncertain.

Tom was escorted by the security officer from the detention building to Erik's cell. With each step, his heart felt heavier, the weight of impending decisions pressing down on him. Time was running out, and he knew he had to make one last attempt to get through to Erik.

"Erik," Tom said, his voice firm yet pleading as Erik slid the door open and looked at him, his expression conflicted but resolute. "Please, reconsider. Let me help you. Let me try to understand your situation and work with you to find a solution."

Erik took in Tom's words, his gaze unwavering. "Tom, I've already told you. There are things I can't talk about, things I can't change."

Taking a deep breath, Tom knew he had to reveal the gravity of the situation. "Erik, Benjamin is in serious trouble. He's been arrested, and the evidence against him is strong. If we don't find a way to clear his name, he could face severe consequences."

Erik's shock was evident, a flicker of concern crossing his face. "What kind of trouble?"

"I can't go into specifics," Tom explained, his voice tinged with urgency, "but he could be court-martialed, even go to prison. Benjamin needs your cooperation to help him, Erik. Please, for his sake and for justice, reconsider."

Erik closed his eyes briefly, a tear escaping down his cheek. After a moment of silence, he nodded resolutely. "Alright, Tom, let's go talk to the Colonel."

With Erik's agreement secured, Tom felt a wave of relief wash over him. He quickly arranged for the interrogation to take place with Colonel Stone present. This would be their final chance to uncover the truth and navigate the complexities that had brought them to this critical juncture.

Tom, Erik, and Colonel Stone reentered the interrogation room, the atmosphere tense with anticipation. Tom took a seat at the table, his eyes briefly meeting Erik's before focusing on Colonel Stone, who sat across from them.

Colonel Stone's gaze was steely as he addressed Erik. "Mr. Müller, thank you for agreeing to this interrogation. We're here to get to the bottom of some pressing matters."

Erik nodded, his expression composed but guarded. "I understand, Colonel. I'll do my best to cooperate."

Tom observed the dynamics in the room, his mind racing with the weight of their mission. He knew that this interrogation could be their last chance to uncover crucial information and clear Benjamin's name.

The Colonel continued, "Sergeant Richardson tells me that you're ready to talk. Well, let's hear it."

Erik leaned back in his chair, a smile peeking from the corner of his mouth, his gaze unflinching. "I believe what you would like me to talk about is the Horten H.XVIII, sometimes referred to as the Amerikabomber. Fascinating piece of engineering!"

"Cut the crap," Colonel Stone snapped at Erik.

"I was directly involved in the development of the Horten H.XVIII, a concept intercontinental bomber designed by the brothers, Walter and Reimar Horten," Erik began, his voice steady but filled with a mixture of pride and resignation. "The aircraft was proposed as part of an initiative by the German Ministry of Aviation (Reichsluftfahrtministerium) called the Amerikabomber, to obtain a long-range strategic bomber for the Luftwaffe that would be capable of striking the United States from Germany."

"Go on," Colonel Stone said, his expression tense, eyes narrowing as he listened intently.

"The Amerikabomber program is an umbrella development project," Erik explained, leaning forward with a serious expression. "Its objective is to create long-range strategic bombers capable of reaching and attacking targets in the United States from Germany as well as other bases in Europe. Many German engineers and aviation specialists have submitted designs to be considered for development."

Erik continued, his tone becoming more animated. "One of the most notable designs came from Messerschmitt. Another design that is being developed is the Horten H.XVIII based on the Horten Brothers' flying wing jet design. The stealth and speed of this experimental aircraft would make interception, prior to bombing, difficult and highly unlikely."

Colonel Stone leaned forward, his gaze sharp. "What is a flying wing jet design?" he asked Erik.

Erik nodded, ready to explain. "A flying wing jet design is an aircraft configuration where the entire structure is a single, unified wing. Unlike conventional aircraft, there is no distinct fuselage or tail. The crew, engines, and payload are all housed within the wing itself."

He continued, "The Horten brothers pioneered this design. It offers several advantages, such as reduced drag, which leads to higher speed and greater fuel efficiency. This design also enhances stealth capabilities because it presents a smaller radar cross-section, making it harder to detect and intercept."

Erik paused for a moment, letting the information sink in. "The Horten H.XVIII is an ambitious project that takes these principles to the extreme. It's meant to fly long distances at high altitudes, evading radar detection and delivering its payload with precision."

Colonel Stone nodded slowly, absorbing the details. "And with the capability to carry atomic bombs, this aircraft could pose a significant threat to the United States."

"Exactly," Erik confirmed. "Its stealth and speed would make it a formidable weapon, challenging to intercept before it reaches its target. This is why the development of the Horten H.XVIII is considered one of the highest priorities within the Luftwaffe's strategic plans."

He paused for a moment, letting the gravity of the situation sink in before adding, "Let's just say, if the Nazis learn to harness a nuclear fission reaction, this airplane could drop atomic bombs all down the east coast of the United States, and your current jets would have an extremely difficult time intercepting it. I can give you all of the general, performance, and armament specifications of the aircraft."

Tom leaned forward, his eyes intent on Erik's. "Alright, Erik, we need specifics. When is the prototype scheduled for completion?"

Erik took a moment to gather his thoughts. "The prototype is scheduled to be completed within the next two months. They're working around the clock, prioritizing this project due to the war's escalating demands."

Tom nodded, his mind racing. "And when will it be tested? We need to know how soon they plan to deploy it."

"Initial test flights are planned for three months after completion," Erik replied. "They're aiming to have it operational by the middle of next year. The tests will start with basic flight capabilities before moving on to bomb delivery simulations."

"Where is it being developed?" Tom asked, his tone urgent. "We need to know the exact location."

"It's being developed at a highly secured facility in the Harz Mountains, southeast of the town of Nordhausen," Erik explained. "The site is well-hidden and heavily guarded to prevent Allied detection. The area is surrounded by dense forests and rugged terrain, making it difficult to approach without being noticed."

"Are there any weaknesses in their security?" Tom inquired. "Anything we can exploit?"

Erik hesitated, thinking carefully. "The site is incredibly secure. An assault on the facility, either by air or by land, would be costly. However, there have been whispers of discontent among the labor force, many of whom are forced laborers. If you could find a way to communicate with them, there might be a chance to gather more intelligence or disrupt their operations from within."

Tom pressed on, "Do you know what kind of defenses they have in place?"

"They have multiple layers of security," Erik said. "Guard towers, patrols, and anti-aircraft guns are positioned around the perimeter. There's also a network of surveillance cameras, barbed wire, and possibly even more rudimentary alarm systems, improvised explosive devices triggered by tripwires, or other mechanical means. Any attempt to infiltrate the facility would be extremely risky."

Tom nodded, absorbing the wealth of information. "This is invaluable, Erik. One last question: Do they have any backup plans if the prototype fails?"

Erik shook his head. "Not as sophisticated as the Horten H.XVIII. As I said before, the Amerikabomber program is developing a few other aircraft designs, but the Horten H.XVIII is their best shot at developing a long-range strategic bomber. If it fails, they'll likely shift resources to other projects, but nothing as ambitious as this."

Tom leaned back, a sense of urgency driving his thoughts. "Thank you, Erik. This information could make a significant difference. We'll do everything we can to use it effectively."

Colonel Stone glared at Erik, his eyes narrowing with suspicion. "I have a few more questions for you on a different topic. Do you know anything about an improvised radio transmission device that was discovered on the premises?"

Erik looked momentarily confused but then nodded slowly. "Yes, I do. I built it," he admitted, his voice steady but resigned.

Tom's eyes widened in surprise. "You built it?"

"Yes," Erik repeated, glancing between Tom and Colonel Stone. "I constructed the device to try and send out a signal. I know it was risky, but I felt I had to try something."

Colonel Stone's expression hardened. "And what was your purpose in building this transmitter? Who were you trying to contact?"

"I was trying to reach out to anyone who could help," Erik explained. "I was hoping to find a way to negotiate my position or at least get a message to someone who could intervene on my behalf."

Colonel Stone's voice grew even more stern. "Was this device used to coordinate the escape attempt that happened a few days ago?"

"No, neither I nor my device was involved in the planning of the escape attempt," Erik clarified quickly. "I only used the device once to try to establish contact with someone outside the facility. I didn't receive any kind of response. After that, I decided it was too risky to attempt it again, so I planned to disassemble the transmitter. That's when Benjamin caught me with it and confiscated it."

Colonel Stone's voice grew even more serious as he leaned forward. "I have one more question for you, and I would appreciate your honesty," he said, fixing Erik with a penetrating gaze. "In your opinion, at any time during your interrogation or detention here at this facility, since being transferred to Sergeant Richardson and Corporal

Steinberg, have you experienced anything that you would consider as unethical, inappropriate, or in any other way inhumane?"

Erik took a deep breath, the weight of the question pressing on him. He glanced at Tom, then back at Colonel Stone, choosing his words carefully. "No, Colonel. While the interrogations have been intense and challenging, I have not been subjected to any unethical or inhumane treatment. Sergeant Richardson and Corporal Steinberg have conducted themselves professionally. Their methods have been firm but within the boundaries of what I would consider acceptable under the circumstances."

Colonel Stone's expression remained stern, but he gave a slight nod. "Thank you for your honesty, Mr. Müller. It's important for us to ensure that all procedures are conducted with integrity. We'll take your words into account as we proceed with our investigations."

Erik nodded in acknowledgment, feeling a slight sense of relief. "I appreciate that, Colonel."

Tom, sensing the gravity of the moment, added, "It's crucial for us to maintain the highest standards, especially in situations as sensitive as this. Erik's cooperation and honesty are vital, and we must ensure that we uphold our own ethical standards in return."

Colonel Stone stood up, his demeanor still resolute but slightly softened. "Indeed. This concludes our interrogation for now. We'll review the information provided and determine our next steps. Mr. Müller, thank you for your cooperation."

As they left the room, Tom felt a renewed sense of purpose. The path ahead was still fraught with challenges, but with Erik's honesty and the newfound information, there was hope that they could navigate through the complexities and ultimately find justice for Benjamin.

Chapter Sixteen

Fort Hunt, Virginia, October 11, 1943

At this time, Allied Aegean Sea Operations were playing a crucial role in disrupting German supply lines and naval operations in the Mediterranean region. One notable event occurred on October 4 when a British naval squadron intercepted a German convoy near the island of Cos. This interception led to the sinking of seven transports and one escort ship, significantly impacting German supply lines in the area.

The British naval action not only inflicted heavy losses on the German convoy but also disrupted their ability to transport vital supplies and reinforcements to their forces in the region. This disruption contributed to the overall Allied efforts to weaken German military capabilities and gain strategic advantages in the Mediterranean theater of operations.

On the Italian front, a pivotal moment occurred when the German 16th Panzer Division retreated behind the Trigno River in Italy. This strategic withdrawal allowed the division to regroup and establish defensive positions to delay the Allied advance.

On October 8, British forces made significant progress by capturing key towns such as Larino and Guglionesi. These victories marked a continued Allied advance through Italy, following the successful invasion of Sicily earlier in the campaign. The capture of Larino and Guglionesi provided the Allies with essential footholds and logistical bases for further operations into Italian territory.

The Allied advance in Italy was part of a broader strategy to weaken Axis forces and gain control of the Mediterranean region. It involved coordinated efforts from multiple Allied nations and required overcoming rugged terrain, strong defensive positions, and determined enemy resistance.

On the Eastern Front, a critical event unfolded with the German evacuation of the Kuban Peninsula, marking a significant strategic shift. The evacuation was completed on October 9, with approximately 255,000 troops and 27,000 civilians successfully withdrawn to the Crimea region. This move was part of the German Army's broader strategy to consolidate their forces and defend key territories against the advancing Soviet forces.

The decision to evacuate the Kuban Peninsula reflected the deteriorating situation for the Germans on the Eastern Front. The Soviet forces, under the command of General

Ivan Petrov, capitalized on their momentum and fully occupied the Kuban Peninsula after the German withdrawal. This occupation symbolized a major victory for the Soviets and a strategic setback for the German military.

The evacuation of such a large number of troops and civilians underscored the challenges faced by the German forces in maintaining their positions against the Soviet offensive. It also highlighted the fluid and dynamic nature of the Eastern Front, where territories frequently changed hands as both sides engaged in intense and grueling warfare.

The Central Pacific Campaign was in its final and crucial stages of planning. The strategy in the central Pacific involved bypassing heavily fortified Japanese positions and capturing less-defended but strategically valuable islands to use as bases for further operations. By capturing strategically important islands the command aimed to advance Allied forces through the central Pacific by "island hopping".

The first in a series of intense battles was set to play out in the Gilbert and Marshall Islands. The capture of these key island chains would set the stage for the invasion of the Mariana Islands, bringing the war closer to Japan and enabling sustained strategic bombing campaigns against the Japanese home islands.

Benjamin's cell at P.O. Box 1142 was a stark, utilitarian space typical of military detention facilities. It was small, measuring about eight feet by eight feet, with concrete walls and a steel door reinforced with a small, barred window near the top. The only furnishings were a simple bunk bed bolted to the wall, a thin mattress, a small table with a chair, and a basic toilet and sink combination unit in one corner. The lighting was fluorescent, casting a harsh, white light that added to the cell's sterile and oppressive atmosphere. Benjamin noted that his new quarters were not unlike Erik's, albeit in a different section of the facility.

Benjamin found himself in the cold, dusty cell, a stark contrast to the freedom and hope he had once known. His mind raced, replaying the events of the attempted breakout. The failed escape attempt had not only led to more extreme security measures being imposed on Eric but had also cast a dark shadow of suspicion over Benjamin. The MPs had been relentless, finding the transmission device and discovering it was partially made from the record player Benjamin had given to Erik. The evidence was damning.

Benjamin's situation became even more precarious with the submission of Staff Sergeant Lewis's report, which included allegations of inappropriate behavior and fraternizing with an enemy detainee. This added another layer of complexity, intensifying scrutiny and suspicion surrounding Benjamin. Now facing a court-martial, he confronted serious charges and the potential for severe consequences, including dishonorable discharge, imprisonment, or other punitive measures.

The tension on the base had only intensified since Benjamin's arrest. Whispers and glances followed him as he was led to one of the interrogation rooms, the metallic clink of handcuffs serving as a harsh reminder of his sudden fall from grace. The energy in the air was charged with suspicion and unease, a stark contrast to the routine of just days ago.

The interrogation room was suffused with a palpable tension as Benjamin faced Colonel Stone and MP Sergeant Harper. The air crackled with unspoken accusations and suspicions.

Colonel Stone's voice was stern as he started, "Corporal Steinberg, we have serious concerns about recent events. The discovery of a radio transmitter hidden in your barracks, amongst your possessions, which is a prohibited device within this facility, coupled with your actions, raises significant questions. We need a full account of the events surrounding the origins and discovery of this transmitter. Explain yourself."

Benjamin took a deep breath. "Sir, I found the transmitter in Erik's possession. I took it from him and hid it."

Sergeant Harper's eyes narrowed. "You hid it? Why wasn't this reported immediately?"

Benjamin met their gazes steadily. "Because if I had turned Erik in, we would have lost all the trust and camaraderie we had painstakingly built. Without that trust, we had no chance of getting the intel we needed from him. Additionally, security measures would have been tightened, making it nearly impossible for me to have access to Erik for further questioning and rapport building."

Colonel Stone's expression remained stern. "So, you chose to keep this a secret? You do realize the implications of such a decision?"

"Yes, sir," Benjamin replied. "But the transmitter had been disassembled. At that point, I didn't believe it posed any further threat to security. My priority was to maintain the delicate rapport we had established with Erik to extract crucial information."

Sergeant Harper leaned forward, his voice sharp. "Do you understand the potential consequences of your actions? The breach in protocol and the risks involved?"

Benjamin nodded. "I do, Sergeant. However, I believed the potential gain in terms of intelligence outweighed the risks. I acted in the best interest of our mission."

Colonel Stone's gaze bore into him, weighing his words. "We will thoroughly investigate this matter. Your actions may have been driven by strategic considerations, but we cannot ignore breaches in protocol and security measures."

Benjamin squared his shoulders, meeting Colonel Stone's gaze evenly. "Sir, I understand the gravity of the situation. However, I need to stress that, with the exception of the escape attempt, everything that transpired was part of a carefully planned strategy. I believed, and still believed that the potential gain in uncovering crucial intelligence outweighed the risks."

"Your opinion has been noted, Corporal," Sergeant Harper responded. "I have some additional questions for you." He paused, visibly uncomfortable with his next line of questioning. "Have you formed any particularly close friendships or alliances during your time here?"

Benjamin took a breath before answering. "I've built professional relationships with several colleagues, but Tom has been the most significant. Our friendship has provided crucial support and insight, helping me navigate the complexities of my duties here."

Sergeant Harper nodded, then pressed on. "Tell us more about your relationship with Erik Müller. How would you describe your level of trust and camaraderie?"

"Erik and I have developed a level of mutual respect and understanding over time," Benjamin explained. "Our conversations have built a sense of camaraderie, which I believe has been crucial in establishing the trust necessary for him to open up about sensitive information."

"According to the security logs in the detention building, you have been spending a lot of off-duty time with Müller," Sergeant Harper noted. "What do you and Erik typically discuss during your off-duty hours?"

"During my off-duty hours, we often discuss broader topics like literature, philosophy, music, and history," Benjamin replied. "These conversations help me understand his mindset and build rapport, making it easier to guide our official discussions toward the intelligence we need."

"Are there any shared interests or hobbies that you and Erik bond over?" the Sergeant inquired.

"We both share a keen interest in literature, which has served as a common ground," Benjamin said. "Discussing books and authors has allowed us to connect on a personal level, easing the tension during our more formal interrogations."

Sergeant Harper leaned in slightly. "Have you noticed any changes in Erik's behavior or attitude that might indicate deeper personal struggles?"

"Yes," Benjamin said thoughtfully. "I've noticed that Erik sometimes shows signs of inner conflict and stress, especially when we touch on topics related to his past and personal beliefs. These moments suggest that he is grappling with deeper personal struggles that might be affecting his willingness to share information."

"In your interactions with Erik, have you ever felt that there are aspects of his life he is particularly secretive about?" Sergeant Harper continued.

"Absolutely," Benjamin confirmed. "Erik often deflects or avoids discussing certain aspects of his personal life, which indicates there are parts of his past or present that he finds difficult to talk about. These guarded areas likely hold significant clues to understanding his motivations."

"Do you believe that Erik's personal beliefs or relationships might be influencing his cooperation or lack thereof?" Harper asked.

"Yes," Benjamin replied. "I believe Erik's personal beliefs and relationships play a crucial role in his cooperation. His loyalty to certain individuals and ideological conflicts seem to be key factors in his hesitation to fully cooperate."

"Is there anything in Erik's background or personal life that you think is crucial for us to understand in order to gain his trust?" Harper asked, leaning back.

"Understanding Erik's mentor relationship with Reimar Horten and his internal conflict regarding the Nazi regime is crucial," Benjamin said. "These elements of his background provide context for his actions and hesitations. Acknowledging and addressing these aspects can help us build a deeper trust and encourage him to share more information."

"Corporal," Colonel Stone's voice cut through the tense air in the interrogation room, "What do you make of the Staff Sergeant's report, and what he claims to have witnessed the night of the attempted breakout? What is your response to that?"

Benjamin remained composed, locking eyes with Colonel Stone in a display of unwavering resolve. "Sir, I acknowledge Staff Sergeant Lewis's account as sincere, reflecting his genuine perception of events. However, given the intense pressure and heightened confusion at that crucial juncture, I respectfully propose that he may have misconstrued a fleeting sequence of events."

He continued with measured precision, "I firmly contend that his interpretation of the events is mistaken, pointing out that, amid heightened tension and confusion, observations can sometimes be misconstrued or misinterpreted. I respectfully assert, sir, that my decisions were driven by the critical need to maintain trust and procure essential intelligence. Any potential misunderstanding on Staff Sergeant Lewis's part could have arisen from the intricate dynamics of the situation, his rapid assessment of a fleeting moment, and could also potentially have been influenced by preconceived notions regarding Erik Müller and myself."

Colonel Stone's eyes narrowed slightly as he listened intently. "I see. Well, Corporal Steinberg, I'll have you know that while you were in the brig, Herr Müller suddenly decided to fully cooperate with us. Sergeant Richardson and I were able to extract some highly classified and critical intel from him. Meanwhile, we've questioned numerous individuals who had the opportunity to observe your interactions with Müller at one time or another, and nobody has come forward to corroborate Staff Sergeant Lewis's claims or offer any related information that would substantiate such allegations. Therefore, I'm inclined to accept your explanation and disregard Staff Sergeant Lewis's report."

"Thank you, sir," Benjamin said, exhaling in relief.

"However," the Colonel continued, "your breach of protocol involving the transmitter must come with some consequence. Therefore, I will be ordering you to attend further training on the importance of procedures and the chain of command. Hopefully this, in addition to your time served in the brig, will give you a renewed appreciation for the importance of protocols. Is that understood, Corporal Steinberg?"

"Yes sir," Benjamin answered, snapping to attention. "Thank you, sir."

"Corporal, you are dismissed," the Colonel said, waving his hand toward the door, indicating that Benjamin was free to leave.

Benjamin saluted Colonel Stone and exited the office, his mind racing with the weight of the reprimand and the relief of having his explanation accepted. He knew the formal reprimand would have lasting implications, but he was grateful to avoid harsher consequences.

Stepping into the corridor, he took a moment to compose himself, leaning against the wall and taking deep breaths. The reprieve felt bittersweet, and the promise of additional training loomed over him. He resolved to face it head-on, understanding the importance of adhering to protocols, despite the complexities of his situation with Erik.

Leaving Colonel Stone's office, Benjamin knew his next stop had to be Tom. Without Tom's unwavering support and loyalty, the situation could have turned out much worse. He made his way to the barracks, hoping to find his friend and share the news.

When Benjamin entered the barracks, Tom looked up a him with a concerned look on his face. "Ben, how did it go?"

Benjamin couldn't contain his relief. "Better than I expected. Colonel Stone accepted my explanation and disregarded Staff Sergeant Lewis's report. I got a verbal reprimand and some additional training for the transmitter, but it could have been much worse."

Tom's expression brightened immediately. "That's great news, Ben! I'm really glad to hear that."

"I couldn't have done it without you, Tom," Benjamin said earnestly. "Your support made all the difference. I owe you a lot."

Tom waved it off with a smile. "You'd do the same for me. We're in this together."

Absolutely," Benjamin agreed. "How about we celebrate? I hear the mess hall has a fresh batch of coffee and some decent pastries today."

Tom grinned. "Sounds perfect. Let's go."

The two friends headed to the mess hall, where they spent the next hour enjoying coffee, pastries, and each other's company. They shared stories, laughed, and for a brief moment, let the weight of their duties fade away. The bond between them, forged through shared experiences and mutual respect, felt stronger than ever.

As they raised their coffee cups in a toast, Benjamin felt a renewed sense of optimism. No matter what challenges lay ahead, he knew he had a true friend by his side.

The following day, Benjamin was overwhelmed by the outpouring of support and joy for his return to the daily grind. Colleagues greeted him with pats on the back and warm smiles, glad to see him back in action. Despite the reprimand and additional duties, he felt a renewed sense of camaraderie that helped him get through the day.

After finishing his full day of duties, including his punitive tasks, he left the interrogation department with one thing on his mind: Erik.

As he walked down the corridor of the detention building, he made a beeline for Erik's cell, hoping to find some answers. Upon reaching the detention area, he was greeted by an unfamiliar guard.

"Corporal Steinberg, what can I do for you?" the guard asked.

"I need to see Erik Müller," Benjamin replied, his voice steady despite the turmoil inside.

The guard hesitated, then shook his head. "I'm sorry, Corporal, but Müller is no longer here. He has been transferred."

Benjamin's heart sank. "Transferred? Where?"

"I'm not at liberty to say, sir," the guard replied. "Orders came directly from Colonel Stone."

Feeling a mixture of frustration and helplessness, Benjamin thanked the guard and walked away. He needed to process this turn of events and decide his next steps.

He made his way to the mess hall, hoping to find Tom. He needed to talk to his friend, to make sense of everything that had happened. As he entered the bustling hall, he spotted Tom sitting at a table, deep in conversation with Private Ortega.

Benjamin approached, and the two men looked up. Private Ortega's expression shifted from concern to relief. "Ben, you're out! What happened?"

Benjamin sat down, lowering his voice. "I got a verbal reprimand and some additional training. But more importantly, Erik's gone. They transferred him while I was in the brig."

Tom's eyes widened. "Transferred? Did they say where?"

"No," Benjamin replied, shaking his head.

The uncertainty of Erik's whereabouts and the reasons behind his sudden cooperation gnawed at him. He needed answers, and he needed them now.

Benjamin decided to pay a visit to the office of Lieutenant Harrison, a mentor who had always been straightforward and supportive since Benjamin and Tom's arrival at P.O.

Box 1142. He hoped the lieutenant could provide some insights or at least point him in the right direction.

Knocking on the door, he waited for the familiar voice to call him in. "Enter," Lieutenant Harrison said. Benjamin stepped inside, finding the lieutenant poring over a stack of reports.

"Ah, Corporal Steinberg," Harrison greeted him, looking up. "Good to see you back. What can I do for you?"

"Thank you, sir," Benjamin replied, taking a seat. "I need to ask about Erik Müller. He was transferred while I was in the brig, and I need to know where he was taken and why."

Lieutenant Harrison leaned back in his chair, his expression thoughtful. "Erik Müller's transfer was classified, Benjamin. However, I can tell you that his cooperation was unexpected and valuable. The higher-ups decided he could be more useful in a different location. That's all I know."

Benjamin's thoughts simmered with frustration as he made his way back to his quarters. The support from his colleagues was heartening, but it couldn't dispel the gnawing worry about Erik. Something wasn't right, and Benjamin had a growing suspicion about where Erik had gone.

Operation Overcast. The name had come up in whispers, hinting at a covert operation to relocate key scientists. Was Erik part of that? The thought was maddening. They had come so far in the past few months, and now, without warning, Erik was gone.

If Erik had been transferred under Operation Overcast, the details would have been buried deep in classified files, inaccessible to someone of his rank. But he couldn't just let it go. Erik wasn't just another detainee; he was everything!

I can't let this drop. Benjamin knew he had to find out more. He needed to be discreet, to ask the right questions without drawing too much attention to himself. Maybe he could convince Lieutenant Harrison to help, or perhaps he could subtly gather information from other colleagues who might know more about the operation. Every small piece of information could bring him closer to understanding Erik's fate.

He took a deep breath, trying to calm the storm inside him. He wouldn't stop until he found out where Erik had been taken. The bond they had formed, the trust they had built, was too important to abandon.

Reaching his quarters, Benjamin sat on his bunk, his mind already formulating a plan. Tomorrow, he would start his search. He wasn't about to let secrecy and red tape stand in his way. He owed it to Erik—and to himself—to find the truth.

Chapter Seventeen

Fort Hunt, Virginia, November 25, 1943

During this period, the Italian Campaign saw some of the fiercest fighting of the war as Allied forces endeavored to break through the formidable German defenses known as the Gustav Line and make their way towards Rome. The campaign was marked by a series of grueling battles and strategic maneuvers that tested the endurance and resolve of both the Allied and Axis forces.

The Gustav Line, also referred to as the Winter Line, was a series of German defensive positions in central Italy. Anchored on Monte Cassino, a historic abbey, the line stretched across the Italian peninsula, leveraging the natural rugged terrain to create formidable defensive positions. The Allies faced significant challenges in their attempts to penetrate these defenses.

The town and abbey of Monte Cassino became the focal points of multiple assaults. The Allies launched several operations to capture the heights, which were strategically important for controlling the surrounding areas and advancing towards Rome. These assaults were met with stiff German resistance, leading to heavy casualties on both sides.

On October 14, 291 B-17 Flying Fortress bombers took off from their bases in England early in the morning, flying deep into enemy territory without the protection of long-range fighter escorts for much of the journey. Their targets were the critical ball-bearing factories in Schweinfurt, Germany, which were essential to the German war machine.

The raid aimed to cripple Germany's ability to produce ball bearings, which were vital components for various machinery, including military vehicles, aircraft, and weapons. The successful destruction of these factories was expected to severely hamper German war production capabilities.

The journey to Schweinfurt was perilous, involving a flight path over heavily defended German airspace. As the bombers approached their target, they encountered fierce resistance from Luftwaffe fighters and anti-aircraft artillery (flak).

The Luftwaffe had anticipated the raid and deployed a significant number of fighter aircraft, including Messerschmitt Bf 109s and Focke-Wulf Fw 190s. These fighters engaged the bomber formations relentlessly, exploiting the absence of Allied fighter escorts.

Despite the intense opposition, the bombers pressed on and released their payloads over Schweinfurt. The bombings inflicted substantial damage on the ball-bearing factories, but the victory came at a steep price.

The losses sustained during the raid were catastrophic. Of the 291 bombers that set out, 60 were lost to enemy action. Additionally, many of the returning aircraft were heavily damaged, with crew members killed or wounded. The high casualty rate among the aircrews earned the raid its grim moniker, "Black Thursday."

On October 15, the Allies launched another significant bombing raid on a highly secured facility and airstrip in the Harz Mountains, southeast of the town of Nordhausen. This facility was believed to be a key site for the development of the advanced Horten H.XVIII flying wing aircraft, a project spearheaded by the Horten brothers, which posed a potential threat to the continental United States and other Allied countries, as well as Allied air superiority.

The raid began at dawn to maximize the element of surprise and reduce the risk of German night fighters. The operation involved 150 B-17 Flying Fortress bombers, escorted by 100 P-47 Thunderbolt fighters to provide protection against German interceptors. The primary targets were the research and development facilities, production workshops, and the airstrip used for testing the Horten H.XVIII.

The Allies lost 20 bombers to anti-aircraft fire and Luftwaffe fighters, with another 30 heavily damaged. The escorting P-47s lost 10 aircraft in dogfights with German interceptors. The raid caused significant damage to the facility, destroying several key buildings and critically damaging the airstrip. Production of the Horten H.XVIII was so severely crippled that the project was eventually scrapped.

Allied casualties included 200 airmen killed or missing. German casualties included both personnel at the facility and defending forces, though exact numbers remain unclear.

Operation Stormfront was considered a tactical success despite the heavy losses. The crippling blow to the Horten H.XVIII project provided the Allies with crucial time to bolster their air defenses and continue their strategic bombing campaigns with reduced threat from advanced German aircraft. This raid also highlighted the Allies' growing capability to strike deep into German territory with significant force.

Driven by an unwavering determination and a deep concern for Erik, Benjamin embarked on a discreet and relentless investigation into Erik's transfer. The stakes were high, and the risks ever-present, but Benjamin's resolve was steadfast. He was acutely aware of the limitations of his position and the dangers of delving too deeply into classified operations. Yet, his determination never wavered. Every dead end and obstacle only fueled his resolve further.

Benjamin knew he had to navigate a complex web of secrecy and discretion, utilizing every resource and contact available to him while staying under the radar. He meticulously planned his approach, knowing that one misstep could jeopardize everything. Conversations with colleagues, careful analysis of recent operations, and discreet inquiries into restricted files became his tools in this covert quest. Despite the inherent dangers, Benjamin was prepared to face any challenge, for he could not rest until he uncovered the truth about Erik's fate.

Benjamin's frustration grew as days passed with little progress. He knew Erik had been transferred under Operation Overcast, but the specifics eluded him.

"Damn it, Erik, where did they take you?" he thought, clenching his fists. "I won't give up. I'll find you, no matter what it takes."

His mind raced through the possibilities, weighing each clue he had gathered. The secrecy surrounding Operation Overcast was a formidable barrier, but Benjamin was resolute. He would continue to navigate the web of secrecy and discretion, driven by his unwavering commitment to finding Erik.

Benjamin began by subtly engaging his colleagues in casual conversations, hoping to pick up any stray bits of information that might lead him to Erik. His approach was cautious, ensuring that his true intentions remained hidden.

One day in the mess hall, he approached Lieutenant Anderson, a fellow officer known for his sharp observations and extensive knowledge of personnel movements. Benjamin tried to sound as nonchalant as possible as he initiated the conversation.

"Have you heard anything about recent transfers?" Benjamin asked, casually stirring his coffee to make the question seem like a passing curiosity.

Lieutenant Anderson looked up, raising an eyebrow. "Just the usual movements. Why do you ask?"

Benjamin shrugged, masking his true intentions with a feigned air of disinterest. "Just curious. We see so many POWs come through here, I sometimes wonder what happens to all of them once we're done with them."

Anderson nodded, seemingly accepting the explanation. "Yeah, it's been a whirlwind lately. But nothing out of the ordinary that I've heard. As for what happens to them or where they go, it largely depends on what they know, how cooperative they are, and whether or not they pose a threat to the Allied war effort. Those who are uncooperative or pose a threat end up in a military prison, most likely. The same goes for high-ranking officers accused of war crimes. If they're not considered high-value targets or threats and aren't privy to valuable intel, they might be sent to a POW camp to be released back into civilian life at some point. The ones with specialized knowledge of military technologies, like scientists and engineers, are integrated into U.S. military projects under programs like Operation Overcast. Are you looking for someone specific?"

Benjamin shook his head. "No one in particular. Just trying to stay informed." He decided to probe further, hoping to gather more specific information. "I've heard about Operation Overcast," he said, keeping his tone light. "What's the deal with that?"

Anderson leaned back in his chair, a thoughtful expression crossing his face. "Operation Overcast is pretty hush-hush, but from what I've gathered, it's a program where the U.S. military brings in German scientists and engineers. They're put to work on our military projects, especially those related to advanced technologies. It's all part of our effort to leverage their expertise and gain an edge in the war."

Benjamin nodded, maintaining his casual demeanor. "That makes sense. Do you know how they decide who gets transferred under Operation Overcast?"

"It's pretty selective," Anderson replied. "Only those with highly specialized knowledge or critical skills are considered. They go through a rigorous vetting process to ensure they're valuable and not a security risk. It's all about what they can offer in terms of military advancements."

"That's interesting," Benjamin said, filing away the information for later. "So, you haven't heard any specific names or details about recent transfers?"

"Not really," Anderson admitted. "Most of what I know is just from bits and pieces I've picked up here and there. They keep a tight lid on those details."

Benjamin smiled, giving a nod of appreciation. "Thanks, Lieutenant. It's good to stay in the loop about these things."

"No problem," Anderson said, returning to his meal. "Just be careful not to dig too deep. Some things are better left alone."

Benjamin acknowledged the cautionary advice with a slight nod. As he finished his coffee, he knew he had to tread carefully. He needed more information, but he couldn't afford to draw too much attention to his search for Erik.

As days passed, Benjamin continued his subtle inquiries, broadening his net. In the officers' lounge, he casually brought up the topic of transfers with Major Thompson, hoping to gain some insights.

"Major, have you noticed an increase in personnel transfers lately?" Benjamin asked, keeping his tone light.

Major Thomp looked thoughtful for a moment. "Now that you mention it, there have been a few more movements than usual. Some of the higher-ups are being pretty tight-lipped about it, though."

"Any idea where they're being sent?" Benjamin pressed gently, careful not to reveal his specific interest in Erik.

Thompson shook his head. "Mostly rumors. Some say they're being reassigned to special projects or other strategic locations. Hard to pin down anything concrete. I would imagine they are being sent to facilitate in U.S. projects that pertain to their specific expertise."

Benjamin thanked him and moved on, his mind racing with possibilities. He knew he needed more concrete information and decided to reach out to some of his trusted contacts who had access to restricted files.

One evening, he met with Sergeant Daniels, a friend from his early days at P.O. Box 1142, in a secluded part of the base. Daniels had a knack for accessing information that was typically off-limits.

"Sergeant Daniels, I need a favor," Benjamin said, his voice low. "I need to know about any recent transfers under Operation Overcast."

Daniels gave him a wary look. "You know that's classified, right? What are you getting yourself into?"

"It's important, sir. I wouldn't ask if it wasn't," Benjamin replied, his tone earnest.

Daniels sighed, then nodded. "I'll see what I can find. But you owe me."

Over the next few days, Benjamin waited anxiously for any word from Sergeant Daniels. He continued to piece together clues from the information he gathered, analyzing recent operations and movements within the base.

Finally, Daniels approached him with a small, folded piece of paper. "This is all I could get. Be careful, Ben."

Benjamin took the paper and unfolded it, his eyes scanning the cryptic notes. It wasn't much, but it was enough to give him a lead.

His heart pounded as he read the details. It seemed that Erik had been transferred to a facility in Texas named Fort Bliss.

Armed with this new information, Benjamin's resolve hardened. He knew the path ahead would be fraught with challenges, but he was determined to find Erik, no matter the cost.

Back in the bustling mess hall of P.O. Box 1142, Benjamin sat with Tom and Private Ortega, their trays filled with standard military fare. Amidst the clatter of cutlery and the chatter of fellow soldiers, Benjamin sat there quietly, a look of bewilderment on his face.

Tom broke the silence, "So, have you gained any new insights into the whereabouts of Erik Müller?"

Benjamin, taking a moment to gather his thoughts, finally broke the silence. "Actually, I did receive a piece of intel that suggested Erik had been transferred to Fort Bliss," he said, eyes flickering with a mix of concern and intrigue.

"Fort Bliss, Texas?" Private Ortega's eyes lit up with recognition, a smile spreading across his face. "That's in my hometown of El Paso!"

"That's right! You're from El Paso!" Benjamin nodded, prompting Private Ortega to continue eagerly, "I grew up near Fort Bliss. It's a big part of life back home."

Tom, intrigued by the conversation, leaned in. "What's it like around Fort Bliss?"

Private Ortega's eyes sparkled with memories. "Well, you've got the desert all around, the Franklin Mountains in the distance. And Fort Bliss itself is like a city within a city. There's always something happening there, from training exercises to community events."

"What's going on at Fort Bliss these days?" Benjamin wondered aloud. His curiosity deepened as Private Ortega shared rumors about the fort.

Private Ortega leaned in, his voice lowered slightly. "I don't know exactly, but my family still lives in El Paso, and I hear a lot of rumors. The military has been sending a lot of German POWs there, but they're not staying for long. My father thinks they're using the base for some sort of orientation for defecting Nazi scientists before reassigning them to other programs around the country."

Benjamin's eyes widened with intrigue. "Defecting Nazi scientists? That's quite a revelation."

Tom, listening intently, added, "It would make sense. Fort Bliss is a strategic location, and it has the facilities for processing and integrating new personnel into military projects."

Private Ortega nodded. "Exactly. And with the war winding down, I've heard talks about leveraging German expertise for American advancements. It's all speculation, of course, but there's definitely something happening at Fort Bliss."

"That's very interesting," Benjamin replied. "Thanks, Javier." Private Ortega nodded as he took a bite of his sandwich. "But if they are only sending POWs there for orientation before transferring them again, then that puts me back at square one."

Tom frowned at Benjamin's admission. "I don't want to bring you down, but maybe it's time to throw in the towel. You know, these matters are classified for a reason, Ben."

Benjamin sighed, the weight of his mission pressing on him. "All I need to figure out is where the most likely place the military would send someone who is an aerospace physicist with specialized knowledge of experimental aircraft."

Tom, ever observant, chimed in. "Well, if they're looking to leverage that kind of expertise, they might send him to a place like Wright Field, in my home state of Ohio. It's a major center for aeronautical research and development. They'd have the facilities and resources to make use of someone like him. My dad used to take us there every year, on the Fourth of July, to watch the air shows."

Private Ortega nodded in agreement. "That makes sense. Wright Field would be a top choice for someone with Erik's background."

Benjamin's spirits lifted slightly, seeing a potential direction in their discussion. "Wright Field…It's worth looking into. Thank you, both of you."

The mess hall conversation shifted again, this time toward brainstorming strategies and possibilities. Despite Benjamin's initial defeat, he was determined to keep pushing forward, knowing that every piece of information brought him closer to uncovering the truth about Erik Müller's whereabouts.

Benjamin found himself at a crossroads, grappling with a formidable dilemma. The task of proving Erik's presence at Wright Field seemed like an insurmountable challenge, leaving him with a scant array of options. His first instinct was to pursue an official avenue, drafting a meticulous request through military intelligence channels. However, he knew this path was fraught with uncertainties. This request would need to be carefully justified, emphasizing the importance of the information for ongoing operations or security concerns. Justifying the disclosure of Erik's whereabouts for ongoing operations or security concerns seemed like a daunting task, casting doubt on the effectiveness of this route.

Another possibility lingered in the air—engaging his superiors or trusted colleagues with access to classified information. Yet, Benjamin couldn't shake off the apprehension that this approach, too, carried a high risk of failure. Presenting a compelling argument for why he needed to uncover Erik's location felt like navigating a minefield of skepticism and bureaucratic hurdles.

Then there was the perilous idea of delving into transfer records and administrative documents, a venture rife with potential consequences. The thought of being accused of espionage sent a chill down his spine, forcing him to discard this option swiftly. To exacerbate matters, Benjamin lacked any contacts stationed at Wright Field who could offer crucial insights.

As the weight of his predicament pressed upon him, a flicker of inspiration sparked in Benjamin's mind—a novel approach, an uncharted path that might just hold the key to unlocking the mystery surrounding Erik's whereabouts. The first thing he would need was a compelling argument.

Benjamin's workspace was a symphony of organized chaos. Papers sprawled across his desk, each one a puzzle piece in his quest for a temporary transfer to Wright Field, Ohio. The hum of the office around him faded into the background as he delved into his research with fervor.

His first task was to understand the intricacies of military protocols and the channels through which such requests were processed. He scoured manuals, regulations, and historical precedents, noting down key points and strategies employed by successful applicants in the past.

Benjamin understood that the more compelling and well-supported his justification was, the higher the likelihood of approval. Clear alignment with strategic objectives and demonstrated expertise would be crucial.

Next, he dove into the specifics of Wright Field itself. He studied its strategic importance, ongoing projects, and areas where his expertise as an interrogator could be of immediate value.

Benjamin meticulously crafted his argument around the operational necessity of his presence at Wright Field. He highlighted the critical role of debriefing German scientists like Erik Müller to gain unparalleled insights into advanced aeronautical technology. By emphasizing the potential breakthroughs in intelligence that his interactions with these experts could yield, Benjamin painted a vivid picture of the invaluable contributions he could make to ongoing intelligence operations.

Drawing from his extensive experience as an interrogator and his successful track record in handling high-value POWs, Benjamin showcased his expertise as a key asset for the mission at Wright Field. He emphasized his familiarity with Erik and other German scientists, positioning himself as uniquely qualified to extract valuable information that could significantly impact strategic decision-making. This personal touch added depth to his argument, highlighting the trust and rapport he had built with these individuals over time.

Benjamin outlined specific goals for his assignment at Wright Field, focusing on conducting detailed debriefings of German scientists. He proposed collaborative efforts with technical experts to decipher the implications of their work, ensuring that the intelligence gathered would be accurately interpreted and effectively utilized. This proactive approach showcased Benjamin's strategic thinking and his commitment to maximizing the value of his presence at the field.

In addition to debriefing missions, Benjamin proposed gathering additional intelligence on other scientists or projects at Wright Field. He leveraged his skills as an interrogator to uncover critical information that could benefit ongoing military operations. By highlighting his role in intelligence gathering beyond individual debriefings, Benjamin demonstrated a comprehensive understanding of the broader strategic landscape and his potential to contribute significantly to national security objectives.

Benjamin understood that the strategic relevance of his mission played a vital role. If his assignment aligned with broader military objectives, such as enhancing understanding of enemy technology, identifying strategic threats, or supporting ongoing defense initiatives, it added weight to his request. Decision-makers prioritized missions that contributed directly to national security interests and strategic goals.

Through meticulous research, strategic planning, and a clear articulation of his expertise and goals, Benjamin crafted a persuasive argument that underscored the necessity and potential impact of his temporary assignment to Wright Field, Ohio. He felt a surge of confidence as he prepared to draft his request, knowing that every detail, every insight gleaned from his research, would strengthen his argument and bring him one step closer to his goal.

While the argument for justification was crucial, Benjamin was also aware that he couldn't do it alone. Strong endorsements from his superiors would significantly enhance his chances. If his request was seen as beneficial to the overall mission, it was more likely to be approved. Benjamin knew he not only needed Colonel Stone's approval, he needed his endorsement.

Colonel Stone's endorsement carried weight and credibility. His support would lend legitimacy to Benjamin's request and signal to other decision-makers that the mission at Wright Field is not only endorsed but also strategically important.

Colonel Stone understood the strategic importance of intelligence operations and the value of extracting information from high-value sources like Erik Müller. His endorsement would highlight the alignment between Benjamin's mission and broader military objectives.

Benjamin had a proven track record under Colonel Stone's command, showcasing his skills, dedication, and effectiveness as an interrogator. This history of success, coupled with Colonel Stone's endorsement, would further strengthen other decision-makers' confidence in Benjamin's capabilities.

Colonel Stone's endorsement could open doors to other influential figures within the military, creating a network of support that amplifies Benjamin's chances of success. His connections and influence could help navigate bureaucratic hurdles and overcome resistance from skeptical parties.

Colonel Stone's endorsement would not just be a formality but a strategic decision based on his understanding of Benjamin's mission, its importance, and the potential impact on military operations. This endorsement would be backed by a clear vision and rationale, adding credibility to Benjamin's request.

The final hurdle, Benjamin realized, would be obtaining the appropriate security clearance to access classified areas and information at Wright Field. His request would be scrutinized to ensure that it aligns with security protocols.

The request would be evaluated for its impact on operational security. Any perceived risk of compromising sensitive information or disrupting ongoing projects would need to be mitigated.

After weeks of meticulous preparation, Benjamin felt a glimmer of optimism creeping in. While uncertainty still lingered, he couldn't help but feel a sense of cautious confidence that his efforts might just pay off.

As he reviewed his meticulously prepared dossier one final time, Benjamin couldn't deny the nervous excitement bubbling within him. The thought of contributing directly to critical intelligence efforts, debriefing high-value sources, and unraveling mysteries at Wright Field fueled his determination.

While bureaucratic hurdles and potential resistance still loomed on the horizon, Benjamin was ready to face them head-on. He had done everything in his power to stack the odds in his favor, and now, all that was left was for him to wait for his scheduled meeting in the briefing room with Colonel Stone and a panel of senior officers.

Chapter Eighteen

Fort Hunt, Virginia, June 03 , 1944

On May 25, the Allies achieved a significant breakthrough in Italy with the success of Operation Diadem. This operation, also known as the Fourth Battle of Monte Cassino, was a coordinated offensive designed to breach the formidable German Gustav Line, a series of heavily fortified defensive positions stretching across central Italy.

Operation Diadem was launched on May 11, and involved a massive and coordinated assault by the Allied forces, including British, American, French, Polish, and Canadian troops. The operation was part of a broader strategy to liberate Rome and push the German forces further north.

The success of Operation Diadem culminated on May 25, when the Allies finally broke through the Gustav Line. This breakthrough forced the German 10th Army to retreat northward, opening the path to Rome. The fall of the Gustav Line marked a turning point in the Italian Campaign, as it enabled the Allies to advance rapidly towards the Italian capital.

The capture of Rome, just days before the D-Day landings in Normandy, provided a significant morale boost for the Allied forces and underscored the importance of the Italian Campaign in the broader context of am the war. The success of Operation Diadem demonstrated the effectiveness of combined Allied operations and set the stage for further advances into northern Italy.

On June 3, the Allies commenced the final preparations for Operation Overlord, the ambitious and meticulously planned invasion of Normandy. Operation Overlord was the codename for the Allied invasion of Nazi-occupied Western Europe, a massive military endeavor that had been in planning for over a year.

Allied forces, including American, British, Canadian, and other Allied troops, had gathered in southern England, ready for deployment. These forces included over 156,000 soldiers who were designated to land on the beaches of Normandy, supported by thousands of ships, aircraft, and vehicles.

Massive logistical efforts were undertaken to ensure the success of the invasion. This included stockpiling ammunition, fuel, medical supplies, and food. Special equipment such as Mulberry harbors (portable, temporary harbors) and PLUTO (Pipeline Under The Ocean) were prepared to support the invasion force once ashore.

Commanders and troops received detailed briefings on their specific roles, objectives, and the layout of the Normandy beaches. Rehearsals and final drills were conducted to ensure that all units were fully prepared for the complexities of the amphibious assault.

The Allies continued to execute Operation Bodyguard, a comprehensive deception plan designed to mislead the Germans about the actual invasion location. This included fake radio traffic, dummy equipment, and the creation of a phantom army group, led by General George Patton, purportedly preparing to invade at Pas de Calais.

Meteorologists played a crucial role in the timing of the invasion. The initial date for the invasion was set for June 5, but due to unfavorable weather conditions, Supreme Allied Commander General Dwight D. Eisenhower made the critical decision to delay the invasion by 24 hours. Continuous weather monitoring ensured that conditions would be suitable for the landing on June 6.

The Allied air forces, consisting of thousands of aircraft, were tasked with bombing German defenses, disrupting transportation networks, and providing air cover for the invading troops. Meanwhile, the naval forces, comprising over 5,000 vessels, including battleships, destroyers, and landing craft, were prepared to support the beach landings with bombardments and troop transports.

General Eisenhower and his top commanders held crucial meetings to finalize the plans and make the ultimate decision to proceed with the invasion. These decisions were based on the latest intelligence, weather reports, and readiness assessments.

The corridors of P.O. Box 1142 seemed unusually quiet as Benjamin made his way to Colonel Stone's office. Each step echoed with a weighty anticipation, mirroring the gravity of the moment. His mind raced, rehearsing possible outcomes, and his heart drummed a nervous rhythm in his chest.

Upon reaching Colonel Stone's door, Benjamin paused for a brief moment to compose himself. He adjusted his uniform, ensuring every crease was sharp and every button aligned—a small act of control amidst the uncertainty that awaited behind that door.

Knocking firmly, Benjamin waited for the customary command to enter. "Come in," Colonel Stone's voice carried a steady authority that Benjamin had grown accustomed to over his time at P.O. Box 1142.

Stepping inside, Benjamin snapped to attention and saluted. "Corporal Steinberg reporting as ordered, sir."

Colonel Stone returned the salute before motioning for Benjamin to take a seat. The office, typically bustling with activity and paperwork, now seemed eerily serene, the only sound the soft rustle of papers as Colonel Stone shuffled through his notes.

"You've been waiting a few months now for this moment, Corporal," Colonel Stone remarked, his gaze appraising but not unkind.

"Yes, sir," Benjamin replied, his voice steady but tinged with a hint of nerves. "I'm eager to hear the decision."

Colonel Stone's words echoed in the confines of his office, carrying a weight of acknowledgment and approval that Benjamin hadn't expected. "I'll admit that when you first presented your request, I thought it was quite unusual," Colonel Stone began, his tone thoughtful as he leaned forward slightly. "But after hearing your argument and reviewing the accompanying documentation, I started to see the merit in the idea."

Benjamin's gratitude swelled, knowing that his efforts to articulate the importance of the transfer had not gone unnoticed. He nodded, a mix of relief and pride coloring his expression. "Thank you, sir. I believe this opportunity will allow me to contribute effectively to our ongoing efforts."

Colonel Stone nodded in return, a small smile of approval gracing his features. "It seems as though the higher-ups agree," he added, emphasizing the collective support behind the decision. "Your track record and dedication to your duties have certainly played a role in this outcome.

"Thank you, sir," Benjamin's chest swelled with a sense of validation, knowing that his hard work and commitment had been recognized at a higher level.

"Your request for a temporary transfer to Wright Field has been under careful consideration," Colonel Stone began, his words measured.

A flicker of hope ignited in Benjamin's chest, tempered by the cautious reserve he had learned to adopt in the face of military decisions.

"After consulting with higher command and assessing the operational needs, I'm pleased to inform you that your request has been approved," Colonel Stone announced, a faint smile playing at the corners of his mouth.

Relief washed over Benjamin, a wave of gratitude and determination. "Thank you, sir," he replied, a genuine smile breaking through his professional facade. "I won't disappoint, sir," he affirmed, his voice reflecting a renewed sense of purpose.

"I have every confidence in your abilities, Corporal," Colonel Stone replied, his tone conveying both expectation and encouragement. Colonel Stone leaned back in his chair, a hint of a smile playing on his lips. His demeanor softened, taking on a more fatherly tone. "You know, Corporal," he began, his voice warm and reflective, "your situation reminds me of something that happened during the Great War."

Benjamin tilted his head slightly, intrigued by the sudden shift in the conversation. "Sir?"

The Colonel's gaze turned distant as he recalled the past. "It was during the early years of my military career, back in the trenches of France. There was a young officer six months out of basic training. He was determined to lead a reconnaissance mission into enemy territory, a task many thought was impossible and foolhardy at the time."

Colonel Stone paused, his eyes meeting Benjamin's with a knowing look. "This young soldier was convinced that the intel he could gather would turn the tide of our operations. He went to his Captain with a well-prepared plan, much like you did. It was unconventional, but his passion and dedication were undeniable."

Benjamin listened intently, sensing the relevance of the story to his own predicament.

"The Captain took a chance on him, approved his request, and he went on that mission. Not only did he return with critical intelligence that helped us secure a significant victory, but he also earned the respect and trust of everyone around him," Colonel Stone continued, his voice filled with a mixture of pride and nostalgia.

"Sometimes, the unconventional path is the right one," the Colonel said, his tone turning more serious. "Your request reminded me of that young soldier's determination and foresight. It's not always about the rank or the position, Corporal. It's about the impact you can make."

Benjamin felt a surge of inspiration, knowing that Colonel Stone saw potential in him. "Thank you for sharing that, sir. It means a lot."

Colonel Stone nodded, the warmth in his eyes unwavering. "Your orders and briefing for the transfer will be provided shortly. Prepare yourself for the challenges and responsibilities that come with this new assignment. Remember, it's not just about proving yourself; it's about making a difference."

With a final salute and a firm "Yes, sir," Benjamin turned to leave, but Colonel Stone's voice stopped him.

"One more thing, Corporal," he said, a twinkle in his eye. "That soldier…that young officer I mentioned. He wasn't just any soldier. He was me."

Benjamin turned back, eyes wide with surprise. Colonel Stone continued, "I shared that story because I see the same determination and potential in you that I had back then. And just like my commanding officer took a chance on me, I'm taking a chance on you. Make it count."

The revelation hit Benjamin with a profound sense of respect and gratitude. "I won't let you down, sir."

Colonel Stone smiled, his expression one of trust and encouragement. "I know you won't, Corporal Steinberg. Now go, and make your mark."

Benjamin left the office with renewed determination. The approval of his transfer marked a significant milestone in his military career, one that he was determined to meet with professionalism, dedication, and a readiness to excel. The Colonel's story served as a powerful reminder that sometimes, taking a chance on an unconventional path could lead to extraordinary outcomes.

As Benjamin made his way to the building's exit, his mind buzzed with plans and preparations. The journey ahead promised new experiences, challenges to overcome, and a chance to prove himself in unfamiliar territory. The corridors no longer felt quiet but charged with the energy of anticipation and readiness. Benjamin was ready to embark on this next phase of his military journey with determination and resolve.

Back in his quarters, Benjamin began packing his belongings with a sense of urgency. The room, which had been his home for so long, now seemed like a temporary stop on his journey. He carefully folded his uniforms, ensuring everything was in order.

A knock on the door interrupted his thoughts. It was Tom, his closest friend and confidant.

"Hey," Tom greeted, his eyes scanning the room filled with half-packed bags. "So, it's happening, huh?"

Benjamin nodded, a determined look on his face. "Yeah, I've got to be at Wright Field in two days. It's all moving so fast."

Tom stepped inside, closing the door behind him. "You ready for this?"

"I think so," Benjamin replied, a mixture of excitement and nerves in his voice. "It's a big change, but it's a chance to make a real impact."

Tom sat on the edge of the bed, watching Benjamin pack. "You know, I'm really proud of you, Ben. Not many people would have the guts to push for something like this."

"Thanks, Tom," Benjamin said, pausing to look at his friend. "I couldn't have done it without your support."

The two shared a moment of silence, the weight of the impending separation hanging in the air. Finally, Tom spoke again. "We'll keep in touch, right? Letters, at least?"

"Definitely," Benjamin assured him. "And who knows, maybe our paths will cross again sooner than we think. I mean, Dayton isn't that far from Columbus, right?"

The next day was a whirlwind of final preparations and goodbyes. Benjamin visited the mess hall one last time, sharing meals and laughter with his comrades. Private Ortega gave him a firm handshake, expressing his hope that Benjamin would find the answers he was looking for.

By the evening, everything was set. Benjamin stood in his quarters, his bags packed and ready by the door. He took a moment to look around, reflecting on all that he had experienced and learned at P.O. Box 1142.

The next morning, just as dawn began to break, Benjamin reported to the transport office. He was met by a transport officer who handed him his travel itinerary. "You'll be on a flight to Wright Field at 0800 hours," the officer informed him.

Benjamin nodded, taking the document. "Thank you."

As he boarded the plane, he felt a surge of determination. The journey ahead was filled with uncertainty, but he was ready to face whatever challenges came his way. The lessons from Colonel Stone's story, the support from his friends, and his own unwavering resolve would guide him as he embarked on this new mission.

The plane's engines roared to life, and as it lifted off the ground, Benjamin looked out the window, watching as P.O. Box 1142 and Fort Hunt, Virginia grew smaller in the distance. His thoughts were already turning to Wright Field and the future that awaited him there. He was ready to meet his destiny.

When Benjamin's plane touched down on the tarmac at Wright Field, the scene was a bustling hub of activity. The airfield was expansive, with long, wide runways that gleamed under the bright afternoon sun. The sky above was a crisp blue, occasionally dotted with fluffy white clouds. Rows of various military aircraft, from bombers to fighters, lined the tarmac, each attended by ground crews in olive drab uniforms. The constant hum of engines, the clanking of tools, and the occasional shout of a mechanic or airman created a symphony of controlled chaos.

As the plane taxied to a halt, Benjamin could see hangars in the distance, their large doors open to reveal the silhouettes of aircraft being serviced inside. Control towers loomed above, their windows reflecting the sunlight, and the American flag fluttered proudly atop one of the buildings. Trucks and jeeps crisscrossed the airfield, ferrying personnel and equipment to and fro. The scent of aviation fuel and the faint aroma of hot food from a nearby mess hall wafted through the air.

Benjamin's heart pounded in his chest as he peered out of the window, taking in the scene. His palms were slightly sweaty, and he rubbed them on his uniform pants, trying to steady his nerves. The enormity of Wright Field, a critical center for testing and research, both excited and intimidated him. He felt a mix of anticipation and trepidation, aware that this was a place where cutting-edge aviation technology was being developed and where his skills and knowledge would be put to the test.

Stepping off the plane, he felt the solid ground beneath his feet and the sun's warmth on his face. His mind raced with thoughts of Erik Müller and what they might accomplish together. The urgency of his mission pressed heavily upon him, mingling with a lingering sense of frustration from not knowing for certain if Erik had even been transferred to Wright Field. He realized the risks he had taken in transferring here. He reminded himself that it was only a temporary transfer.

As he walked across the tarmac, Benjamin couldn't help but feel a pang of awe at the sheer scale of the operations around him. He wondered what secrets lay hidden within the walls of the hangars and laboratories. His thoughts drifted to the conversations he'd had with Erik, the subtle hints and guarded revelations. He knew that unlocking those secrets could be crucial for the war effort.

Benjamin's determination solidified with each step. He resolved to find a way to contribute to the war effort, to delve into the minds of Erik Müller and the other newly arriving German scientists, and to uncover the wealth of knowledge and expertise they held within. His thoughts were a whirlwind of strategy and hope, mixed with a profound sense of duty. The future felt uncertain, but Benjamin knew that this place held the key to his destiny, shaping the path he was meant to follow. As P.O. Box 1142 was slowly winding down its operations, Wright Field was ramping up theirs.

Once Benjamin had made his way to the opposite side of the tarmac, he was directed toward a designated processing area, a small temporary structure near the tarmac, serving as an initial point of entry for incoming personnel. Inside, he encountered a flurry of activity as clerks and officers processed arrivals, verified identification, and provided initial briefings.

Benjamin presented his orders to a clerk behind a wooden desk stacked with paperwork. The clerk, after scrutinizing his documents and checking his name against a list, directed him to a nearby waiting area. This area, filled with rows of metal chairs, was occupied by other new arrivals—pilots, engineers, and intelligence officers—each awaiting further instructions.

While waiting, Benjamin had a chance to observe his surroundings. The walls of the processing building were adorned with maps, notices, and bulletin boards filled with memos and schedules. The atmosphere was a mix of urgency and routine, a testament to the airfield's critical role in the war effort, and the development of advancing aviation technology.

Soon, a young lieutenant with a clipboard called Benjamin's name, motioning for him to follow. They walked through a series of hallways to a briefing room. This room, equipped with large maps, a projector, and a long conference table, was where new arrivals received their initial orientation.

Here, Benjamin met with a senior officer who provided a detailed briefing on the current operations at Wright Field, emphasizing the importance of their work and the need for absolute secrecy. The officer outlined Benjamin's immediate tasks and introduced him to a liaison who would assist him in integrating into the field's activities.

After the briefing, Benjamin was escorted to his temporary quarters, a barracks building near the heart of the base. The barracks were modest but functional, with rows of bunk beds and personal lockers. Benjamin quickly stowed his gear, feeling the weight of his new assignment settling in. He knew that his time at Wright Field would be challenging but crucial, and he was ready to immerse himself in the work that lay ahead.

After stowing his gear and acclimating to his new living quarters, Benjamin took some time to rest and review the materials provided during his initial briefing. He organized his thoughts and prepared for the days ahead.

The next morning, Benjamin rose early, eager to take charge of his new duties. He reported to his liaison officer, who provided him with a detailed schedule and a comprehensive tour of the base facilities. This tour included key locations such as the intelligence offices, research labs, briefing rooms, and the mess hall. The liaison officer introduced Benjamin to various personnel, including scientists, engineers, and fellow intelligence officers, emphasizing the collaborative nature of their work.

During the tour, Benjamin kept a watchful eye, hoping to catch a glimpse of Erik going about his daily duties, but he was nowhere to be seen.

Despite this, Benjamin paid close attention, noting the layout of the base and familiarizing himself with the critical areas where he would be spending most of his time. He met several colleagues who welcomed him and offered insights into the current projects and challenges they faced.

The tour and introductions set the stage for Benjamin's integration into the operations at Wright Field, ensuring he was well-prepared to contribute effectively to the war effort.

Next, Benjamin attended a series of orientation meetings and briefings tailored to his specific role. These sessions were comprehensive and meticulously organized, designed to ensure that new arrivals quickly understood the critical aspects of their assignments and the overall mission at Wright Field.

The first session covered the base's security protocols in extensive detail. Security officers emphasized the importance of maintaining strict confidentiality about all operations conducted at the base. They outlined the procedures for accessing secure areas, handling classified information, and the stringent measures in place to prevent unauthorized disclosures. Benjamin was briefed on the protocols for reporting any security breaches and the severe consequences of failing to adhere to these guidelines. This session underscored the high stakes of their work and the paramount importance of maintaining operational security.

Following the security briefing, the focus shifted to the latest developments in aviation technology. Leading scientists and engineers presented the cutting-edge advancements being made in aeronautics, including new aircraft designs, propulsion systems, and materials science. Benjamin was fascinated by the intricate details of these innovations, which represented the forefront of aviation research. The presenters highlighted the potential impact of these technologies on the war effort, demonstrating how they could enhance the capabilities of Allied forces. The room was filled with excitement and anticipation, as everyone understood the significance of staying ahead in the technological race.

In subsequent sessions, senior officers and strategic planners outlined the broader objectives of their mission at Wright Field. They provided an overview of the key projects currently underway and the strategic goals they aimed to achieve. This included improving aircraft performance, developing more effective reconnaissance methods, and enhancing the overall efficiency of air operations. The officers discussed how each department's work contributed to the larger mission, fostering a sense of unity and shared purpose among the attendees.

One of the most crucial aspects of these briefings was the detailed information about the newly arrived German scientists. Laisons presented comprehensive dossiers on these individuals, outlining their backgrounds, areas of expertise, and previous work. Benjamin flipped through the stack of folders, each containing valuable insights into the expertise brought by these scientists. However, as he scanned through the folders, one dossier stood out among the rest. It was the dossier of Erik Müller, a scientist whose contributions to experimental aircraft designs and knowledge of advanced propulsion systems made him a key figure of interest. The briefers emphasized the strategic importance of extracting and utilizing the knowledge these scientists possessed, particularly focusing on techniques for building rapport, gaining trust, and effectively interrogating them to elicit valuable information.

Throughout these sessions, Benjamin took meticulous notes, absorbing the wealth of information being presented. He formulated questions and strategies, mentally preparing himself for the complex task of working with the German scientists. The briefings also provided him with an opportunity to meet and interact with other intelligence officers and researchers, fostering a collaborative environment where ideas and insights were freely exchanged.

By the end of the day, Benjamin felt a mix of exhaustion and determination. The orientation meetings had provided him with a clear understanding of his role and the vital importance of their mission at Wright Field. He was now equipped with the knowledge and resources to begin his work, ready to contribute to the war effort by unlocking the secrets held by scientists like Erik Müller. What's more, he now had confirmation that Erik was, indeed, somewhere in this facility.

As Benjamin reflected on the day's events, he felt a surge of excitement knowing that Erik, the man he had come this far to find, was present at Wright Field. The thought of finally getting to interact with Erik again, to delve into his expertise and glean insights that could shape the course of their mission, filled Benjamin with renewed energy.

The future, though uncertain, held a sense of purpose and direction that Benjamin was eager to pursue. With Erik's dossier in hand and a plan forming in his mind, Benjamin looked forward to the challenges and discoveries that lay ahead. He was determined to make a meaningful contribution to the war effort and to unravel the mysteries hidden within the walls of Wright Field, with Erik Müller at the center of it all.

Chapter Nineteen

Wright Field, Ohio, June 09 , 1944

The Battle of Normandy had begun. Allied forces, including American, British, and Canadian troops, landed on the beaches of Normandy, France, marking the beginning of the liberation of Western Europe from Nazi occupation. Allied troops encountered intense resistance as they pushed inland from the beachheads.

On June 6th, D-Day, also known as Operation Neptune, was the largest seaborne invasion in history. It involved around 156,000 Allied troops landing on five beachheads (Utah, Omaha, Gold, Juno, and Sword) along the Normandy coast. The operation included extensive naval and air support.

Allied forces consolidated their positions on the Normandy beaches, expanding their beachheads and reinforcing their troops. German counterattacks were repelled as the Allies worked to establish logistical support and infrastructure for the ongoing campaign.

That morning, in the Pacific Theater, the Battle of Saipan began when U.S. forces launched an ambitious amphibious invasion of Saipan, one of the Mariana Islands located in the central Pacific Ocean. This operation was part of the larger strategy to push Japanese forces out of key territories and establish a strategic foothold closer to Japan itself.

Saipan was of immense strategic importance due to its airfields, which, if captured, could be used by Allied forces to launch devastating air raids against Japan's home islands. Additionally, control of Saipan would deny the Japanese a crucial defensive position and allow the Allies to exert greater naval and air power in the region.

The amphibious assault on Saipan involved a coordinated effort by U.S. Marines, Army units, and naval forces. Troops landed on Saipan's beaches under heavy enemy fire, facing fierce resistance from well-entrenched Japanese defenders. The terrain, characterized by rugged cliffs, dense vegetation, and fortified positions, posed significant challenges for the advancing Allied forces.

Despite these obstacles, the U.S. forces managed to establish beachheads and push inland, engaging in intense and brutal combat with the Japanese defenders. The battle quickly turned into a protracted and grueling campaign, marked by close-quarters fighting, artillery barrages, and fierce counterattacks from the Japanese.

As the battle raged on, both sides suffered significant casualties. The Japanese, determined to defend Saipan at all costs, fought tenaciously and inflicted heavy losses on the advancing Allied forces. However, the superior firepower, air support, and logistical capabilities of the Allies eventually began to take their toll on the Japanese defenses.

As Benjamin settled into his role at Wright Field, his anticipation grew for the pivotal task ahead—interviewing captured German scientists. The first week passed in a whirlwind of orientation sessions, additional training in interrogation techniques, and familiarization with intelligence analysis tools. Each day brought him closer to the moment he would step into the interrogation room.

By the second week, Benjamin had absorbed a wealth of information about ongoing projects, key objectives, and the intelligence landscape. He pored over intelligence reports detailing the expertise of captured German scientists, including Erik Müller. The urgency to extract valuable information was palpable, driving Benjamin's focus and determination.

With a deepening understanding of the landscape, Benjamin worked closely with senior officers and intelligence analysts to assess the strategic importance of initiating interviews. Plans were meticulously crafted, taking into account the sensitive nature of the information sought and the delicate balance of rapport-building and strategic probing required during interrogations.

It was during the third week that Benjamin finally initiated the interview process. Each interview would be a carefully orchestrated dance of questions and observations, as Benjamin sought to establish trust and extract critical intelligence. He delved into the task with enthusiasm.

Benjamin's first scheduled appointment arrived, and Erik Müller, escorted by the front office personnel, made his way to Benjamin's new office at Wright Field. The office itself was a modest yet functional space, reflecting Benjamin's organized and efficient work style. The walls were barren, giving the space a minimalist yet functional look. A large wooden desk occupied the center of the room, accompanied by a comfortable chair for guests.

As Erik entered the office, he observed Benjamin sitting at his desk with his back turned, engrossed in setting up a new filing cabinet. The morning sunlight filtered through the window, casting a warm glow on the room. Erik cleared his throat and spoke, "Good morning, I was told that I should report to this office to meet my new handler."

At the sound of Erik's voice, Benjamin slowly turned around, a warm smile crossing his face. "Mr. Müller," he greeted, rising from his chair to welcome Erik. "It's nice to hear your voice again."

"Benji?" Erik's face was full of shock, his voice tinged with disbelief. "What are you doing here? I feared I would never see you again."

Benjamin stepped out from behind the desk, his smile widening. "Aren't you excited to see me?" he asked, a hint of playful warmth in his tone.

"Excited doesn't even begin to cover it," Erik finally said, a mix of relief and astonishment evident in his expression. "I thought our paths had diverged for good."

Benjamin nodded, the gravity of the moment settling between them. "After you got transferred, I did everything I could to try to find you. When I was pretty sure you were here, I fought the system to get a transfer. I came after you, Erik."

Erik's eyes widened, a flicker of hope lighting them up. "Benji…"

"The last time we spoke," Benjamin continued, his voice soft but steady, "you told me that you loved me. Tell me now, do you still feel that way?"

Erik's breath caught, his expression shifting to one of vulnerability and yearning. "Yes, Benji," he whispered. "I do. I never stopped."

Benjamin felt a rush of emotions, a blend of relief, joy, and determination. The bare walls of the office seemed to fade away, leaving only the two of them standing at the threshold of a new beginning, ready to face whatever lay ahead together.

"Come, sit with me," Benjamin gestured toward the cozy chair beside him. "We have so much to talk about."

As Erik took a seat, Benjamin motioned towards the empty walls. "Please excuse the lack of decoration at the moment. I have plans for maps and charts; I hear they are all the rage in these places. They'll be up soon."

Erik chuckled, acknowledging Benjamin's attempt at humor.

"Let's get started," Benjamin said, returning to his desk. "There are many things we can discuss regarding your role here and how we can work together effectively."

The conversation shifted towards their partnership, setting the stage for a productive and collaborative working relationship between Benjamin and Erik at Wright Field. They delved into the specifics of Erik's expertise, discussing the projects he would be involved in and the strategic importance of his knowledge. Benjamin outlined his expectations and goals, emphasizing the significance of their mission.

Erik listened intently, appreciating the clarity and structure Benjamin provided. The bare walls seemed less significant as they delved into the details of their collaboration, their shared purpose bringing a sense of focus and direction to the room.

As they continued to talk, it became evident that their connection was not just professional but deeply personal, their past intertwining with their present roles. The future, though uncertain, held a renewed sense of purpose and hope, as Benjamin and Erik prepared to navigate the challenges ahead together.

Over the next six months, Benjamin found himself at the heart of a whirlwind of innovation and collaboration at Wright Field. His office, though initially bare, gradually filled with charts, maps, and reports detailing the myriad of projects he oversaw. Each day brought new challenges and breakthroughs, with Benjamin playing a crucial role in facilitating the integration of Erik Müller's expertise into the American war effort.

Erik was immediately immersed in the development and refinement of jet propulsion systems. His knowledge of advanced propulsion, honed in the laboratories and test fields of Germany, was invaluable. He collaborated closely with American engineers on the General Electric J31, the U.S.'s first operational jet engine, providing insights that accelerated the engine's development. Benjamin ensured that Erik had access to all the necessary resources and that communication between teams was seamless.

Simultaneously, Erik's experience with experimental aircraft designs was put to the test. He worked on high-speed and high-altitude flight projects, contributing to the design and testing of advanced fighter and bomber aircraft. His input was particularly crucial in projects like the North American P-51 Mustang and the Boeing B-29 Superfortress. Benjamin's role was pivotal, coordinating efforts between different departments, and making sure Erik's suggestions were implemented efficiently.

Erik also delved into the aerodynamics and materials research, applying his deep understanding to improve aircraft performance. Wind tunnel testing, computational simulations, and studies of new materials became routine, with Benjamin ensuring that these tests were integrated into the broader project goals. Together, they pushed the boundaries of speed, maneuverability, and structural integrity.

A significant portion of Erik's work involved reverse-engineering and integrating captured German technology. The Messerschmitt Me 262, the world's first operational jet-powered fighter aircraft, became a particular focus. Erik's familiarity with its design allowed him to provide critical insights, which Benjamin facilitated by organizing dedicated teams to study and adapt these innovations into American designs.

The collaborative environment at Wright Field fostered an exchange of ideas that was instrumental in driving progress. Benjamin ensured that Erik worked closely with American engineers and scientists, creating an atmosphere of mutual learning and respect. This synergy was evident in the rapid advancements they achieved together.

Erik also took on a mentoring role, training American personnel to understand the complexities of jet propulsion and advanced aerodynamics. His sessions were highly valued, and Benjamin made sure they were well-attended and supported, recognizing the long-term benefits of building a knowledgeable and skilled workforce.

Some of Erik's work was classified, involving innovative and experimental technologies aimed at giving the Allies a technological edge. Benjamin was often the liaison, managing the sensitive information and ensuring that these projects received the focus and protection they needed.

Throughout these months, Benjamin's dedication never wavered. His ability to navigate the complexities of the various projects, his knack for bringing together the right people, and his relentless pursuit of excellence were instrumental in the success of their endeavors. The collaboration between Erik and the American teams, facilitated by Benjamin, led to significant advancements in aviation technology.

By the end of the six months, Wright Field had transformed into a powerhouse of innovation, with Erik's contributions deeply woven into the fabric of their success. Benjamin looked back on their journey with a sense of accomplishment, knowing that their work had not only advanced the war effort but also forged a bond that transcended their individual roles. The future, though still filled with uncertainties, now held a promise of continued collaboration and breakthroughs, thanks to the foundation they had built together.

During these six transformative months, Benjamin and Erik spent endless hours together, not just working on cutting-edge aviation projects, but also discovering new and exciting things about each other. Their professional partnership soon blossomed into an even deeper personal connection. They fell deeper and more in love every day, their bond strengthened by shared goals and mutual respect.

In the quiet moments between their intense collaborative sessions, they would steal away to secluded corners of the base, sharing their hopes, dreams, and fears. Erik spoke of his childhood fascination with flight and his conflicted feelings about his past. Benjamin, in turn, shared his struggles with acceptance and his unwavering desire to serve his country while staying true to himself.

Their relationship was a delicate dance, balancing their public roles with the private sanctuary they found in each other's company. Benjamin's office, initially a place of strategic planning and briefings, became a haven where they could let their guards down. They found comfort in simple gestures—a shared glance, a fleeting touch, a whispered conversation late at night.

Erik's laugh became a cherished sound to Benjamin, a reminder of the man beneath the scientist, while Erik found solace in Benjamin's unwavering support and understanding. Their love grew in the stolen moments between the chaos of their work, each discovery about the other deepening their connection.

As they worked on integrating German technology, refining jet propulsion systems, and designing experimental aircraft, their partnership evolved into something far more profound. They challenged and inspired each other, pushing the boundaries of what was possible both in their work and in their hearts.

Despite the secrecy surrounding their relationship, their love was an open secret among those who worked closely with them. The quiet understanding and respect of their colleagues created a space where their bond could flourish. Together, they faced the uncertainties of the future with a sense of purpose and a shared vision.

By the end of those six months, their professional achievements were remarkable, but it was the love they had nurtured that truly transformed their lives. Benjamin and Erik had found something rare and beautiful amid the turmoil of war—a connection that gave them strength, hope, and a reason to look forward to each new day.

Finally, one remarkable evening, the air was palpable as the personnel at Wright Field gathered on the tarmac for the unveiling of the newly redesigned Lockheed P-80 Shooting Star. The sun was beginning to set, casting a golden hue over the assembled crowd and the sleek jet fighter hidden beneath a large canvas.

Benjamin stood beside Erik, feeling a mix of pride and excitement. Over the past several months, their collaboration had been intense and fruitful. Erik's deep knowledge of jet propulsion and aircraft design had significantly contributed to the improvements made on the P-80. Benjamin had facilitated the integration of Erik's ideas with the American engineers, ensuring a seamless and productive partnership.

As the senior officers made their way to the front of the crowd, the chatter among the gathered scientists, engineers, and military personnel hushed. Colonel Franklin O. Carroll took the podium, his authoritative voice carrying over the assembled group.

"Ladies and gentlemen, today we stand on the brink of a new era in aviation history," Colonel Carroll began, his voice resonating with pride and conviction. "The Lockheed P-80 Shooting Star represents not only a technological marvel but also the relentless spirit and innovation of our team here at Wright Field."

He paused, allowing the weight of his words to settle over the crowd. "This project has been a testament to our dedication and collaboration. In the face of adversity, amidst the challenges of war, we have come together—military personnel, scientists, and engineers—united by a common purpose: to secure the future of our great nation."

Colonel Carroll's eyes swept over the assembled group, each face reflecting the determination and resilience that had brought them to this moment. "The P-80 Shooting Star is more than just an aircraft. It is a symbol of American ingenuity, of our unwavering commitment to innovation and progress. It embodies the courage and tenacity that define our nation."

He gestured towards the canvas-covered aircraft. "This jet fighter stands as a beacon of hope and a testament to what we can achieve when we work together towards a common goal. It is a product of countless hours of hard work, late nights, and the brilliant minds who refused to give up in the face of seemingly insurmountable challenges."

Colonel Carroll's voice grew more passionate. "In this aircraft, we see the future of aerial combat, a future where our pilots have the advantage, where our skies are protected by the very best that technology has to offer. The P-80 Shooting Star will give our forces the edge they need to bring this war to a successful conclusion and to ensure the safety and security of our nation for generations to come."

He looked directly at the crowd, his gaze intense and unwavering. "Let this aircraft be a reminder of what we are fighting for: our freedom, our way of life, and the principles that make America the greatest nation on earth. Let it inspire us to continue pushing the boundaries of what is possible, to never settle for anything less than excellence."

Colonel Carroll's voice softened but remained powerful. "Today, as we unveil the Lockheed P-80 Shooting Star, let us remember the sacrifices made by those who came before us, the bravery of our pilots, and the unwavering support of the American people. Together, we will soar to new heights, and together, we will secure victory."

With a final, sweeping gesture towards the aircraft, Colonel Carroll concluded, "Ladies and gentlemen, I present to you the Lockheed P-80 Shooting Star—a symbol of our triumph, a testament to our resolve, and a beacon of hope for the future."

With a dramatic flourish, the canvas was pulled away, revealing the gleaming jet fighter. The crowd erupted into applause and cheers as they took in the sight of the sleek, aerodynamic design. The P-80 was a stunning example of modern aviation, its clean lines and powerful stance a testament to the hard work and ingenuity of everyone involved.

Erik glanced at Benjamin, a proud smile on his face. "We did it," he said softly, his voice filled with awe.

Benjamin nodded, his eyes never leaving the jet. "We did. And this is just the beginning."

As the crowd moved closer to get a better look at the P-80, Colonel Carroll continued his speech, outlining the capabilities and advancements of the aircraft. He highlighted the improved turbojet engine, the enhanced aerodynamics, and the increased speed and maneuverability that would make the P-80 a formidable presence in the skies.

Benjamin and Erik were soon surrounded by their colleagues, all eager to congratulate them on their contributions. The atmosphere was electric, filled with a sense of accomplishment and camaraderie.

After the formalities, Benjamin and Erik found a quieter moment near the aircraft. Benjamin placed a hand on the cool metal surface of the P-80, feeling a surge of pride. "This jet is going to change the course of the war," he said.

Erik nodded, his eyes shining with excitement. "And it's a symbol of what we can achieve when we work together."

Their conversation was interrupted by Colonel Carroll, who approached them with a broad smile. "Gentlemen, your work has been nothing short of extraordinary. The P-80 is a testament to your dedication and expertise."

Benjamin shook the colonel's hand. "Thank you, sir. We're honored to be a part of this."

As the evening drew to a close, the crowd slowly dispersed, but the sense of accomplishment lingered. Benjamin and Erik stood together, looking out at the P-80, knowing that their efforts had made a significant impact.

Over the next few weeks, the P-80 would undergo rigorous testing and evaluation, but this night was a moment of celebration. Benjamin and Erik had not only advanced aviation technology but had also deepened their bond, both professionally and personally.

As the evening settled in, casting a gentle glow through the windows of Erik's living quarters, Benjamin and Erik found themselves enveloped in a moment of intimacy and reflection. The echoes of the day's events lingered in the air, mingling with the soft strains of music playing on the record player.

Benjamin lay across the sofa, his head cradled in Erik's lap. Erik's fingers traced the line of the pale scar above Benjamin's left eyebrow, a tender gesture that spoke volumes of their unspoken connection.

Erik asks softly, "How did you get this scar?"

Benjamin laughs nervously and replies, "Oh, that? I tried to show off some dance moves at a party. Unfortunately, I didn't realize how close I was to the coffee table. Let's just say, the coffee table didn't appreciate my fancy footwork."

Erik giggled, then decided to level the playing field by offering an embarrassing story from his past. "Well, if it makes you feel any better," he began with a sheepish smile, "I once tripped and fell flat on my face in the school cafeteria while trying to impress a crush. The whole tray of food went flying, and I became the talk of the school for a few days."

They both shared a laugh together. They shared other triumphs and challenges, their journey intertwined in ways that words could scarcely capture.

The music provided a backdrop to their quiet conversation, a conversation that didn't need words. They spoke of how far they had come together, from the uncertainties and hesitations of their first meeting to the seamless collaboration and deep understanding they now shared. They reminisced about the challenges they had faced, the obstacles overcome, and the victories celebrated.

In that moment, surrounded by the warmth of each other's presence and the soft melodies filling the room, Benjamin and Erik found solace in the simple act of being together.

They didn't need grand gestures or elaborate words to express what they felt; their connection spoke volumes in the shared silence, in the gentle touch of fingers and the quiet exchange of glances.

As they lay there, lost in their thoughts and the comfort of each other's company, they knew that whatever the future held, they would face it together, their bond a source of strength and resilience that would carry them through any challenge that lay ahead.

Chapter Twenty

Wright Field, Ohio, September 03, 1945

In the spring of 1945, the world witnessed a series of dramatic events that would shape the course of history and bring World War II to a decisive end. These events unfolded in rapid succession, marking the final chapters of the war and the beginning of a new era.

As the cherry blossoms bloomed in the Pacific, signaling the onset of April, the Battle of Okinawa erupted on April 1. The lush island of Okinawa became the stage for a grueling struggle between Allied forces, primarily American and Japanese defenders. The battle, marked by fierce ground combat, naval clashes, and relentless air attacks, inflicted heavy casualties on both sides. The rocky terrain and determined Japanese resistance prolonged the fighting, but by June 22, Okinawa was firmly under Allied control, paving the way for the final push towards Japan.

Amidst the unfolding battle in the Pacific, the world mourned the loss of President Franklin D. Roosevelt on

April 12. His passing marked a somber moment in American history, and Harry S. Truman stepped into the role of President of the United States during a critical juncture in the war.

While the Pacific Theater raged on, the Soviet Union launched its Berlin Offensive on April 16. This massive offensive spearheaded the Battle of Berlin, as Soviet forces closed in on the heart of Nazi Germany. The fierce urban warfare that ensued culminated in the fall of Berlin, and on April 30, Adolf Hitler, the architect of Nazi tyranny, took his own life in his bunker as Soviet forces encircled the city.

The month of May brought a pivotal moment as Germany surrendered unconditionally to the Allies on May 7, marking Victory in Europe (VE) Day. The guns fell silent in Europe, and the world rejoiced in the long-awaited victory over Nazi Germany.

But the war was far from over. On July 16, the United States achieved a scientific breakthrough with the successful test of an atomic bomb in New Mexico, a culmination of the top-secret Manhattan Project. The world had entered the nuclear age, and the devastating power of atomic weaponry would soon alter the course of history.

On August 6 and 9, the United States dropped atomic bombs on Hiroshima and Nagasaki, respectively, bringing unparalleled destruction and prompting Japan's surrender. The bombings ushered in a new era of warfare and diplomacy, with the world grappling with the implications of nuclear weapons.

Finally, on September 2, aboard the USS Missouri in Tokyo Bay, Japan formally surrendered, marking the end of World War II. The signing of the Japanese Instrument of Surrender brought a fragile peace to a war-torn world and set the stage for the challenges and opportunities of the post-war era.

As the first rays of dawn gently kissed the horizon, Wright Field stirred with a sense of quiet anticipation. The morning after the surrender brought a mixture of relief, reflection, and renewed hope to all who gathered to commemorate Victory over Japan Day (V-J Day) on September 2. On this historic morning, the airbase was bathed in a soft golden light, signaling the dawn of a new era.

At the heart of the field, a platform adorned with the American flag stood tall and proud. A lone trumpeter, his instrument gleaming in the morning light, stood poised to sound the familiar notes of "To the Colors." The solemn melody echoed across the base, a poignant tribute to the sacrifices made and the triumph of Allied forces.

As the last strains of the trumpet faded, the flag began its ascent, unfurling majestically against the backdrop of a sky painted with hues of pink and gold. It was a moment frozen in time, a symbol of freedom and the collective spirit of a nation that had endured and prevailed.

The sight of the flag fluttering proudly in the morning breeze stirred the hearts of those gathered. Veterans, civilians, and military personnel stood side by side, their eyes fixed on the symbol that represented so much—courage, sacrifice, and the promise of a brighter future.

Cheers broke out as the flag reached its zenith, a chorus of voices united in celebration and gratitude. The air was filled with the sound of applause, mingling with the distant hum of aircraft taking to the skies in a display of aerial prowess.

The morning after the surrender was a time of reflection and remembrance. It was a day to honor the fallen, to acknowledge the resilience of those who served, and to look ahead with optimism and determination. Wright Field, like countless other places across the nation, was alive with the spirit of V-J Day, a testament to the enduring strength of the human spirit in the face of adversity.

Benjamin and Alex stood together amidst the festive crowd, their faces lit up with smiles that mirrored the joyous atmosphere around them. As the American flag soared high above, marking the morning after Japan's surrender, they exchanged a meaningful glance, their thoughts echoing the collective relief and sense of accomplishment that permeated the air.

Their day began with attending the solemn ceremony of flag-raising and morning trumpeting, a poignant reminder of the sacrifices made by their comrades-in-arms and the triumph of Allied forces. They stood side by side, their hands resting on their hearts as they paid homage to those who had fought bravely and the lives lost in the pursuit of freedom.

After the official ceremonies, Benjamin and Alex joined the festivities, exploring the various activities and attractions scattered across Wright Field. They wandered through displays of military equipment, marveling at the technological advancements that had contributed to victory in the war. Erik, with his keen interest, and continued involvement in aviation, eagerly shared insights into the aircraft and innovations showcased at the event.

The duo also took part in social gatherings, joining fellow servicemen, veterans, and civilians in a grand barbecue, and an impromptu dance party. Laughter and chatter filled the air as people of all ages and backgrounds came together to celebrate the end of hostilities and embrace a future of peace and prosperity.

Amidst the revelry, Benjamin and Alex found moments of quiet reflection, discussing the significance of the day and their hopes for the post-war world. They shared memories of their experiences during the war, reminiscing about the challenges they had faced and the bonds they had forged with comrades and friends.

As the sun set on V-J Day, casting a warm glow over Wright Field, Benjamin and Alex stood once again beneath the fluttering flag. They exchanged a silent vow to never forget the lessons learned, the sacrifices made, and the enduring spirit of resilience that had brought them to this moment of celebration and remembrance.

A few months later, another surprise warmed their spirits. Tom knocked on Benjamin and Erik's door in Fairborn, Ohio, his face beaming with excitement. As Benjamin opened the door, he was met not only by Tom's familiar grin but also by a radiant woman by his side.

"Tom!" Benjamin rushed in to give his good friend a big hug. "I can't believe you're here! I have missed you so much, my friend!" Erik came to the door as well, a look of surprise on his face.

"Benjamin, Erik, meet my wife, Nancy," Tom exclaimed, introducing his newly married wife with a proud gesture.

Benjamin and Erik exchanged surprised glances before breaking into welcoming smiles. "Congratulations, Tom!" Benjamin said warmly, extending a hand to Nancy. "It's a pleasure to meet you, Nancy."

Nancy returned their greetings with genuine warmth, her eyes sparkling with happiness. "Tom has told me so much about both of you," she said, stepping into the cozy living room.

As they settled in, Tom and Nancy shared stories of their wedding day and the joys of newlywed life. Benjamin and Erik listened attentively, sharing in their friends' happiness and celebrating this new chapter in Tom's life.

"And then," Tom chuckled, "Nancy decided to surprise me with a dance performance she had been secretly practicing for weeks!"

Nancy blushed but laughed along. "I couldn't resist adding a bit of flair to our special day," she admitted, her eyes sparkling with fond memories.

Erik raised an eyebrow playfully. "A dancer, huh? Tom, you've truly found yourself a gem," he remarked, earning a playful nudge from Benjamin.

As the conversation flowed, they transitioned to discussing their honeymoon adventures, from scenic road trips to unforgettable experiences in exotic destinations.

"It's incredible how travel opens your eyes to new perspectives," Benjamin reflected, his gaze drifting to a framed photo on the mantelpiece from one of their own memorable journeys.

Tom nodded in agreement. "Absolutely. Every adventure brings us closer together and creates lasting memories," he said, wrapping an arm around Nancy's shoulders.

The evening was filled with laughter, shared memories, and a sense of camaraderie that warmed the hearts of everyone present. It was a delightful surprise and a reminder of the enduring bonds of friendship that had been forged in the midst of challenges and triumphs.

"So, Benjamin," Tom asked, leaning back in his chair, "How are your parents doing these days?"

Benjamin's smile faltered slightly, but he quickly composed himself. "They're...adjusting," he replied, choosing his words carefully. "It's been a bit of a journey for them to accept who I am, but they're getting there. We've had some good conversations lately, and I think they're starting to understand."

Erik reached over and gave Benjamin's hand a reassuring squeeze. "It's never easy," he said softly. "But I'm glad you're talking."

Nancy, sensing the gravity of the topic, offered a supportive smile. "It's important that you're giving them the chance to understand," she said. "Sometimes it just takes time."

Tom nodded, his expression thoughtful. "I remember when I first told my parents I was joining the military," he said. "They were worried, of course, but eventually, they saw how much it meant to me. I think, in the end, what matters is that they see you're happy."

Benjamin smiled, grateful for the support. "I think so too," he agreed. "And honestly, having Erik by my side has made all the difference. We're building our life together, and that's what's most important to me."

Erik's eyes softened as he looked at Benjamin. "We've come a long way," he said quietly. "And I wouldn't trade any of it."

Tom adjusted his focus onto Erik, "And what about your family, Erik? Have you gotten any word from them since the war ended?"

Erik's expression softened with a mixture of relief and hope. "Yes, I was finally able to get some information about them, however small. It seems they immigrated to Argentina towards the end of the war. My father, mother, and little sister Emma. I don't have any information about where in Argentina they are living now, but just knowing that they got out of Germany before the end, and they are still alive, is enough to keep me going. Perhaps one day I will find out more."

Nancy's eyes widened with sympathy. "That must be such a relief, Erik. I can't imagine the weight of not knowing."

Erik nodded, a small smile playing on his lips. "It is. For the longest time, I feared the worst. But now, there's a glimmer of hope, and that's something I hold onto."

Benjamin squeezed Erik's hand, offering silent support. "We'll find them, Erik," he said with determination. "One day, we'll find them."

Tom leaned forward, his voice earnest. "If there's anything we can do to help, you know we're here for you. The world may be vast, but connections like ours make it feel a bit smaller."

Erik's gratitude was evident in his eyes. "Thank you, Tom. And thank you, Nancy. Knowing I have friends like you makes all the difference."

The conversation paused for a moment, the weight of Erik's words settling over them. It was a reminder of the far-reaching impact of the war, the lingering uncertainties, and the importance of the bonds they had formed.

Nancy broke the silence with a gentle smile. "It's amazing, really, how life can bring us together in the most unexpected ways. I'm grateful for the chance to know you all."

Benjamin nodded in agreement. "We've all faced our own battles, but together, we've found strength. And now, as we move forward, we do so with hope."

Erik looked around the room, his heart full. "Hope, and the support of good friends. That's all we need."

Tom raised his glass again. "To acceptance and understanding," he toasted. "And to the bonds that keep us strong."

They all clinked glasses, the sound a gentle reminder of the strength and support they found in one another. The conversation flowed on, touching on lighter topics and shared memories, but the warmth of their connection lingered, a testament to the journey they had all undertaken together.

As the evening drew to a close, they sat in comfortable silence, reflecting on the paths that had brought them to this moment. The challenges they had faced, the victories they had celebrated, and the friendships they had forged had all led them here, to this night of camaraderie and connection.

"We've been through so much," Benjamin mused, his voice filled with gratitude. "But we've come out stronger on the other side."

Erik nodded, his hand still intertwined with Benjamin's. "And we'll keep moving forward," he said. "Together."

Tom and Nancy smiled, their hearts warmed by the strength and resilience of their friends. It was a night they would all remember, a celebration not just of their individual journeys, but of the enduring power of love and friendship.

As the evening progressed, the conversation took a reflective turn, delving into their shared experiences and the paths they had taken since their days at P.O. Box 1142.

"You know," Tom began, a nostalgic smile playing on his lips, "I still remember the day we first met at Camp Ritchie. It feels like a lifetime ago."

Benjamin nodded, a reminiscent glint in his eyes. "Those were challenging but formative times," he recalled. "We were all finding our footing in a world filled with uncertainties."

Erik leaned forward, his expression thoughtful. "It's remarkable how our paths intertwined, leading us to where we are today," he remarked, his gaze shifting to Benjamin. "I never would have imagined back then that we'd be sitting here, sharing stories and celebrating each other's milestones."

Nancy, listening intently, chimed in, "Your bond is truly special. It's evident how much you've all been there for each other, through thick and thin."

The conversation turned to the lessons they had learned along the way and the challenges they had faced, both individually and as a group. They discussed moments of triumph and moments of doubt, finding strength in their shared resilience and unwavering support for one another.

"It's the people in our lives who make the journey worthwhile," Benjamin reflected, a sense of gratitude in his voice. "The friendships we've built, the laughter we've shared—it's what keeps us going."

Erik nodded in agreement. "And it's not just about the good times. It's about weathering the storms together, knowing we have each other's backs no matter what."

Tom raised his glass again in a silent toast, a silent acknowledgment of the bond they shared and the enduring friendship that had stood the test of time.

The night continued with stories of triumphs and challenges, laughter and reflection, creating a tapestry of memories that strengthened their bond and reaffirmed the value of true friendship.

As they bid farewell to Tom and Nancy later that evening, Benjamin and Erik felt grateful for the unexpected visit and the joy it brought to their home. The warmth of friendship and the love shared among them left an indelible mark, enriching their lives with moments of connection and happiness.

The golden hues of the setting sun cast a warm glow over Fairborn, Ohio, where Benjamin and Erik had built their life together. As they sat on the porch of their quaint home, overlooking a serene landscape, they reflected on the journey that had brought them to this moment.

"I never imagined we'd come this far," Benjamin mused, his gaze drifting to the horizon where the last traces of daylight lingered. "All those challenges we faced, and yet here we are."

Erik reached for Benjamin's hand, their fingers intertwining in a silent affirmation of their bond. "It hasn't been easy," he admitted, "but every hurdle we've overcome has only made us stronger."

They recalled the early days of their relationship, navigating a world that often felt unwelcoming and judgmental. Despite the external pressures and internal doubts, their love had remained unwavering, a beacon of hope and resilience.

Benjamin, having completed his novel, achieved his dream of becoming a writer. Meanwhile, Erik went on to become a U.S. citizen, continuing to work at Wright Field for the next four decades, and contributing to the development of several other aircraft including the B-17 Flying Fortress, the P-51 Mustang, and the Boeing B-29 Superfortress.

"We've accomplished something special," Erik remarked, his eyes filled with warmth as he looked at Benjamin. "We've created a place where we can be ourselves, a life together where we have fund acceptance and understanding."

Benjamin chuckled, a sense of nostalgia washing over him. "We've come a long way since those days at P.O. Box 1142."

As they reminisced about their shared experiences and the friendships forged in the crucible of wartime, they marveled at the strength of their endurance. Despite the challenges and sacrifices, they had built a life filled with love, laughter, and purpose.

The scene faded into the tranquility of the evening, with Benjamin and Erik basking in the comfort of each other's company. In that moment, they knew that no matter what the future held, they had each other and the enduring power of their love to guide them.

Seventy love-filled years passed by with Benjamin and Erik's bond still as strong as ever. After June 26, 2015, following the landmark Supreme Court ruling in Obergefell v. Hodges, which legalized same-sex marriage across the United States, Benjamin and Erik celebrated by renewing their personal commitments to each other and formalized their bond by finally getting legally married. Benjamin was ninety-six, and Erik was ninety-eight.

Their wedding was a quiet, intimate ceremony, surrounded by close friends and family who had witnessed their enduring love over the decades. They exchanged vows with the same passion and dedication they had felt in their youth, their hands trembling with age but their hearts as steadfast as ever.

Eight months later, Erik passed away in Benjamin's arms, a peaceful smile on his face. Two months later, Benjamin joined him, their love story concluding as beautifully as it had begun.

In recognition of their extraordinary lives and their unwavering commitment to each other and their country, they were both posthumously awarded the Congressional Gold Medal. Their love, bravery, and dedication served as a testament to the power of resilience and the enduring strength of the human spirit.

Their story became an inspiration to many, a reminder that love knows no bounds and that true devotion can withstand the test of time. Benjamin and Erik's legacy lived on, celebrated by those who cherished their memory and the profound impact they had on the world around them.

About the Author

Lancer Gareth's passion for storytelling ignited during his childhood, filling countless spiral notebooks with imaginative short stories, plays, and poetry. His talent quickly garnered recognition during his teenage years, earning him numerous awards for his creative prowess. At just 17, Lancer Gareth achieved a significant milestone by becoming a published author after clinching a college writing competition while still in high school.

Since then, Lancer Gareth has embarked on a multifaceted journey, expanding his creative horizons. Building on his literary achievements as a teenager, he has evolved into a record-producing musician, a self-published novelist, content creator, and business owner. Based in Texas, USA, Lancer Gareth continues to captivate audiences with his diverse talents and entrepreneurial spirit.

Thank you for joining Benjamin and Erik on their journey through history as they explore the depths of duty and desire in "P.O. Box 1142."

If Benjamin and Erik's story touched you, I would greatly appreciate your feedback. Reviews on Amazon help other readers discover stories like this and support authors in continuing to create

new works.

Amazon.com: Lancer Gareth: books, biography, latest update

www.amazon.com

Please consider leaving a review on Amazon at https://www.amazon.com/stores/author/B0CSWPBM51.

You can simply scan the QR code below to go directly to my Amazon Author website.

For more updates, exclusive content, and a peek into future projects, visit my Facebook author page at: **https://facebook.com/61561131429900**.

Thank you for your support, and I look forward to sharing more stories with you in the future!